THE BRIDE PRICE

She was Welsh, he was English. They had been brought up as enemies and taught to hate each other, but Cadfael needed a guide into the wild mountains of Snowdonia. Sioned seized the opportunity to escape from the marriage about to be forced on her by her treacherous brother. She also had her own quest in the mountains and had no intention of falling in love with a man she suspected of being a spy for the English. Once in his hands she had no choice but to follow wherever he led.

THE BRIDE PRICE

The Bride Price

by

June Francis

Dales Large Print Books
Long Preston, North Yorkshire,
England.

British Library Cataloguing in Publication Data.

Francis, June
The bride price.

A catalogue record for this book is available from the British Library

ISBN 1-85389-875-9 pbk

First published in Great Britain by Mills & Boon Ltd., 1987

Published in Large Print 1999 by arrangement with Judith Murdoch Literary Agency.

Dales Large Print is an imprint of
Library Magna Books Ltd.
Printed and bound in Great Britain by
T.J. International Ltd., Cornwall, PL28 8RW.

All the characters in this book have no existence outside the imagination of the Author, and have no relation whatsoever to anyone bearing the same name or names. They are not even distantly inspired by any individual known or unknown to the Author, and all the incidents are pure invention.

CHAPTER ONE

'You will do as you are told, Sioned. I will stand no argument in this matter!'

Sioned and Hywel ap Rowan stood on opposite sides of the table in the empty hall.

'Is that why you never told me the real reason why we have come to this cantref of Perfeddwlad?' Sioned glared angrily at her brother. 'You should have asked me first—prepared me. But no! You leave it until we are here in Govan's hall!' She folded her arms across her breast.

'Angharad thought it would be better this way,' muttered Hywel, not meeting Sioned's glance.

'Angharad!' Sioned almost spat the word out. 'I should have known that Angharad was behind this. She has wanted to be rid of me ever since you wed her!'

Sioned began to pace the rush-strewn floor with barely controlled impatience. 'Well! I will not do it. I will not wed Govan, even though he is prepared to pay my amobr for me. He is gross, and leers at me, and I do not care for him.'

'Keep your voice down,' growled Hywel,

his head shooting up. 'I tell you that you will do as I command you—you will not be returning to Gwynedd with me.' He stared at Sioned, his brown eyes as dark and determined as hers. 'Forget any thought you might have had about wedding Dafydd.'

Sioned returned his stare and her hands clenched. 'He would have wed me if you and Angharad would have allowed it! He would have paid the amobr you spent that was rightly mine after our sire was killed,' she choked. Money her mother had given.

'It wasn't enough. Besides, Angharad has other plans for her cousin.' Hywel shrugged his shoulders.

'So, instead you chose Govan! A fine choice, brother. He is as fat as a flawn and has pawed me almost continually since I have been here!' Sioned came to a halt on the other side of the table again, leaning on it with outspread hands. She gazed at her brother, despair written clear on her face. 'You do not have this right—you know that, Hywel. If Owain were here, he would not let you do this to me!'

'Owain!' Hywel threw back his handsome head and laughed. 'Our dear, beloved older brother? He is most likely dead, or else we would have seen him before now. It is six years since he sailed from Deganwy—remember, Sioned? Your amobr belongs to me now, and I will have it. Angharad has expensive tastes.' Hywel smiled, staring into space a moment before his eyes fell on Sioned again. 'Also I must buy weapons. Govan says that the English are already in this cantref.'

'The English!' Sioned's brown eyes widened. 'And you would leave me here so near the border?' Her bronze braids swung forward, brushing the bare sunburnt throat revealed by the low-cut scarlet linen cotte.

'You have nothing to fear from the English,' grunted Hywel impatiently. 'Every move they make is being watched. Govan has his men out even now. But it would be best if you do not wander from this keep into the hills and forest, as you have been wont to do at home. You have heard often enough what sort of beasts the Normans are when it comes to women. They take what they want without asking or paying. You would be best to content yourself with learning from that wench who holds house for him, just how Govan likes things done.'

'That wench is his whore!' Sioned's eyes sparked, as she flushed on meeting her brother's gaze.

'So the man has a mistress.' Hywel tossed his lank black hair, and shrugged.

'Do you expect him to be a saint? You should be glad. Once he has got you with child, he will most likely return to her bed if you are so unwilling, sister.'

Sioned gasped and then gave a bitter laugh. 'You think that makes it easier for me?' She turned from him angrily and began to pace the floor once more.

Hywel frowned, staring at her moodily. 'Govan has made comment on the way you dress,' he snapped. 'He does not approve of your going about barefoot. You are not among the mountains of Snowdonia now, Sioned. Having lived so close to the border, Govan knows much about what is fashionable.' He gave a sneering laugh. 'He has sampled the best that the palatinate of Chester can offer!'

'You mean that he has plundered over the border. That, I suppose, is why he is so rich! Rich enough to satisfy you and Angharad.' Sioned came to a halt in front of her brother.

'You will not fight me over this, Sioned,' said Hywel, his voice dangerously level. 'You cannot remain unwed for ever, and will regret it if you make matters difficult for me.'

Sioned lowered her eyes, swallowing the sudden tightness in her throat as she stared down at her bare toes peeping from beneath her skirts. The weals from the beating her brother had given her after Angharad's first coming to the hafod in the mountains had lasted almost a fortnight. She suddenly yearned for the days before her father had died and Owain had gone away. She had been happy then. Angharad had changed all that. Brought up used to having the finer things, by a father who was one of the best and fiercest raiders in the mountains, Angharad had disapproved of the economies Sioned had needed to enforce after her father's death. She had encouraged Hywel to leave his cattle and fields and to raid more daringly. It was a sure way of ensuring that disharmony flourished among the tribesmen of Gwynedd under the rule of Llewelyn ap Gruffyd, pendragon of Gwynedd in the year 1277. Yet it had not been all unhappiness—there had been Dafydd.

'Well! You will do as I bid, Sioned?' said Hywel impatiently. 'Be pleasant to Govan—try to please him. You are not stupid, sister. Use the wiles that you have been given, and you might find that there is much that is pleasurable in living under the care of a rich man.'

'Money! That is all you care for,' said Sioned in a low voice. She lifted her eyes to Hywel's face, tears sparkling on her thick lashes.

'You have forgotten what it was like to be without it. I have not!' Her brother turned his back on her. 'You will become accustomed to this place and to Govan. No more dispute now. Go and put on that gown Angharad gave you, and some hose.'

Sioned stared at Hywel's broad determined back before whirling away from him abruptly to run across the stone floor. The door was heavy in her hands as she wrenched it open and shot down the steps. She ran like a hare across the clearing and was in the trees before Hywel had even reached the top step.

'Sioned! Come back, you little fool!'

She took no heed of her brother but dodged and weaved between the trunks of the trees, running and running until she could run no more and all sound of her brother's voice and steps had faded. Panting for breath, she was forced to slow to a walk as she neared the summit of the wooded hill. Here the trees huddled closer together, their branches tangling overhead. She paused, listening intently, but the only sound that came to her ears was that of a bird. She listened to its trilling cascade of notes, and the ache of despondency inside her eased. Only the lightest flurry of air stirred the leaves on the bushes that grew thickly about her. It was warm. So warm that sweat trickled between her breasts.

As Sioned walked on, her anger still burned within her. She scuffed the leaves that mouldered beneath the trees, heedless of the fact that the way now led downhill, and not conscious of the men's voices that came on the breeze from the river below.

She would walk back to Snowdonia over the drovers' path, the way they had come with their cattle to Govan's. Dafydd would marry her. She doubted he was aware of his cousin's and Hywel's plans for her to marry Govan. The thought of how Dafydd had kissed her on a cold night, hard as iron, last winter thrilled her suddenly. Ay! She would go back home to the mountains.

Suddenly she came to a halt. She had not seen the dark green fronds of bracken that blocked her way, head-high and thick. Which way to go? Which way to the drovers' path? For a moment she felt panic tighten her stomach, for she knew little about the ways in this cantref. When she crept forward, she caught a stir of movement beyond the bracken-stems, and was aware of men's voices calling to one another and answering. Curiously but with cautious tread Sioned moved, parting the crowding bracken with unsteady fingers.

She caught the gleam of the river beyond, and remembrance stirred again. Why had

Owain gone away? Even on the tail of the thought, she knew the answer. The sea was in his blood, descended as he was from one of those pirate princes who had crossed the water from Ireland. Then her eyes caught the flash of metal, and she stared.

Men were falling out of line, spreading out like honey when it spills from the pot. Soon they filled the clearing with a bustling order; erecting tents, lighting charcoal fires. Some were dressed in full chain mail, others in leather tunics and woollen hose. Cartloads of provisions and equipment were being unloaded, causing Sioned's eyes to widen in amazement at such bounty. Here, then, was the army of Edward I of England. They were making camp, despite the delaying tactics of the Cymri raiders on the woodsmen widening the road through the forests of Perfeddwlad.

Sioned nervously fingered the knife at her girdle as she watched the seemingly unending columns of foot soldiers, bowmen, and mailed riders on warhorses continue to fill the clearing. One paused as he entered, pushing back his mail coif. His dark hair, which curled under in a roll on his neck, stirred in the breeze from the River Dee. His eyes scanned the tree-clad hillside.

Sioned stretched herself flat, her cheek pressed closely to the woven stems of grass.

She lay still, listening, praying. Eventually, after several minutes, she ventured to lift her head.

The man's back was to her now, and the army men seemed unaware of her presence, so she relaxed, her dark eyes scanning the clearing. On the air came the appetising odour of cooking meat. Her stomach rumbled, and she realised that she had not had dinner. She resolved to move as soon as the handful of troopers, taking their ease not so far from her, finished their meal and went about their duties.

Without warning came the swift thud of rushing feet, and men emerged from the trees, clad in red homespun, with bare legs. They charged towards the knot of troopers, barely pausing before loosening their spears. Several of the English slumped forward, spears jutting from between their shoulder-blades. There was frantic movement about the dead, and several bolts and arrows were sent speeding after the fleeing raiders. Not all gained the cover of the trees.

Sioned did not hesitate. Her heart was pounding heavily as she began to worm her way backwards through the bracken, conscious of the shouts of men searching, and the crashing in the undergrowth. Would she be safer lying still in the bracken? If she reached the trees, she might be seen more easily than where she was. She lay motionless in the bracken and grass, the warm somnolence of the summer day encompassing her. Bees droned and a caterpillar humped its way up a swaying stem next to her cheek, tickling her. She scrubbed a hand across her face, not realising she left a trail of grime. Then she stiffened as the soft tread of feet approached her hiding-place.

Peering through the stems, her stomach twisted as she caught sight of the mail-clad legs a few feet from her, and slowly she raised her eyes. He was tall, this one ... big boned, and upright of bearing with broad shoulders. His mouth was firm, his nose straight. The hazel eyes were large and expressive and seemed to be gazing straight at her.

Sioned's mouth went dry, but the hazel eyes barely flickered. The dark brows arched as his glance seemed calmly to wash over her prostrate form. Then he turned and went in another direction. She set free a trembling breath, not believing that he—that English warrior—had see her and let her lie. But perhaps he had not seen her? She puzzled over the matter, staying still. Flies now joined the bees to create a continuous buzzing and itching about her ears, but still she did not move. She waited seemingly for hours, until all was quieter in the camp. Then she began to wriggle backwards through the bracken.

She reached the edge of the forest and, swiftly crouching, darted up among the branching pillars of the trees. No sound of pursuit followed her, and soon she had to resort to scrambling, her skirts tripping her when she had to use both hands to heave herself up and over banks of tangled scrub. It did not take her long to reach the top of the hill, where she paused and took stock.

Which way lay the drovers' path? It would be to the west. If she kept the estuary in her eye, she would know the right direction, and sooner or later she was sure to come to the path. Once on it, she would find the way home. She would have to be careful, on her guard, not only for the English but for her brother and Govan. Warily she began to walk down the other side of the hill.

Hywel pounced just as she reached an outlying stand of trees. 'By the saints, where have you been?' he rapped, seizing Sioned by the hair and cuffing her across the head.

'Walking,' she gasped, attempting to wriggle out of her brother's hold, her heart plummeting.

'Walking? You are untidy and dirty—and I do not believe you!' Hywel's black brows drew together and his narrow face lengthened in furious disapproval. 'But I will not go into that now! Our host returned but an hour since and is in a foul mood because several of his men have been killed by English bowmen. You did not see any men on your—walk?' He shook her by the shoulder. 'Answer me!'

'I saw no one.' Sioned wrenched her shoulder out of his grip, knowing it would only make her brother angrier still if she told him she had seen the English camp. 'I tripped over a root. That is why I am so—dirty. I will go straight to my chamber. Govan will not wish me to dine with him in this state, will he, dear brother?'

Hywel stared at her grimly and let out an impatient breath. 'He will be angrier if you are not at table, sister.' He frowned in thought. 'There is a spring not far from here, dedicated to the saint. We will go there, and you will wash your face and hands.'

'I would rather go to my chamber,' said Sioned stubbornly, beginning to walk towards the keep. If he went to dine, there might be a chance for her to get out of the keep again.

Hywel grabbed her tightly by the arm. 'You will do as I say, Sioned! Do not argue with me. The bare feet will anger Govan, but ...' he frowned again, 'the gown will not do—it is filthy. I will need to get you one, but I do not wish for Govan to see you in this state.' He dragged her along not giving her a chance to get free or to protest.

When they came near the spring, they met one of the maids who helped in the dairy. Hywel called her over and exchanged a few low-voiced words with her, smiling into her eyes and kissing her rosy mouth before sending her on the way. Sioned puckered her brows. It seemed that her brother was not going to let her out of his sight!

The water was sweet and cold, but Sioned drank sparingly to quench her thirst. The liquid was chilling as it went down her throat. She washed her face and hands, conscious of her brother's eyes on her. There was a shrine with a pot of clover set in a niche next to a roughly carved and painted figure of St Winifrid. This was one of many shrines dedicated to the saint, but the original holy well was a few miles away at the monastery of Basinwerk, near the camp of the English king. She bowed her head, and murmured a few short prayers, barely conscious of the actual words, but of a need, a desperate need, for intervention from the saint.

'Your hair could do with rebraiding.' Her brother wrenched at the ribands that bound the plait-ends, even as she prayed. Sioned let out a painful gasp, but her brother ignored it. 'Shoes—I hope the girl remembers the shoes.' He whirled her round and gazed at her face—clean, heart-shaped, the nose tip-tilted, the cheeks smooth and flushed from exertion and anger.

'You think of everything, brother,' hissed Sioned in a hoarse voice.

'I need to,' he said stiffly. 'I have no intention of letting your amobr slip through my fingers!'

There was no time to answer, for just then the maid came with some garments and shoes in her arms. Hywel took them from her, chucking her under the chin, and slapping her bottom as she turned away with a giggle. Sioned felt sick. Not only was she hungry, but her brother's actions sickened her: to sell her to the highest bidder, as he would sell his cattle.

'Here—make haste.' Hywel thrust the garments into Sioned's arms.

For a moment she hesitated, but he made a threatening movement towards her and she stepped quickly behind the shrine. She dropped the grubby red cotte on to the ground and dragged the silken gown over her linen shift, fastening the gown slowly as Hywel impatiently watched her. The fabric was smooth and soft where it touched her skin, and she had never worn a gown so fine or expensive. It was only now that she realised why Angharad had been so generous. She stepped from behind the shrine.

Hywel's glance took in her elegant statuesque form, and he nodded. 'That is better. You are rather on the tall side for a woman, but Govan will not mind that, being a large man himself!'

'Too large,' murmured Sioned, as she began to braid her hair. 'I will not wear the hose.'

'You will!'

'I will not—it is too warm. And how will he know if I wear them or not? I shall wear the shoes.' She gave him a cool smile.

He smiled, suddenly in a good humour. 'So be it—but make haste, Sioned. I will say that we are late because you wished to spend some time in prayer at the shrine, reflecting on your past life and on what joys lie ahead for you now that you are to be wed.'

'It will not be the first untruth you have told, Hywel!' Sioned smiled back sweetly at her brother as she took the shoes, and turned away, balancing against the shrine while she pulled them on. They were of soft red leather sewn with tiny jewels at their fronts. Another gift from Angharad! How had she not realised that they were a bribe to behave, to be obedient, to do as she was told—or else! She straightened, smoothing down her skirts, and gazed at her brother.

'You do not realise how different you look now, sister! No one would take you for the unruly maid from the mountains you looked half an hour ago.'

Sioned's eyes frosted. 'I would still rather be that unruly maid,' she declared, tossing her braids back. 'But I accept that there is no persuading you otherwise, Hywel.'

'There is not,' Hywel agreed placidly, 'so let us go in. There will be many such gowns if you learn to be amenable, Sioned.' He took her arm and forced her forward. 'So let me have no more disagreement from you, or you will pay for it.'

Sioned went with him, her feet dragging, her mind busily searching for a way out of her brother's scheme for her future.

CHAPTER TWO

Sioned spared no glances for the men who ate of Govan's meat as she walked beside her brother up the middle of the hall between the crowded trestle tables. Her attention was on Govan and Annest. Especially Annest, as she could not bear more than a fleeting glance at her proposed husband. She could not dislike Annest, Govan's mistress. She was small and rounded of figure, with a gentle plump face and the softest wide-set blue eyes she had ever seen. She wondered what she thought of Govan's intention to marry.

'We will forgive your lateness, Sioned, now that your beauty has come to grace our table.'

Sioned's eyes shifted unwillingly from Annest to Govan. 'I thank you, and beg your pardon for delaying your meal.' Her voice was stiff and cold.

'I found my sister praying at the shrine, Govan,' interposed Hywel, giving Sioned's arm a squeeze. 'She tells me she was thanking the saint for her good fortune in your offering to marry her.'

Sioned cast her brother a glance of scorn.

He was determined to have everything settled as quickly as possible, it seemed!

'Gratitude is a virtue the saint, like myself, much appreciates,' said Govan. Was there a hint of warning in the soft, smooth tones? He patted the intricately carved chair set on his right at the high table, and held out his other hand to Sioned. She ignored it and sat down, knowing she might pay for the gesture later, aware that her brother and Govan exchanged glances. She slanted a look at the others who sat at the high table: a couple of local chieftains, their wives, Annest, the bard, and Hywel and herself.

'You will enjoy your supper, Sioned.' Govan's fleshy hand rested on hers before she could pull her fingers away. 'It is good English beef.' He smiled broadly, revealing large yellow teeth.

Hywel laughed, and Sioned smiled politely, attempting to pull her fingers free as she stared down at her trencher of thick wheaten bread. A serving-man placed several slices of beef dripping with juice on the trencher. She was suddenly remembering her brother's words.

She barely waited for her host to be served as soon as he had released her hand to eat. Her mouth watered as she took the knife from her girdle, and she speared one of the slices of beef, raising it speedily to her mouth. She began to tear at it hungrily with her strong but small teeth. That slice eaten, she took up another.

'Little savage!' Govan muttered against her ear. 'I will tame you, if you were thinking of setting your will against mine.' His elbow brushed her breast as he picked up his cup.

The colour was suddenly high in Sioned's cheeks, and the meat dropped from her knife on to her trencher. 'The bard ...' she said in a stammering voice. 'Is he going to entertain us? I ... I would hear of the old days of glory ... when Llewelyn the Great ruled nearly all Wales and drove the Normans out.'

Govan's small eyes almost disappeared in his fat cheeks as he scrutinised her flushed face. 'If that is your wish, little dove.' He leaned forward and kissed her on the mouth before she could withdraw. He signalled to the bard.

'Does ... does he play the harp?' Sioned tried to ease the dryness in her throat. 'I ... I would have the tale with music, if I may.'

'I will fetch my harp, lady.' The elderly bard rose to his feet with some reluctance.

'I have a harp if you wish to make use of it, man.' The voice came from the trestle table nearest to the high table.

'Who spoke there?' Govan peered from

small round eyes at the group of raiders, who all looked much alike, clad as they were in red plaids, unless one looked closely for a familiar face.

'I did.' A tall man unfolded himself from one of the benches and got to his feet. His bare legs were long and sinewy as he strolled towards the high table, a harp under one arm. He stopped, and bowed slightly before Govan.

Sioned stared at his bent head. The hair was dark, and it curled crisply on his neck. He straightened and, as he did so, his eyes rested for a moment on her countenance. Surprise registered in the hazel eyes, even as her own heart seemed to jolt against her ribs.

'I would sing to you of Nest, the daughter of Rhys ap Tewdwr, if you would wish it, lady,' he murmured, amusement and admiration replacing the surprise. 'Of how Owain, son of Cadwgan ap Bleddyn, hearing of her beauty, fell madly in love and stole Nest away from under her husband's nose.'

'I ... I am desiring to hear that tale again.' Sioned's voice was as low as his had been. 'But to whom do I address myself?'

'I am Cadfael ... ap Glyder,' he replied after the barest of hesitations. 'My mother is from the mountains, my father from

... the Marches.' The broad shoulders straightened, and he ran tapering fingers lightly over the harp-strings.

'Well, now we have that settled, man—play!' commanded Govan in a sharp querulous voice, hitching a fold of dark blue velvet over his plump knees.

'Certainly.' Cadfael began to pluck the strings and to sing in a light tenor voice that was easy on the ear. Sioned tried to place his accent, but could not. Was that because he was not as Welsh as his name? Absently she cut her meat into small pieces, her eyes not leaving Cadfael's tall form. She was certain he was the man she had seen when hiding in the bracken. Yet should she cry 'Spy!'? It could be that he was a spy for the Welsh in Edward's army. But then it could be that he was a spy for the English. There were many Welsh 'friendlies' in Edward's army, she had heard. Men who had accepted money from the king after their chieftains were defeated earlier that year. Yet what could he discover in Govan's hall? She doubted that Govan knew Llewelyn's whereabouts or his plans.

The tale came to its unhappy end and Cadfael bowed, his eyes holding Sioned's. 'I have pleased you, lady?' he murmured.

'Ay, you have pleased me,' she responded, unsure of what to do.

'Sing to us of Llewelyn the Great!' shouted one of the men. 'Those were the days when Welshmen crossed the border and captured Shrewsbury.' He tossed a bone to a dog behind him, and Sioned's attention was distracted. A fierce battle ensued that threatened to drown all their voices, followed by a kick at the dogs under the table.

'Ay! Tell us of those days!' shouted Hywel. He shot to his feet, his eyes shining, his horn brimming with ale. 'They will surely come again! Here's to the pendragon. He has not been named after his grandsire for nothing! Other chieftains may fall beneath the English yoke, but Llewelyn ap Gruffyd will not. Once the English are lured into the mountains, we will destroy them as we have in the past.'

'Do you think it will be so?' The question was softly spoken, and directed at Sioned.

'It is a certainty.' Sioned's voice lilted sweetly. 'The English cannot defeat our warriors—or our mountains.' Her eyes challenged Cadfael to deny her words. For a moment her fierce gaze held his cool stare—then he smiled.

'It will most likely be as you say, lady. The English have always been defeated by the mountains of Snowdonia—and did not the pendragon seize these cantrefs of

Perfeddwlad from Edward's control fifteen years ago? I was a raw youth then, but I remember it well.'

'Ay, that is true,' muttered one of the men nearest the high table. 'And now Edward seeks to get them back.'

'That I cannot permit!' growled Govan, slamming his gold cup down on the table, while his fat cheeks turned purple.

'Ay, it would put an end to our raiding if Edward's rod ruled here,' grunted a chieftain.

Soon the air was filled with talk about the invasion and what one or the other thought Edward's plan would be to bring Llewelyn to heel. Cadfael quirked a brow at Sioned and inclined his head. She returned his stare, her eyes cool and appraising. Then Annest spoke to her, and her gaze wavered.

Cadfael turned and went back to his place at table, still unsure whether the lady would mention having seen him. He sat down and prodded at a piece of beef, which might just have come on the hoof from his brother's manor. Good English beef! He sank his teeth into the meat, wondering if he would manage to return to Edward's camp as easily as he had followed the raiders' tracks to this keep. He supposed it would all depend on the lady remaining silent—or was she even now speaking of him?

He glanced up. The fat Govan was stroking the lady's shoulder with his thieving hand, and Cadfael was not sure if the lady liked it or not. He thought of how she had appeared when first he saw her. He had considered her a child with her tangled hair and dirty face, and he did not make war on children! No child, he mused, staring openly at Sioned's well-formed figure in its yellow silk. On closer inspection, the dirty face appeared petal soft. He watched her extremely kissable mouth form some answer to Govan's remarks. Perhaps it would be best if he left soon, before the lady changed her mind. Very soon, he decided, as he saw her look away from Govan and straight at him, her face angry and flushed.

It was as Sioned was combing her hair in the bedchamber that she remembered she had left her scarlet cotte behind the shrine. If she left it, the dye might run if it rained. Her years of thrift would not allow her simply to leave it. Besides ... she rose, unsure of what to do. She had thought of trying to go in the morning, but maybe now would be best, to try to get away before her brother, or Govan or any of his men realised her intent. If she were stopped, she could say that she had left something behind at the shrine when she had gone to pray.

It was already dark on the stairway outside her chamber when she passed like a shadow down the stone steps. Her heart jumped as a man came from beneath the archway leading into the passage to the door outside.

'I have left something at the shrine,' she said coolly, pushing past the man before he could prevent her from going. 'If my brother asks for me, tell him where I have gone.'

'It is getting dark, mistress,' the man called. 'Would you like me to accompany you?'

'No ... No, I will not be gone long.' Swiftly she pulled the door to and was gone with a whisk of skirts.

The light breeze had strengthened since the afternoon into a strong cool wind, heavy with the tang of the sea. Sioned shivered but sniffed pleasurably, moving swiftly in the direction of the shrine. She came to the spring and bent to pick up her cotte.

'So this is where you changed from child to woman!'

She whirled round, her heart racing, and stared into the bushes behind the shrine. 'Who—who is there?' she demanded, although she guessed the answer.

'Not so loud, lady Sioned! I do not want all your mighty Cymri warriors on my tail.' Cadfael came into view from behind the elder tree growing at the side of the spring. He still wore the red plaid of the raider but had donned a black cloak. He seemed immensely tall to Sioned, and she was not small.

'Who are you?' Sioned snatched at her cotte, clutching it, almost defensively, against her breast.

'Sir Cadfael Poole from the palatinate of Chester.' He bowed slightly, and she caught the gleam of his eyes as he straightened.

'So you are not Cymri.' She realised suddenly that the shrine was a lonely spot at that time of evening, and he must be a Norman.

'I am half Cymri,' he drawled, leaning against the trunk of the elder. 'My mother is from Gwynedd, like you and your brother. It was from her I learnt the language, and from a certain Welsh harpist on crusade I learnt my music and tales.'

'Why are you here? Are you a spy for the English king, then?' Her eyes flashed. He was the enemy; she was suddenly certain of it.

'If you thought I was, why did you not tell Govan or your brother I might be?' He stood up, easing the strap that held his harp on his back.

'At first I was not sure,' Sioned responded slowly, glancing about her for any sign of Govan's men. 'I—I thought maybe you were a Welsh spy in the English camp—but I think you are not.'

'You are right,' he murmured. 'I do hope you are not going to scream for help! It would be a foolish act at this moment.' He smelled the slight scent of flowers that perfumed her hair.

She looked up at him. 'You would kill me? If you would do such a thing, why did you not act when you saw me by your king's camp?'

The hazel eyes narrowed. 'I thought you were a child—and I do not fight children. But if I had known ...' He did not finish.

Sioned's eyes dilated, remembering the tales of Norman rape and pillage. She wanted to move away from him, but his eyes seemed to hold her frozen. Her limbs felt heavy.

'Why do you look at me like that?' Cadfael reached out a hand, and she shrank back. 'Do you think me a ravishing wolf?'

Sioned laughed shakily. 'You are not? Perhaps not! After all, you are not a Norman. Maybe ... it is because you are part Welsh that you let me go, I deem.'

'It has nothing to do with it at all. I

have spent most of my life fighting Welsh raiders, who are feared over the border as much as the Normans are here,' said Cadfael, so softly. 'It is time that peace came between our countries.'

'Peace? While your king seeks to bring Llewelyn to heel by invading our land!' she retorted with spirit and made to move away from him, but his fingers suddenly curled about her hand.

'Edward bid him come at least thrice to pay homage, but Llewelyn refused, not even appearing at the coronation at Westminster. There is a limit to my king's patience. But these matters are for men, not for women. You should leave them to your brother or the gross Govan.'

Sioned's eyes sparkled and there was a flush high on her cheeks as she wrenched her hand from his grasp. 'Just because I am a woman, it does not mean that my heart is not loyal or hot for my pendragon's cause! But you are like all men in ...'

'I have no time to argue or debate causes, lady Sioned,' he interrupted ruthlessly. 'I must go before your voice brings Govan's men about my ears.'

He looked down at her, and some mischief caused him to reach out and pull her close before she could retreat. Sioned had no time to prevent him having his way. He kissed her hard on the mouth before saying, 'I would that you will not forget that this part Norman wolf did not come ravishing, lady!' Then he was gone, vanishing in the gloom beneath the trees.

Sioned clutched the trunk of the elder, angry that he should dare to kiss her. His mouth still seemed to burn its impression on her lips. Then, as she stood there, voices could be heard.

'She said that she had left something by the shrine.'

Sioned's stomach seemed to twist as she heard an answering growl. Nowhere to run now. She could not chance running into the spy and, besides, it was much, much too late. When she lifted her eyes, she met Govan's suspicious gaze.

'I heard voices,' said Govan in a sharp voice. 'Have you been meeting one of my raiders here, woman?'

'I have not!' Sioned drew herself up to her full height and faced him. 'I was praying aloud.'

'Thanking the saint for your good fortune, no doubt,' Govan sneered, taking her arm in a painful grasp.

'No!' gasped Sioned. 'I have no desire to wed you, whatever my brother might have said to you.' She tried to pull away from him, but his fingers tightened so cruelly on her upper arm that she desisted.

'You would speak so to me, your future

husband? You little fool!' Govan began to force her back towards the keep.

'I do not want to be your wife,' she whispered, tears of pain starting in her eyes.

'But I want you!' he hissed. They had come to the door, which he forced wider with his foot. 'Your qualities are those I seek in a wife—and if you were to show a little sense, Sioned, it would be better for you.' He pushed her along the passage towards the stairs that led up to her chamber. She tried to resist, but he dug his fingers into her back with such viciousness that she cried out, stumbling forward to the foot of the steps.

Govan grabbed her arm and propelled her up the steps. In the darkness, she was forced against his fat belly when the stairs twisted dangerously, and almost lost her footing. His breath was hot on her face and she tried to pull away from him, but he pressed her against the stone wall, giving a sudden deep gurgling laugh, kissing her throat and neck and fondling her body. Revulsion surged inside her and she tried to push him away, but he was too heavy for her. She began to feel a paralysing terror numbing her will to resist. It was hopeless to fight him. She felt and heard the silk tear at her shoulder and began to struggle, digging her elbow into his side, but he made no sign of having felt the blow. Sioned despaired. How could Hywel have involved her in such a predicament? As Govan tore her gown down, faintness overcame her body so that she was suddenly limp in his grasp. As if from a great height, she caught the sound of footsteps and a voice calling from the top of the steps.

'Sioned? Is that you?' It was a woman's voice, soft and caring, and Sioned found herself suddenly released. Govan's hands worked feverishly about her bodice, pulling the ripped silk together, covering her breasts.

'It is I, my sweeting.' Sioned could barely believe that it was Govan speaking. 'I found the poor child outside by the shrine. She had been set upon by one of the English, no doubt.'

'Oh, by the saint!' A light suddenly appeared round the bend of stairs, showing Annest's kind face. 'Bring her up to her chamber, my lord.'

Sioned tried to speak but the hard pinch on her arm was a warning. She was helped to rise to her feet by Annest's firm but gentle hand on one side, and Govan's on the other. Within minutes she was up the stairs and on the bed in her chamber.

'You will leave us now, my lord.' Annest's voice was insistent. For an instant

Sioned thought he would resist, but Govan looked down at her lying on the bed, half smiled a full-lipped smile, and went from the room.

'He—he tried to ...' began Sioned in a harsh whisper, trying to sit up.

'I know. There is no need for you to tell me.' Annest's tone was sad and resigned.

'You know? You know the sort of beast he is, yet you pretended to believe ...'

'Ay.' Annest sat down on the bed, pulling her scarlet robe tightly about her plump figure. 'It is safer to pretend that I do not suspect his cruelties. He is not cruel with me, you see. In his way, I think Govan loves me.'

'Loves you?' Sioned gave a reluctant laugh. 'Dear God!' She could think of no more to say.

'You find it hard to believe that he could love me, and yet still wish to marry you?' Annest's sober eyes met Sioned's. 'I have been Govan's woman for over ten years. He took a fancy to me on a raid over the border. But I cannot give him the son he desires.' She paused. 'Tolerate his advances—let him get you with child. Then leave him to me if you find him so—so not to your taste.'

'He is to yours?' Sioned gazed at Annest incredulously. A great cold fear gripped her at this calm suggestion.

'He was not always so,' said Annest defensively, getting to her feet. 'Once he was young and handsome, and I was thin as a reed. I learnt to please him, and grew fat in so doing. Although he loves me in his way, you must do as I say if you are to lead a life that will be tolerable here. You will adjust to our customs, child.'

Sioned stared at her. Adjust? Adjust to living with Govan's bestial demands on her? He wanted her for breeding purposes, that was all. Dear God, what had Hywel done to her when he brought her to this place! Surely—surely there must be some way out of what he so ruthlessly had set his mind to do to her? She doubted if even the spy from Edward's army could have treated her so unkindly.

CHAPTER THREE

Cadfael passed swiftly through the trees. He had roamed this cantref as a boy, before his family had been swept back over the border during the uneasy years in England between Henry III and his barons. Llewelyn had taken full advantage of an England divided, and a ruler in the Palatinate who was a raw youth. Cadfael's father was dead, and his brother Ralph now had possession of the manor in Cheshire. Cadfael's own land, much smaller, lay in the Wirral, a happier distance from the border.

It took him less than an hour to reach the camp. He gave the password, and went in search of Reginald de Grey, hoping he was not asleep yet. The tents, billowing in the wind blowing from the Dee estuary, all looked alike against the night sky. There was a man on guard outside the one he wanted, who recognised Cadfael immediately.

'Sir Cadfael! Praise the saint,' said John in his gruff voice. 'I was beginning to worry about what I would tell Gwenllian and your mother when I got home. Letting you go off without me!'

'You had no need to worry,' grinned Cadfael. 'There was no mighty warrior presenting any threat—only a lady! Is Master de Grey waiting for me?'

'Ay, and growing impatient.' John rubbed his bulbous nose vigorously, and wondered. A lady?

'I'll go in then, without delay.' Cadfael let his hand rest briefly on his man's shoulder before passing into the tent.

A rush light burned low in a bowl, dimly showing de Grey's face. He was sitting on a stool, drinking a horn of ale, and looked up quickly as Cadfael stood before him.

'Well, Cadfael?' His voice was rough and slurred with tiredness.

'They have no idea, Reginald.' Cadfael sank on the other stool, watching as his friend poured him a horn of ale. He took it and drank it off in a couple of gulps. 'I needed that!' He sighed, and extended the horn again.

'They do not guess at all?'

'I doubt it. They seem to have no inkling of the kind of man our king is, despite his having gained conquests in the south of Wales and the Marches. They are certain that Edward comes to repossess Flint and Denbigh, and that he means to call Llewelyn to heel. But they still think he is going to invade the mountain valleys in search of the tribesmen who vanish into the mists.'

'Good! The longer they think like that the better. Surprise is vital in this campaign. Cadfael, as you know.' De Grey's eyes gleamed. 'Have you eaten?'

Cadfael nodded. 'Well, and of English beef!' he murmured lazily. 'God willing, it will not be for much longer that they will be stealing our beef ... Any news?'

Master de Grey grinned. 'You have been gone only half a day, friend. As it happens, there is a visitor for you ... off one of the ships from Chester. Your sister Matilda's husband. I put him in your tent. It is a wonder your man did not tell you.'

'I did not give him time. Best go and see Ned, I suppose.' Cadfael downed the rest of his ale and, bidding de Grey good night, went from the tent.

John looked up as Cadfael paused outside the tent. 'He has told you, then?'

Cadfael nodded. 'I wonder why he has come.' He rubbed his unshaven chin. 'The only way is to find out, I suppose.' He yawned. 'Do not bring me breakfast too early in the morning, John.'

The elderly man nodded his grizzled head. 'You will be talking into the night I suppose,' he grunted. 'Still, we will not be on the move for a while, will we, sir?'

Cadfael nodded. 'The king intends

rebuilding the castle at Flint, and it will take some time to widen the road to Rhuddlan.' His voice was low as he turned away and went in the direction of his own tent.

Ned, a man of average height and slender build, looked up as Cadfael approached. He stood in the doorway of the tent, gazing across the estuary. 'So—you have come at last,' he murmured in his pleasant, unhurried tones. 'John said you had gone on some mad escapade.'

'Not mad, Ned.' Cadfael smiled and held out his hand, gripping Ned's fingers hard. 'It is good to see you. Matilda and the lad are in good health, I hope?'

'Both blooming,' Ned said calmly, not quite managing to hide his fondness for his wife and son. 'Matilda sends her love—and news, which will not please you, Cadfael. I am sorry to bring it to you, but Matilda insisted that you should know. You only can bring to pass that which your mother desires.'

'Mother?' Cadfael's tone was sharp. He gazed keenly into Ned's narrow, rather lugubrious, face, which showed only as a pale blur. 'What is wrong, Ned? Tell me, man.'

'Let us go in. The night air grows cool.'

Cadfael nodded impatiently and pulled

the flap aside, ducking as he entered the darkened tent. He did not bother to seek a light, but pulled out stools and bade Ned be seated. 'Well?' He leaned forward, his hands resting on his knees.

Ned took a deep breath. 'Your mother is dying. She has a growth in her belly, and there is nothing the physicians can do.' He paused, hating his task. Cadfael only, out of all the children, understood his mother's fiery, stubborn but loving temperament, with her strange visions and the unexpected fey moods that would take her.

'I see,' muttered Cadfael in a taut voice after a long silence. He rose and moved over to the tent opening, pulling the flap aside. He looked up into the star-sprinkled night sky. 'How long do they think she will live?'

'Until Christmastide—perhaps not as long. They are not certain. She says that she will not die until she has seen Rhys again.' Ned's voice was a shade apologetic.

'Rhys?' Cadfael turned slowly and faced Ned. 'But we have not seen Rhys for over fifteen years.'

'Your mother realises that, I think, but she wishes you to seek him out, now that you are to go to the mountains anyway.'

'Go to the mountains! That is not ...'

Cadfael stopped abruptly and let out a hiss of breath. 'God's blood! Does she think I am here for my own pleasure?' He paced the trodden-down grass. 'Dear, foolish mother! How, in God's name, do you think I will find Rhys?' Cadfael spun round. 'Ned—you know Rhys went back to the mountains when I was only a lad. He insisted on returning with grandmother after grandfather was killed on another of those blood-feuds. I have no idea where he is, or how to find him!'

Ned cleared his throat in a slightly embarrassed fashion. 'Your mother seems to think you will find him, saying that you will find help in your search.'

Cadfael gave out a groan, seeing the gleam in his brother-in-law's eyes. 'Her sight? What has she seen?'

'A woman—young—darkish and in distress. Also a cowled figure. But she is not so sure if he is the angel of death or not.' There was a sudden tremor in Ned's voice.

Cadfael gave a bark of laughter. 'Is he seeking her or me? What does she think Llewelyn's men would do if they got their hands on me? To spy on a small band of raiders in a part of the country I know is one thing, but to go into the stronghold of Llewelyn, which I know not at all is another. I would lose myself in a day!'

'This young woman will guide you—so your mother says.' Ned's voice was bland as he spoke the words Matilda had insisted he should also tell Cadfael. 'She will save your life, as well!'

'What?' Cadfael's brows drew together and he gave an exasperated sigh. Instantly he remembered Sioned. Had she saved his life by remaining silent? He tried to shrug off the unwilling conviction that perhaps there had been an inevitability about their meeting. Why had he alone searched in her direction? Was it because it was predestined? And what had made him pause to drink at the spring earlier that evening? He had ignored his mother's 'sight' in the past, and still rued the day. He could not ignore her request now—not now that she was dying—whatever the danger to himself.

'What are you going to do?' Ned peered at Cadfael curiously, wondering what he made of his mother's words. 'I must return in the morning, as I have another shipment from Gascony due. Is there such a woman?' The words slipped out.

Cadfael lifted his head. 'Ay,' he muttered harshly. 'Almost I wish there were not. I will ask leave to go, although I have no need. Edward has well had my quota of days of service this year. All I ask is that someone will not think up some task for me to perform while I am in the mountains—to find Llewelyn, perhaps—hog-tie him singlehanded and bring him back in my train!' He ran an impatient hand through his hair, causing it to stand up in a crest. 'I'm for bed. You can tell Mother and Matilda I will do what I can, Ned. That is all I will promise.'

'That is all they ask.' Ned grinned and gazed about him in the gloom. 'Now what do I sleep on? How you can live in these conditions, Cadfael? When are you going to give up this life, and ...'

'And marry?' Cadfael laughed sardonically. 'I have tried marriage, Ned, and it was not to my liking.'

'You were unfortunate. Isabella was not the right woman for you.'

'I was in love with her. And she ... She swore undying love to me as she waved me off on crusade.' Cadfael's voice was bitter. 'Let us not talk about it, Ned.'

Ned shrugged and accepted the pallet and blanket from Cadfael's hand. To see her brother married, and with children, was his wife's dearest wish; but he thought there was little likelihood of it being granted.

The two men settled to sleep. They were woken by John with ale, bread, and meat to break their fast, and they sat outside the tent to eat. The camp was full of bustle. Already the axemen were chopping trees to widen the road and lessen the chance of surprise attacks. On the river floated several ships. Their goods had been unloaded—planks, nails, food, wine, ale and many other burdensome necessities.

After they had finished eating, Cadfael walked with Ned to the harbour.

'You will give them my message and my love.' Cadfael said quietly. 'Does Kate know what ails our mother?'

'No.' Ned frowned in answer, turning his cap over between his hands. 'We have not seen her since you left. Your mother does not like to make the journey, and Kate will not come.'

'I see it is still the same between them.'

'Kate will not forget, says Matilda, and your mother refuses to understand how she hurt Kate. Women!' Ned smiled wryly. 'I must go, or I will miss the tide. Take care of yourself, Cadfael. If the task is too dangerous, bring yourself home the earlier to see your mother instead. It would do her much good.'

'We shall see.' Cadfael pressed Ned's arm and bade him farewell. He stood back watching the ship until Ned was but a blur in the stern, before going back towards his tent, thinking deeply.

Sioned watched as Annest demonstrated to the new dairymaid how to churn butter.

She was young and nervous, but Annest was patient. Would she herself ever learn such patience and acceptance? She turned and strolled out of the byre, glad that Hywel had gone off with Govan to gaze down on the English camp and see the ships in the estuary. Her brother had told her before he left that he meant to discuss with their host a date for the marriage ceremony.

'The sooner it takes place the better, Sioned,' his tongue had cajoled. 'What is the use of putting off the time when you will no longer be a maid? As matters lie, I wish to be back in the mountains soon. Angharad bade me not to be absent for long.'

'Bade you to do the task of getting rid of me swiftly, so that you can forget you ever had a sister, whose amobr you spent, brother!' taunted Sioned, braiding her hair with angry movements.

Hywel's thin mouth tightened, and his eyes narrowed. 'You were not averse to giving me the money, sister. I did not have to beg for it, or steal it,' he rapped, folding his arms across his chest.

'I never thought you would sell me,' she said with quiet sarcasm. She rose to her feet and smoothed down her blue linen skirts. 'Now, if you do not mind, I am going with Annest to see over the keep and the outhouses. I do not care when you arrange my wedding, Hywel. The sooner I am rid of your company, the happier I will be.' With a swiftness that took her brother by surprise, she shut the door in his face, almost causing him to bump his nose on the wood.

The satisfaction of shutting the door in her brother's face had soon evaporated, but her anger had not. He cared little what happened to her, since he had wed Angharad. Why was Angharad so unwilling to allow her cousin to marry her husband's sister?

Sioned stared moodily at a bed of leeks, their green spears tall now. Beans and peas also were well grown in the garden, and she could see Annest's hand in their tending. She had never met a woman so careful and thorough in looking after a household. Perhaps she needed to be, when the man she lived with was not her husband.

Apprehension tightened her stomach, and she glanced over her shoulder, aware that Govan had set a man to watch her movements. Bruises had shown up on her skin that morning—on her arms and throat. It would be no better living here than in Snowdonia. Ay, she would be free of Angharad's haughty ways and sharp tongue, but suffering Govan's attentions would be far worse. She was not made like Annest, a woman from the border. A serf, so Annest had told her, who before Govan's abduction of her had often gone hungry. But pleasuring Govan had changed all that. After a morning spent in Annest's company, Sioned suspected that Annest loved the gross Govan. She might not realise it, but there was affection for him in her voice and the tending of his home. Was that what love did to a woman?

Did she herself love Dafydd? She lifted her eyes and gazed about her, realising that her musings and aimless strolling had brought her to the spring and the shrine of St Winifrid. Crouching and cupping her hands, she drank of the water. She found herself remembering the man who had kissed her at this spot last evening. Almost she could feel his arms about her and his lips against hers—if she thought about it. She flushed and pushed the thought aside. When she went back towards the hall, she was aware that the man still followed her.

She hardly heard Hywel's and Govan's voices as they rose and fell about her ears, talking, talking of Edward's army and fighting tactics. The shock of Hywel's earlier words still hurt and frightened. Her fingers trembled as they curled tightly on the stem of the gold cup. Tomorrow!

Hywel had arranged for the ceremony to take place in the morning. She could not take it in, or accept that there was no way out.

Sioned cast a surreptitious glance at Govan, seeing the small eyes, the short nose and full, thick-lipped mouth. His plump body was encased in a tunic, and a surcoat of green and yellow velvet. She shut her eyes briefly, trying not to dwell on the thought of him touching her, kissing her, possessing her. Panic surfaced. She must have a chance to compose herself. Could she go to some place of solitude? Could she ever become accustomed ... Could she accept her fate?

She rose to her feet abruptly, only for Govan instantly to put out a hand and grasp her arm. 'Where are you going, my lovely? I do not wish for you to leave us yet.'

'I ... I wish to spend some time in prayer—please, Govan.' Her voice trembled, and her hand shook beneath his fingers.

'I see.' He hesitated. 'You may go, but I will have Annest prepare a draught for you that will give you rest this night and strength for the morrow.' He squeezed her fingers before releasing her hand and beckoning one of the men forward.

'You will watch the lady Sioned and see

that she comes to no harm.' The man gave a brief nod, and her spirits sank even lower. There was to be no escape.

Almost of their own accord, her feet took her to the shrine of St Winifrid. She bowed her head, and then decided to kneel in the grass. Her blue skirts made a bright splash of colour on the turf. Soundlessly, as her lips moved in prayer, the words seemed to come of their own accord from the depths of her being. A cry for understanding of the ways of God, and a rebuke to him that he should let her suffer such a fate. She was fearful, and did not wish to show her fear on the morrow. It would not be fitting for a daughter of a chieftain. She was barely aware of the sudden muffled cry of her guard as he crumpled to the ground behind her.

She stood up at last, taking a long, steadying, breath. At the sound of footsteps, she turned, expecting to see her guard.

A strong hand covered her mouth, and she was swung off her feet by an arm clamping her waist so firmly that before she was able to kick out at her assailant, she was dragged backward into the cover of the trees.

CHAPTER FOUR

Sioned struggled, attempting to bite the hand covering her mouth.

'Keep still!' Cadfael ordered in a low terse voice, his temper, not easily roused, firing as he held Sioned's wriggling body. 'I do not intend you harm.'

Sioned stiffened, and surprise stunned her thinking.

'I will set you down and take my hand away if you give me your word not to call out. Nod your head if you agree.'

She nodded her head jerkily, aware of the heavy, quick pumping of her heart. Cadfael removed his hand and lowered her to the ground, not taking his arm from about her, but twisting her about to face him.

'You! How dare you handle me in such a manner,' she whispered furiously, gazing up into Cadfael's sombre expression.

'I beg your pardon, but there was no other way. I did not think they would let me come into the keep and talk to you—or that you would come without making a tirade.' His hazel eyes gleamed apologetically.

'Of course! But why do you want me to come with you at all?' Sioned attempted to remove his arm from her waist, but the muscles tautened, resisting all her attempts to free herself. 'Will you release me, Sir Cadfael, at once!' she panted.

'Keep your voice down,' he murmured, 'or I will quieten you myself, and I know only one way of effectually doing that to a woman.'

Sioned stilled and blinked up at him. 'Why should I? I have but to scream, and I will most likely bring half of Govan's men about your ears,' she lied. Only the guard would hear her from here.

'And I could slit your throat, or ...' Cadfael lifted her off her feet, forcing her chin up with his own. Slowly he brushed her lips in a tantalising caress before his mouth covered hers in a kiss that was complete in its thoroughness and that silenced her utterly. He let her slide through his hands until her feet touched earth again. 'The choice is yours, lady Sioned.' He smiled.

'Then it is no choice,' she retorted, breathlessly angry, not only with Cadfael, but with herself for being stirred by his kiss. 'I have heard how men like you take what you want without asking or paying!'

'Have you, indeed?' His smile vanished. 'Then be warned, and do not gainsay me,' he told her, holding her firmly again.

Sioned bit back several insults. 'What do you want? I can tell you nothing of Govan's plans.'

'I know all I wish to know of Govan. It is you I am interested in.'

'Me?' Sioned's throat tightened. 'There is nothing I can tell you about any matter that would further your king's plans.'

'It is for my own cause I would speak with you,' he said, releasing her. 'There is no need for you to look so outraged. I am not what you think! I do not need to force a maid if I want one.'

Sioned flushed and, hunching a shoulder, turned from him slightly. 'What is it that you want from me, then? If it is not to act the spy or ... aught else.'

'I perceive you are a devout maid, Sioned, and perhaps given to Christian charity. I pray you will not be averse to performing such an act for a woman of your own race.'

'What do you mean?' Sioned's dark brows puckered. His words surprised her. 'Your act of snatching me away from my devotions is hardly a Christian way of asking me to do a favour!'

'You had finished your devotions.' Cadfael came closer to Sioned. 'I have been watching the shrine for some time, hoping you would come—but we will talk on the way. I have hidden my pack in the hollow of an oak some half a mile on.' He took her by the arm.

'By the saint! What is this about?' Her eyes widened, and she tried to shrug off his hand. 'On what way? Where are you taking me?'

'To Gwynedd, of course. I wish you to act as my guide,' said Cadfael in an easy manner. 'You know the road, I think, and the trackless ways of your mountains?'

'Gwynedd!' Sioned's heart leapt into her throat and she dug her heels into the covering of dead leaves, folding her arms across the bodice of her blue gown. 'Explain yourself! I will go no further until you do.' She looked up at him, her heart beating jerkily. He must be crazed to think she would go so calmly with him. And what did he mean about a woman of her own race? But to go to Gwynedd!

'I told you,' he replied in a low voice. 'I will explain. If you are concerned for your safety, I assure you I have no designs on your person. I give my word that if all goes well I will bring you back safely to this place.' He urged her forward again.

'You must have lost your wits,' she whispered, giving a reluctant laugh. She could not believe that this was really happening. 'Why should I believe you?'

'I assure you that you are safe with me.'

He pressed her arm. 'It is your craft in the mountains that interests me.'

'But I was to be wed in the morning,' she cried, her relief almost choking her, even as he jerked her on again.

'Wed?' Cadfael came to an abrupt halt, staring down at her with an arrested expression on his angular countenance. 'That is sudden, is it not? I heard no mention of it last evening.'

'My brother and Govan arranged it to be so.' Sioned's voice was strained as she sought to conceal her bitterness and apprehension from him. 'Govan is prepared to pay my amobr for me.'

There was a sudden silence but for a bird chattering in a hornbeam near by, and the wind rustling in the branches overhead.

'Amobr? Your bride price! Is that not a fine a woman has to pay her protector for her virginity? We deal with such matters differently in England. Have you no money of your own?'

'I have no money.' Loyalty forbid her to lay the blame on Hywel, and she gazed down at the gemstone in the ring on the middle finger of her right hand and twisted it nervously. It was the only jewellery she possessed, and it had belonged to her mother. 'Govan is extremely wealthy, according to my brother,' she added after a long silence.

'Is he, indeed?' Cadfael's voice was dry. 'So you are selling yourself to the highest bidder!' He rubbed the curve of his chin. 'If he wants you badly enough, he will be prepared to wait for you, then.'

Sioned's bronze head shot up. 'You still intend to force me to go with you?'

Cadfael nodded. 'Of course. My need is great, lady, or else I would not take the risk.' His mouth curved into a grim smile. 'You need not fear that I will not return you to your future husband. I give my word I will. You will not have to explain anything. I will ransom you, and Govan will think that you have been my prisoner all the days we are away.'

Sioned stared up into his stern face. 'You think that is the right thing to do?' She laughed hysterically, wrenching herself out of his slackened grasp, but she had barely moved away from him when he grabbed her shoulder.

'Hush!' He shook her slightly. 'You are coming with me whether you like it or no.' He paused, then shrugged, giving a wry grimace. 'Besides, it is foretold that you will come with me, so accept that you have no choice.'

'Foretold?' Sioned felt suddenly bemused. It had bee a wearisome, frightening, day, and now this enemy wished her to go with him on the eve of her wedding to Govan ... to the mountains. Her mountains! The realisation of what that meant blossomed in her mind's eye. To see Yr Wyddfa again—its head drifted with cloud—to breathe mountain air. Perhaps to escape this man and see Dafydd again, as she had planned.

'My mother sees visions—she dreams dreams.' Cadfael's voice was gently affectionate, and sad. 'She is dying, and desires to see my half-brother Rhys before she goes. We have not had word from him for many a long year, and the last we heard, he had gone back to Snowdonia.'

'Your half-brother?' Sioned was interested, despite her reluctance to show it. 'And this woman you mentioned earlier—she is your mother and has the sight?'

'Ay.' His fingers tightened on her shoulder, aware of the change in her; she had a very expressive face. 'You will come willingly? It would not be pleasant having to force you each step.' His voice was eager, persuasive even.

'You could not force or watch me all the time,' she murmured, excitement stirring within her.

'No. But I could use questionable persuasion.' His voice was determined.

She was about to protest at his words, but she remembered the strength in his arms and how he had kissed her, and she knew that words would be wasted. Besides, did she not want to go to Gwynedd—and would it not be best to have an escort—a male escort, whom she was certain would give her his protection if needed?

'I will go with you,' she said at last, wrenching her shoulder from beneath his slackened grasp.

'It is best we go quickly. Night will not fall for some hours yet, and we could cover several miles by then. If there be a moon tonight, we could go further.' Cadfael's hand slid down her arm and grasped her hand, and he began to hurry her on through the trees. He had talked with her too long, and it must have only been providence that had kept listening ears and prying eyes from this part of the forest.

The girl was pulled forward at speed, but she did not speak. Now that she had a chance to study him, she realised that Cadfael was dressed like a peasant. Clad simply, he wore a brown homespun tunic, and a coif cap of the same colour covered his curling hair. He would have passed without notice but for his height. That would always set him apart. She wondered what explanation he would give if they were stopped by raiders or an invader. And herself? How would he explain her presence with him? Sister? Sweetheart?

Wife? The thought caused a quiver to race through her. She was mad to go with him, for all his words of reassurance. Had he not kissed her twice?

They came to a halt on the hilltop. Far below them lay the camp of Edward of England, hidden by the trees. Sioned's eyes scanned the estuary as Cadfael bent and tugged a pack from a hollow in a tree. He swung it up to his shoulder before coming over to her. For a moment he stood, his arm warm against hers, looking down at the ships on the Dee. Then he pressed her arm and urged her westwards.

Sioned went with him in silence. Her mood of excitement had been replaced by a sense of unreality brought on by the sight of the English ships on the river. How did she know that this knight had told her the truth? All that talk about her going with him being foretold—was more likely a lot of nonsense, and he must think her a gullible maid to believe it! It could be that he was the spy he had said he was, and that his aim was to discover what Llewelyn was up to. Yet it was true that some people did seem to have powers beyond the understanding of men and women. Besides, what did it matter? She could lose him in the mountains and go to Dafydd.

After some time they came to a vale.

They would need to cross the river, and she knew of a ford, but so far Cadfael had not asked for her guidance—would he, once they were on the other side of the vale? It would be then that he would be in her hands.

'Which way will you take once we are across the river?' His voice made her jump, although she had expected the question.

'Over the drovers' road,' Sioned replied absently, praying she could find it.

'I thought you might. I have heard that they are frequented, despite the dispute between our countries.' Cadfael's pack bumped on his back as he swept aside a tangle of overgrown ferns with an ash staff. 'Ned is not averse to buying Welsh wool from the monastery at Aberconwy. Although he does not have a licence to export it to Flanders, he can find a market.'

'Ned?' Her voice barely showed interest, as her eyes scanned the countryside for a landmark.

'Ned is a merchant who is married to my elder sister Matilda. They live in Chester, and my mother is in their care.'

'I see.' Sioned gave Cadfael a glance. 'You live in Chester, too? I have heard that it is a great city.'

'It is, but I live in the Wirral, overlooking the Dee. My sister keeps house for me.'

'You are not wed, then?' She had not meant to ask!

'No.' There was a sudden stiffness in his voice. 'I was once, but she died.' He broke off, and she did not like to interrupt a silence that seemed suddenly tangible.

They walked on for some time without speaking. The river shone before them in an unexpected shaft of dying light. Then the sun went behind clouds, and by the time they reached the ford, it was gone. Once they had crossed the river, Sioned took the lead. White deadnettle in flower brushed her skirts and specks of pollen clung where the fabric had been dampened in the river. They had almost reached the lower slopes that lay ahead when she heard the sound of men's voices, and she paused and looked towards Cadfael. Their eyes met, and swiftly he paced the few feet separating them, his face sharply alert as he gazed ahead.

About a dozen men burst from the trees, and they were clad like the raiders who had taken the camp by surprise the day before. They quickly surrounded Cadfael and Sioned.

'And who might you be?' demanded one of them in a deep musical voice, prodding Cadfael in the midriff with the butt of his spear. 'Whence have you come and where do you go? These are hazardous times for travellers.'

'It is really none of your affair, man,' retorted Cadfael, his eyes bright as he swept aside the spear with his staff. 'Yet I will tell you, for I can see that you must be about Llewelyn's business, and I would not hinder you.'

There was a babble of sound, but by merely raising his hand the man silenced his companions. 'It would be wiser, my good fellow, if you were to tell us! If your words please me, I will let you and the maid ...' He bowed slightly in Sioned's direction. She met his dark, bold eyes coolly, having often come across his sort in her brother's hall.

'My sister,' said Cadfael promptly, standing erect, his hand gripping his staff more tightly. 'I am a messenger sent from the abbot of the monastery at Aberconwy to discuss terms with a merchant of Chester concerning wool. We are on our way back to the monastery now. Somewhere, man, I have papers.'

Cadfael patted his tunic, feeling the pouch which hung from his girdle. He looked suddenly worried. Then his face brightened, and he reached for the pack on his back. 'Somewhere I have them, if you would but wait a moment.'

'Your name, man. Your name! Leave

the papers,' rumbled the leader, his black brows meeting above the short hump of his nose, and forming a thick V.

'Cadfael ap Glyder,' replied Cadfael, hastily ceasing his search for the non-existent papers. 'And my sister Sioned.'

Sioned stared at him, wondering if now was the time to denounce him to these men, but she did not recognise any of them, and was uncertain whether she would be any safer in their hands.

'Sister?' The leader winked at Sioned. 'She is not like you!'

'She is my half-sister. We share the same sire.'

'Not wed?' The leader walked slowly round Sioned, taking in the trim waist and well-formed bosom. Her hand itched to slap his face.

'She is spoken for, thank God,' said Cadfael fervently. 'A shrew like her mother, man. You have no idea of the sharpness of her tongue!'

'Comely wench, still.' The leader stopped in front of Sioned and planted a kiss full on her mouth. She stepped back, annoyed, and Cadfael's arm went about her shoulders.

'Would you take advantage of two travellers, man?' Cadfael's voice was angry and affronted.

'Don't get bold with me!' The leader

scrubbed at his black beard, his eyes narrowing. 'Have you seen aught of the English? We have heard there is an army ahead led by Edward himself.'

Sioned's eyes went swiftly to Cadfael's face, but she could not tell from his expression how he felt about the question.

'Maybe.' Cadfael nodded his head slowly. 'You would let us pass for the information?'

The man's eyes darkened, and the other men gathered closer about the two travellers hemming them in. 'I will drag out your entrails if you don't give us the information!'

'Then I will give it to you. I have a fondness for my stomach.' Cadfael smiled suddenly. 'A great mass of men there are, camped not far from Basinwerk. We did not venture too near in case we were spotted. We have heard that they have men combing the woods near at hand with a new longbow that is deadlier and swifter than the crossbow or spear.'

There was a buzz from the men gathered about them. Their leader nodded thoughtfully, his thick brows drawing together.

'I do not doubt your words, but ...' He slit the ties that held Cadfael's coif cap with his spear. Sioned's heart jumped into her throat.

'But what?' Cadfael stared back arrogantly. 'It would be best if you saved your weapons to spend on the English and not two poor Welsh folk, man!'

The leader gazed back at Cadfael, meeting his defiant stare, and he laughed suddenly. 'I like you!' He lowered his spear and slapped Cadfael on the shoulder. 'You must spend the night with us.'

He cast a glance towards Sioned, then met Cadfael's gaze again. 'Tell us—what did you see of the English pigs? It is said that Llewelyn's brother might be with Edward. What say you? I deem that you are not a peasant—perhaps you are a spy for Llewelyn and are on your way back to Aber?'

'Perhaps.' Cadfael's face eased into a grin. 'Maybe we can learn from each other.' He turned to Sioned. 'What say you, sister? Shall we spend the night with these brothers?' There was the merest flicker deep in his eyes.

Did he really expect her not to give him away? thought Sioned. She hesitated, having little liking for his suggestion, but she could see, as he had done, that they had little choice. She felt uneasy whenever the bold eyes of the chieftain rested on her.

'We might as well,' she agreed at last. 'The night is almost upon us, and I have no desire to break my neck just because you are in a hurry, brother.' Only by the slightest freeing of his breath did she guess that her words satisfied Cadfael.

They were escorted up the hill and into the trees, along the path beaten smooth by the hooves of animals and the tread of men without number. The drovers' path! Sioned gave a sigh of relief, despite her weary trepidation. Cadfael's arms still lay across her shoulders, and she found herself having to lean on him as they stumbled on through the darkness. The trees thinned out, and before them lay fields where cattle still showed as dark humps. Ahead, the outline of a house could barely be seen, set as it was into an outcrop of grey rock on the hill.

'We will spend the night there,' grunted the leader, 'now that we know how far ahead the enemy lies.'

Cadfael nodded. He would have preferred a camp in the open, but he would just have to see how matters lay before making his move to escape. He hoped that Sioned would not change her mind and betray him to them once they were inside.

CHAPTER FIVE

Leading up to the house were a great many steps, roughly hewn and set into place awkwardly. Cadfael took Sioned's hand, ignoring her protestations, and pulled her up so that they kept up with the leader. They stood at last in front of a massive oak door.

The leader took his spear and banged hard on the wood, letting out a great bellow as he did so.

'My cousins might have gone to bed, Llwyd,' muttered one of the men, shifting from one foot to the other.

'Then we will just have to waken them,' growled the leader, continuing to thunder at the door.

The darkness seemed to wrap about them as they stood waiting on the steps, some of the men muttering that they would just as soon sleep out in the open. They had their plaids. Llwyd hushed them as there came the sound of footsteps and the murmur of voices.

'Who ... Who is there?' called a trembling voice.

Sioned's eyes went quickly to Cadfael's

face, and he smiled down at her. She was suddenly aware of the warmth of his hand and hastily pulled her fingers from his, as one of the men called out his own name.

They heard a loud squeak and the sound of bolts being drawn back hastily. The door swung open, and in the doorway crowded several women. One carried a heavy stick, another a long spear. The other two women bore knives.

'Gruffydd!' The one carrying the spear dropped it and flung her arms about her kinsman.

'Desist, woman!' The young warrior's voice was husky as he held off his cousin, who was small and pretty with slanting dark eyes. 'I ask shelter for my chieftain and brother warriors.'

The girl's eyes widened as she took in the crowd of men on the step. She reached for her spear hastily, but Gruffydd was before her.

'He is my chief, Agnes,' he muttered. 'Tell your sisters to let us in.'

'All of you?'

'Agnes, do as your future husband tells you,' grunted the chieftain. 'We are hungry, and would have shelter.' He pushed her aside, putting her within Gruffydd's arm. Then he felt one of the women's knife-points before twisting it swiftly out of her hand. When he laughed and chucked her under the chin, she looked at him with cold eyes, turning abruptly and going on ahead of the men through a long, unlit room.

Sioned was prodded in the back by one of the men, and she moved forward slowly, sniffing as she went, realising that there were animals in the room: a cow certainly, and several fowls. She stumbled as she came to the stone steps that led up to the living quarters of the women who lived there.

In the centre of the large hall stood a brazier, a fire barely smouldering. It gave little warmth in a room that struck chill. A rush light cast a soft yellow glow over a trestle table and two benches. Against opposite walls of bare rock stood two enormous wooden-framed beds, their brightly-coloured covers flung back showing signs of the haste in which the women had left them.

Sioned sank down on to a bench wearily, while Cadfael sat astride it, so that his body formed a bulwark against the other men. The women hastily set about bringing food: cold beef, oatcakes, barley bread, and several jugs of ale.

'Your hospitality is good, Agnes,' called the chieftain, ramming a slice of beef into his mouth and chewing it noisily. 'I thank you and your sisters for it.' He reached into a pouch at his belt, and flung several coins on the table. 'Do not say that we came empty-handed and took all you had!'

The sister from whom he had taken the knife darted forward, sweeping the money from the table and into her skirts, almost as if she feared he would take it back again. Sioned, watching her, caught her eye, and she smiled. The girl smiled back shyly and came over to her.

'Do you wish for aught else to eat, lady?'

'I thank you, but I have had my fill. I am Sioned. What is your name?'

'Nest.' She bobbed slightly, almost curtsying as Cadfael's eyes fell upon her.

'You have a famous namesake, and I doubt she was any prettier than you, Nest.' Cadfael smiled, and the girl blushed, giving a tiny giggle.

'I would not wish to be carried off in such a manner, sir.'

'No? Then you must try and not be so beautiful,' he responded promptly, taking the girl's hand and kissing it.

Sioned stared at him, suddenly irritated. What was he thinking of, flirting with the girl? He should be trying to devise a way out of this situation. She sighed in exasperation as Cadfael continued to talk to Nest, unaware that the chieftain's eyes were on her.

By the time the meal came to an end,

Sioned's eyelids were heavy, and she was having a hard task to keep them open. The men had asked Cadfael several probing questions, which he had answered with not unsurprising ease and knowledge, but which in no way revealed Edward's real plans concerning Llewelyn's downfall.

Several men now left the table and curled up on the floor, their plaids round them. Gruffydd had gone with Agnes to one of the beds and now lay on it with her, his arms fast about her, as he kissed her passionately.

Sioned looked away, wondering where she was to sleep. A couple of the men had made advances to the sisters, but had promptly had their faces slapped. They had accepted their rebuke in good part.

'You must come with me, Sioned,' whispered Nest, coming to blow out the light. Sioned nodded thankfully, and rose hastily.

'Goodnight, Cadfael. I will see you in the morning.'

'I pray so, sister,' he murmured, staring at her out of narrowed, drowsy eyes. 'Sleep well—but lightly.' Sioned thought she had mistaken the words, they were so low.

The lamp went out, leaving them in complete darkness. Sioned jumped as a hand fastened on her arm, but it was only Nest. The girl took her hand and led her over to the bed she was to share with the other sisters. Sioned did not undress, but only took off her shoes before climbing, fully clothed, into the large bed. She lay on her back, staring up into the darkness of the room, glad to be on the outside. It was sticky and uncomfortably hot beneath the covers.

How was it possible that she should be lying in this place instead of the bedchamber that Annest had allotted her? Would Hywel and Govan be searching for her now? What would they be thinking had happened to her? She smiled slightly. It would perhaps do her brother some good to worry about her! She thought of her mountain home, and smiled as she dozed.

There came a movement beside her and a sudden sharp wrench at the covers. Sioned was instantly awake, thinking that perhaps it was Cadfael come to say they would try to escape. She could hear the heavy slumbering of the men. She pushed back the blanket and whispered Cadfael's name. Instantly she was rammed back against the edge of the wooden frame of the bed as the heavy weight of a man crushed her beneath him. Shock caused sweat to prickle all over her, and for a moment, her limbs were paralysed. A wet mouth came down over hers, and a beard scratched her face.

Sioned lashed out, digging her nails into the man's face. He let out a growl, and banged her head against the wooden frame. She moaned as the darkness seemed to spin round. There came the sound of a bitten-off oath, and the next moment she felt the monstrous weight lift as he was pulled from her. For a brief second she simply lay there, the pain in her head was so great. Then feet moved, and she heard the sleepy mutterings of the sisters, and curses as the men began to wake. She eased herself up in the bed, trying to peer through the darkness.

'Who is it?' whispered Nest against Sioned's ear.

'Cadfael and the chieftain, I think,' she gasped, sliding from the bed.

'Why do they fight?'

'It was the chieftain. He tried to ...' Sioned's voice trailed off as there came a sudden crash as one of the benches went over. A man yelped as his fingers were trodden on.

'Your brother cannot win,' said Nest in a low voice, standing next to Sioned, 'even if he kills the chieftain. His men will kill your brother for so doing and punish you as well. You must get away.'

'How?' Sioned reached out a hand to where Nest's voice was moving away. Her fingers fastened on fabric. 'Nest!' she whispered desperately.

'I am here.' Nest's fingers held hers tightly now. 'Come, Sioned, before the men are fully awake and call for a light.'

'But what about Cadfael?' She gasped, almost losing her footing as they skirted Cadfael and the chieftain who were heaving and panting in their attempt to gain the upper hand.

'Your brother will have to just take his chances,' sighed Nest.

Sweat trickled down Cadfael's cheek, mingling with the blood that the point of the unseen blade had drawn. He only wanted the fight over with now. It seemed incredible to be struggling in the dark for his life in defence of the honour of a wench he barely knew! Yet he had got her into this pass. He dragged the chieftain round, and unexpectedly he saw two figures as the darkness began to lift. Then there was the stench of animals in his nose. In that instant, he realised that they were women. Desperately he twisted his opponent round again and hooking his foot about his ankle, he pulled hard.

The Welshman went over, almost taking Cadfael with him. Just in time Cadfael freed his foot, stumbling backwards as he did so. He made for the direction of the smell and flung himself through the open doorway. He dragged the door shut and stood up, only to stumble headlong down the three steps that led to the lower room. Regaining his balance, he slithered to a halt in a swirl of straw. A hen clucked sleepily, then another, and another.

'Do you have to make so much noise?' hissed Sioned. 'They will know where we are, now!'

'Perhaps,' muttered Cadfael, breathing heavily. 'But it will not be because of any words I spoke—that door is as thick as a whole tree-trunk. But let us not argue now. We must get out of here.'

'Ay, you must!' Nest's voice held a hint of laughter. 'Go quickly, I have not had so much fun for a long time.'

'Nest! I should have realised that Sioned could not have escaped on her own.' There was a smile in Cadfael's voice as he took the girl's outstretched hand. She had already unbolted the door, which stood ajar. Cadfael squeezed her fingers, and Sioned saw him lean forward and kiss the girl's cheek.

'Thank you, Nest. You deserve someone very rich, very handsome, and kind to come and carry you away.'

'I have someone in mind,' said Nest mischievously.

'I see.' Cadfael kissed her again.

'No! 'Tis not you, Cadfael! But you

remind me very much of him.' Nest laughed and turned to Sioned. 'Go with your brother now. Perhaps one day we will meet again.'

'I pray so.' Sioned hugged her, then turned towards Cadfael. He lifted a mobile brow. 'Let us go then, sister.'

'Let us.' Sioned's voice was cool.

Cadfael took her arm, and without further delay they ran down the steps into a darkness that was lighter than the room they had left behind. The sky was clouded, but a moon flitted fitfully now and then from behind the clouds.

It was not until she reached the bottom of the steps that Sioned realised that she had left her shoes behind. She would have to do without them, for it was impossible to go back.

'Which way now, Sioned? Forward or back? I have left my pack behind, which means we have no food or blankets.'

Sioned hesitated but a moment. What had she to go back to, this day? Her stomach twisted. 'To the mountains is west.'

'Let us go swiftly, then, before we are caught. Nest said that there were some caves further along near the drovers' road.'

Sioned felt strangely irritated by his mention of Nest. It seemed that he gave his kisses freely! 'I know of them,' she muttered, easing her shoulders. She reached up and touched the bump on her head, and let out a gasp.

'Are you all right? That swine did not hurt you too much?'

'A bump on my head. It could have been much worse if you had not come.' She did not look at him as they walked along at a brisk pace.

'I was aware of his interest.' Cadfael's voice was bland. 'But it was hard to keep an eye on him in that room, black as pitch.'

'It seems that the saints were on our side! How did you escape the chieftain? Did you kill him?'

'No!' Cadfael grimaced. 'But he nearly killed me.' He rubbed at the sticky blood on his face. 'At least we both escaped without too much difficulty.'

Sioned nodded, and after that they travelled on for some time without speaking, until light, pale as mist, grew in the sky. Birds twittered and swooped. Morning had come, and they were both hungry. They came to a small river and, lowering themselves on to the bank, drank deeply from their cupped hands.

'We could try catching some fish,' said Cadfael, washing the blood from his cheek.

'How?' Sioned stared across at him.

Cadfael smiled, and taking his coif cap from his tunic where he had placed it when the chieftain had slit all the ties, he unwound from its brim a length of line with a hook.

'You cut me a branch from that tree—a narrow, whippy one. I will see if I can dig some worms.' He handed her his knife. She looked up at him and then laughed. 'Let us pray that our luck is in!' For a brief moment their glances held, then Cadfael turned away.

It was restful on the river bank, and Sioned almost dozed off. Cadfael's sudden shout woke her just in time to catch the silvery-grey flash as he pulled in his line, and after that she stayed alert, finding as much pleasure as he in each fish caught. At last he called a halt when he pulled in his third. Soon he was striking flint into a heaped pile of wood-chips. Sparks flew and soon flames leapt, greedily consuming the wood. While the fish cooked, they sat on the bank with their feet in the water. Sioned gazed from beneath her lashes at Cadfael's sunburnt profile. She had enjoyed the last hour.

Cadfael lifted his eyes from his contemplation of the river and met her glance. 'You are hungry?' He smiled.

'Ay! But I can wait.' She hesitated, then spoke again. 'I was just wondering how a knight in Edward's army knew about lighting fires and cleaning fish. I thought you would have a man to do such tasks.'

'I have.' He drew his knees up to his chin and rested his arms across them. 'A knight has to know many things, especially when he follows his king—or prince should I say, as Edward was then—to the Holy Lands.'

Sioned's eyes gleamed with interest. 'Is that where you were kissed by the sun? I have heard that it is hot—hot as fire, some say.'

'Uncomfortably hot, I found it. Often under Syrian skies my mind turned to the cool green garths and leafy forests of my own land. But I had made a vow, and had to keep it.'

'I heard that the lord Edward almost died, after being struck down by a poisoned dagger of the enemy.'

Cadfael nodded. 'The lady Eleanor, his wife, helped to nurse him back to health.'

'She must be brave to have gone with her husband.'

'She is a noble, stately-looking lady, with long dark Spanish tresses. She only left her husband to go home to have their child.'

'Do many women go with their husbands on crusade?' Sioned pushed back her braids which were swinging forward, almost touching the water.

'Some. My wife chose not to.' He rose abruptly and without speaking went over to the fire.

Sioned uncurled and slowly went after him, sensing that his moment of revelation was over. They ate the perch slowly. It burnt their fingers, but they did not care, so crisp and delicious was it. When they had finished, Cadfael stamped out the smouldering embers of the fire, then wrapped the rest of the fish in some leaves before putting it into the bodice of his tunic.

Leaves hung motionless on tree and bush, and the weather had turned sultry. Clouds were piling up slowly, soiled yellow, slate-grey and black. Suddenly a flash lit the hills. There was a crack, and a moment later a growing rumble of thunder rolled angrily about the hills.

'Are those caves far?' called Cadfael, reaching out for Sioned's hand. 'It looks as if we are in for a soaking!'

'Not too far.' Sioned attempted to push away a tendril of damp hair which kept falling into her eyes. 'They are beyond the next hill.'

They scrambled swiftly over rocks and rough scrub, forcing their way through ferns and tangled wild roses. Outcrops of bare rock showed like bones through the covering of earth and thin coat of turf.

Trees clung precariously to the slope, roots humping up out of the ground. At last the dark opening of the cave came into view ahead. The grass in front was thin and beaten down with the passage of feet. Of any other living being there was no sign. Even the birds were silent and invisible. Clambering over a last huddle of rock, they came to the entrance and went in.

The cold struck chill, and Sioned shivered. 'I wish we had a fire.'

Cadfael frowned as his eyes scanned the rock walls. They were dry, except in one corner where the rock glistened damply. 'I will need to gather kindling and wood swiftly, then.' He kicked at the blackened remains of a fire near the mouth of the cave. 'We might be here for some time, and a blaze would cheer us.' He turned swiftly and was gone before she could say a word.

She dropped down upon a heap of rustling dried grass that someone had placed there, listening to the rumble of the thunder. Then, unexpectedly, she heard a murmur of sound in the cave. Her hands stilled in her lap and she strained to listen to the sound again. There was an uncanniness about the whisper. She moved forward slowly on hands and knees to where she thought the sound came from. She stiffened abruptly, and pressed her lips tightly on the scream that rose in her throat as she saw the snake.

Its lidless eyes seemed to bore into her, and its tongue kept flicking in and out as it watched her. Even as she kept her eyes on the reptile, her hand was frantically searching for a weapon. The thought that the snake might be as scared of her as she was of it did not occur to her. Her fingers fastened on a slab of flint. She did not pause to think, but swung her arm forward, the stone a heavy dragging weight as she smashed it down on the snake's head.

CHAPTER SIX

The snake seemed to twist and writhe for an age before at last it lay still. Sioned dropped the flint from nerveless fingers and covered her face with her hands. She did not hear the soft flapping of Cadfael's sandals, or see him until he stood immediately in front of her.

'Sioned!' Cadfael dropped the kindling on to the ground as he took in the bloodied remains of the snake. 'Did it bite you?' he demanded, kneeling down before her and pulling her hands gently from her face.

Sioned shook her head. Her face was pallid, but glistened with perspiration. He squeezed her hands and then, as she swayed, his arms went round her and he held her close.

'I hit it and hit it ... but it ... would not lie still,' she stammered.

'It is still now. You made a thorough end of it. I am glad that you do not run with the warriors, if that is how they taught you to defend yourself,' Cadfael teased.

Sioned shivered, but did not answer. She was aware of warmth dispelling the inner tremors that shook her. He rocked her gently to and fro, his cheek resting against her bronze hair. Her head lay against his chest and she could smell the warm maleness of him. As the tremors subsided, an unaccustomed lethargy seemed to hold her still in his embrace. She closed her eyes, and they stayed like that for a few moments until they became aware of the lashing rain outside and the crackle and rumble of the storm overhead.

She blinked and yawned, then lifted her head to look into Cadfael's face. There was a hard-to-read expression in his eyes, and she was conscious of the strength in the arms holding her and the warmth of the flesh beneath the fabric under her hands. His face was only inches away, and she felt as if she were teetering on the edge of a crag, waiting, waiting.

With an almost violent movement, he released her. 'I will light the fire,' he muttered, rising to his feet. He kicked the dead snake into a far corner of the cave with the side of his foot.

Sioned scrambled to her feet and went to look out of the mouth of the cave. She should not have come with him. He was a man, and an enemy. She felt resentful, unreasonably so, that he should have brought her comfort in such a manner. Yet, had she not come with him, at this moment it would have been

Govan's arms round her in a far from comforting way. She shivered again, staring unseeing out at the rain for a long time.

She rubbed her ears suddenly. She could hear singing. The words were in Latin and the song was low and monotonous, almost a chant, one might say. It *was* a chant!

She whirled, and met Cadfael's startled glance. He was snapping twigs and gathering them into a pile before he lit the fire. Daggers of flame darted up through the kindling. When the monk entered, they both had their hands held out to the fire.

He was garbed in white, and when he saw the flames he pushed back the rain-darkened cowl, and a smile of pure joy creased his plump weatherbeaten face.

'God grant you all your petitions if you will let me share your fire,' he said in a merry voice, coming forward slowly, leaning heavily on his staff.

'It is our pleasure.' Cadfael rose to his feet, unable to resist the friendly warmth in the monk's face, but wary.

'I am brother Thomas from Aberconwy, and I am on my way to the holy well of the blessed saint,' he said expansively, holding out his hands to the crackling fire. His habit began to steam gently.

'I go to drink the waters for the good of my stomach, although the physician says that it is too much food and not enough labour!' His eyes twinkled as he took a package from his scrip.

'Would you care to share my supper in exchange for the heat of your fire?' He held out a napkin, and even before he unfolded it, the smell of ripe sheep-cheese rose in Sioned's nostrils.

She and Cadfael took some cheese and a chunk of the barley bread he offered. The monk bowed his head and muttered a few words of prayer before they began to eat.

'You will find the English are not so far from the well, brother.' Cadfael reached into his tunic and brought out the remains of the fish. They were rather squashed, but edible.

'I doubt the English will be disturbed by one monk and his donkey,' said the brother peaceably. Then he put down his napkin. 'Dear God, I have forgotten about the poor creature! Would you mind her sharing our cave?' He did not wait for their answer, but scrambled to his feet and hurried outside, pulling his cowl over his head.

Cadfael exchanged a smile with Sioned, and the stiffness about her mouth eased as he offered her some of the fish. She took it with a murmur of thanks and began to eat hungrily.

There came a braying and a smothered expletive, and brother Thomas came back into the cave with his donkey. It took him some time to settle the beast, and by the time it was done to its satisfaction, the good brother had cause to resort to the contents of a flask he took from his habit.

Cadfael threw more wood on the fire as at last the brother dropped to the ground and carried on with his meal. Lightning flared outside and lit up all their faces. It was only late noon, but already it seemed as if night was about to fall. The monk began to talk again and to pass round his flask.

'Have you been at Aberconwy long?' Cadfael took the cup and the flask, and poured out some of the mead.

'Some thirty years or more,' replied brother Thomas, giving a loud burp. He looked slightly nonplussed.

'Have you ever met a man named Rhys ap Glyder, brother? It might have been recently or some time ago.' Cadfael handed the cup to Sioned. She took it and sipped cautiously. The liquid was sweet, tasting of honey, but good as only the monks made it.

'I have not.' The monk stared intently at Cadfael. 'But then there are many of the tribes I do not know, who live deep in the mountains.'

'Of course.' Cadfael frowned slightly,

chewing his bread and cheese absently. 'Your abbot ... Would he know?'

The monk shrugged. 'It is doubtful, but ...' He looked thoughtful.

'But ...?' prodded Cadfael, leaning forward towards the monk.

'There is a woman you might ask concerning him. She knows many people, and has lived in the mountains all her days.'

'Has she a name?' Cadfael threw some more wood on the fire.

The rain still dripped from tree and rock outside. Sioned stared at him. It seemed that his tale might be true, after all!

The brother began to speak again. 'Some say she is a witch, but I think she has done too many good deeds to be a mere tool of a devil. Megan is just old—only God knows how old. Yet she is clear in her mind and her memory is good.'

'Megan? Has she another name?' asked Cadfael eagerly.

'If she has, it has long been forgotten,' replied the monk.

'Does she live far from your monastery—which lies the other side of the inlet, where Deganwy stands, does it not?'

'Ay, that is true. It is a beautiful spot, and ships sail to Ireland and Ynys Mon across the straits,' agreed the monk.

'Now Ynys Mon!' He smiled rapturously.

'There is one of God's chosen places in this land. Anglesey is warmer than in the mountains and the corn grows well there, as Llewelyn knows to his benefit.'

Sioned felt Cadfael's elbow jolt against her knee and she shot him a glance, sensing his unease. Was it due to a realisation that he was going with her into the heart of Llewelyn's mountain stronghold?

'You have been to Anglesey, brother?' Sioned asked with interest. Owain had once proposed to take her there, but he had sailed on a ship bound for Ireland before she could take up his offer.

'Several times, daughter. Our order has a priory there.'

When she was about to ask another question, Cadfael spoke before her, anxious to get back to the subject of Megan, it seemed. She yawned. She knew a couple of Megans, but he had not thought to ask her, and if he chose to ignore her, she had no reason to speak. Besides, the monk would likely tell him where to seek. Her eyelids began to droop as the gentle rumbling flow of conversation carried on.

Sioned's head felt as if it floated, and several times she nodded off. But her feet were cold, and they kept her from falling asleep completely. Yet when Cadfael's arm slid about her shoulders as her body sagged against him, she offered no resistance—and she took no heed at all when he lay down to sleep and her head found a resting-place against his shoulder.

It was only when she woke the next morning, alone, that she suffered a strange sense of not being comfortable. She stumbled sleepily out of the cave. The rain had washed clean sky and rock. The sweet scent of flowers and grass rose like incense.

Cadfael turned towards her.

'Here she is, brother! Just in time to bid you farewell.'

'It must have been the mead,' Sioned excused herself.

'You were tired. I made you travel too far, too swiftly.' Cadfael took one of her hands and pulled it through his arm. Sioned made to pull it away, but he held it tightly.

The monk smiled upon them. 'I must be on my way and you on yours, Cadfael. I pray that God will bless your search. And you and your lady wife.' He mounted his donkey, blessed them, and lifted a hand in farewell before he was gone behind an outcrop of rock.

'Wife? I have change roles now?' She made to drag her hand away, but he released it without fuss.

'I thought it best to pretend that it

was so,' he responded in a lazy voice. 'Especially as you spent the night lying in my arms.'

'What?' Sioned felt warmth suffuse her face. His eyes gleamed gold.

'Nothing happened!' His smile mocked her. 'It was cold in the cave when the fire burnt low. Let us be on our way, woman. The quicker my search is accomplished, the swifter you will be rid of my presence.'

'That is true,' she retorted promptly, moving away from him. 'Did you find out where Megan lives?'

Cadfael grimaced and stroked his cheek. 'The monk had a bad habit of failing to make himself clear and sticking to the point.'

'Perhaps if you thought to ask me—I might be able to help you,' she murmured, smoothing down her crumpled skirts.

'You! You know of this Megan's whereabouts?' he demanded, his eyes narrowing as he gazed at her thoughtfully.

'I know of several women called Megan. I wonder how many you will have to visit before you find the right one.' There was a sparkle in her eyes. 'It could take some time, I imagine, and I could lose you in the mountains, perhaps.'

'So you could.' Cadfael eyed her measuringly. 'But what good would that do you? It could hardly further your own cause—or Llewelyn's.'

Sioned made no answer. She was not going to let him know her cause, as she saw it. There was no need to antagonise him, and his protection had proved useful when the tribesmen had captured them. Why had he fought for her? Was it solely because he needed her to guide him? They began to walk towards the outlying slopes of the mountain range.

'Have you not thought of being on Llewelyn's side?' she asked. 'There is much you could do to help him. Surely you know something of your king's plans?'

'You would have me become a traitor?' Cadfael spoke softly, though his eyes were suddenly hard and shining cold.

'You are part Welsh—do you not owe some loyalty to this land?' Sioned flushed, and her voice was heated.

'I was at Edward's crowning in the abbey at Westminster, where I paid him fealty. He is my lord and king. I do not come on this campaign only because of him though. I wish to rid my palatinate of harassment from raiders. My own father was killed in one such raid. I desire peace so that both our lands can prosper. Instead, it spends its young men in senseless fighting.' He aimed a swipe at a low branch with a stick he had found. 'And it will come ... Llewelyn will give in and pay homage to Edward.'

'Never!' Sioned exclaimed violently. She could not understand why his words disappointed her so much that they left a bitter taste in her mouth.

'You do not want peace?'

'Ay!' she cried, twisting the end of a braid round and round between her fingers. 'But why should a prince of Gwynedd bow to Edward of England? If Edward truly wished for friendship with Llewelyn, he should not have given the prince's brother shelter when he fled from Llewelyn.'

'If Llewelyn had not banished one brother and imprisoned another, this country would not be divided, perhaps,' said Cadfael, in an obviously patient voice.

'But they tried to kill Llewelyn years ago. He had no choice!' Sioned's voice was exasperated.

'Choice or no, only unity will serve Wales. It is rich in men who are as proud and stubborn as they are brave.'

She shook her head, even though she knew there was much truth in his words. Her throat was tight with a fierce emotion and she felt she could not bear any more. Turning from Cadfael, she picked up her skirts and ran headlong down the hill.

'Damn!' he muttered. 'That's what comes of trying to explain to a woman.' He broke into a run, hastening along the almost invisible path, which twisted round bushes and trees. When eventually he caught up with her, he saw the signs of tears on her face.

'I can see why you love this land.' Cadfael's voice was friendly. 'My own Wirral has few hills, but the air is soft and warm in the summer, and across the Dee we can see the hills of Wales on a clear day.'

'Can you?' Her voice was cool.

'Some days when it is misty, it is as if they floated in a dream—a far distant land, not quite real.'

Sioned noted his curved lips and straight nose, and she felt a sudden constriction in her throat.

'Sometimes ...' she began hesitantly, scuffing the dust with her bare toes. 'Sometimes Mon mam Cymru looks like that—as if it could float away on the sea.'

'Mon mam Cymru—Mother of Wales,' repeated Cadfael softly. 'That is another name for Anglesey. But what of your mountains? It is sad there is gold to be dug—and iron. Your people have much they could trade, besides wool and cattle, with England—substantial goods that would not float away.' He half smiled and she knew he was trying to coax her into a good mood. 'Now tell me of these Megans you spoke of, Sioned, if you would, please?'

She decided that there would be no harm in helping him to find Megan and his half-brother. 'I know of only two Megans who are old. One is always wandering the hills collecting herbs, talking to animals, helping sick folk. The other never moves from her son's hafod and is constantly falling asleep before your eyes.'

Cadfael grinned, sure in his own mind which one brother Thomas had meant.

'You know where the first one lives?'

'Ay, I visited her when Owain was sick unto death years ago, before he went away. She has a small hafod not far from a river on the side of a mountain.'

'Owain?' Cadfael realised that her voice had contained a hint of sadness.

'Owain went to sea. He always wanted to be a mariner, and I have not seen him since, and miss him still.' Sioned half turned from him for a moment. 'Megan cured him—she is crafty with herbs. If you wish me to take you to her, there will be climbing to do.'

Cadfael studied his bare toes protruding from his dusty sandals, and Sioned's naked feet. He pulled a face.

'There is also food to think on, and I am hungry now.'

'We shall just have to tighten our girdles!

Even if you have some money, Cadfael, it might not be wise to let others know of it. We might find some wild berries, and we could fish again. The streams and rivers coming down from the mountains abound with fish: trout, salmon and eels. The monks at Aberconwy have a great sea weir at Llandrillo yn Rhos, where salmon are caught.'

'I doubt we will sup of their salmon, but at least we shall not go thirsty!'

'No.' Sioned's eyes danced. 'That is one commodity Gwynedd is not short of—rain!'

'So I have heard.' Cadfael remembered the tales of bogs and marshes, sudden driving rain that blinded and caused men to be lost for ever in the mountains.

They travelled on, finding a few wild strawberries and raspberries, drinking from streams, and managed to catch a couple of trout in one small river, which they ate ravenously before going on. Cadfael noticed that the inclines were becoming steeper, the peaks higher, and that there were more times when both hands were needed to drag themselves up.

'We will not get there this night,' panted Sioned, flinging herself down amid a patch of brackets.

'No.' Cadfael frowned, looking down into a valley where smoke curled. Sheep grazed below, and black cattle could be seen as dots. 'We are fortunate that the weather has turned fine.' The clear sky was already tinged orange and pink in the west.

'It will not last,' muttered Sioned, gazing towards one of the peaks where cloud curled. 'Tomorrow it will rain, but if the good God is with us, we will have reached Megan's by then.'

'You have done more for me than I thought you might when first I asked ...'

'Asked?' Sioned laughed. 'Forced!' She watched him stretch himself out upon the ground.

'I have used little force since, woman,' he said lazily, his brow puckering slightly. 'You would throw my thanks back in my face.' His expression was serious as he reached out and took her hand. He brought her fingers up to his mouth and kissed them gently.

For a moment Sioned was strangely moved, and her hand lay in his warm grasp. Then she remembered why she had come with him and snatched it away, caught up in a strange panic.

CHAPTER SEVEN

Sioned sat up, clasping her arms about her knees and staring westwards to where the sun was setting behind a distant mountain. Soon it would be dark.

'We should try to find shelter.' Her voice was expressionless. 'It will be cold tonight.'

'Where do you suggest we go? The only shelter I can see is the hafod below, and did we not agree to stay away from those who might recognise you, but for Megan?'

She nodded. 'But you do not know how cold the mountainside can be.'

'So what do you suggest?' repeated Cadfael patiently. 'The byre, when it is dark?'

'Perhaps.' She shrugged her shoulders, shivering slightly.

'So be it.' Cadfael wondered if this would be the night she might betray him. 'Should we make a move now? I should imagine this slope will be dangerous when it gets darker.'

Sioned nodded and rose to her feet. Shadows deepened and spread, filling crevices and gullies with patches of gloom. She was glad of the cover, for there might be eyes scanning the slopes in the house below.

They stepped carefully. Cadfael's sandals slipped on the loose scree even as Sioned's bare toes sought a hold on the sharp stones. She winced as she stubbed her little toe, and he looked at her over his shoulder, holding out a hand. For a moment she hesitated, then she placed her hand into his strong one. They came down gingerly, setting loose a shower of small stones, Cadfael having to brace himself to slow their pace so that she would not cut her feet. Despite his efforts they finished their descent with a sudden rush, slithering into the hollow not far from the house with a speed that set them running hand in hand before slowing gradually. Sioned was laughing when he swung her to a halt.

Cadfael looked at her and grinned. 'Not the best way to come down a mountain!'

'It would not have done if there had been a hidden drop at the bottom, or a lake.' Her cheeks were rosy with exertion, and her eyes sparkled. For a moment they smiled at each other.

Cadfael dropped her hand and looked up at the sky, where evening was giving way to night. Clouds scurried across a star-flung sky.

'Do you know the folk who live here?'

'Slightly.' She could barely see his expression. 'The husband is no friend to my brother, but many men are away at this time. Either they are on a raid—or now it might be that they are with Llewelyn preparing your king's fate when he attempts to penetrate these mountains.' She shivered, rubbing her blue-clad arms, trying to infuse some warmth.

'Shall we go, then?' Cadfael started to move towards the outbuildings.

No light showed as they crossed a stretch of low ground. They came to a gritstone building that was rough beneath their hands as they worked their way towards the door. He felt for the latch and lifted it, ushering Sioned in before him.

It was warmer instantly—and dark, much darker without the starlight. His hand searched for hers in the dark, and gripped it tightly as there came the sudden restless movement of a beast to their left.

'Right, I think,' murmured Cadfael. 'I have no wish to be trodden on in the night!'

'A cow—and maybe a calf,' she responded. 'It might be best if we do not go too far from the door.'

'Hmmm.' Cadfael felt the ground with his foot, and heard a rustle. 'There is a mound of hay here. It is quite dry.' He pulled Sioned down with him, then let go her hand as he eased himself on to the mound with a relieved sigh. He intended only to rest and watch.

Sioned wormed her way deeper into the hay a foot or so from him. She began to feel warmer, and prayed that sleep would come swiftly, so that she would not be so conscious of her enemy so close to her. His presence disturbed all her thinking. Dafydd—she would concentrate on Dafydd and how he would look when she surprised him. Would he still be at Hywel's hafod, or would he have returned to his father's? She found it hard to picture his face. Cadfael shifted in the hay and instantly she was awake fully again, but he did not approach her. Slowly her eyelids began to droop as the exertions of the day took their toll. Soon she slept, while he watched.

Cadfael awoke with a start, forcing his eyes open. What had woken him? Hair tickled his chin, and he could feel Sioned's soft warmth nestling into the curve of his arm. She stirred, but she was so comfortable that she lay still for a while in that hazy boundary between sleeping and waking. Then she was suddenly aware that the heart she could hear beating in her ear was not her own, and that her hand curled on Cadfael's chest. She lifted her head swiftly and looked straight into his face. There was a warm golden sparkle in the hazel eyes that caused her pulses to jump in a nervous excitement. She made to move away, but his arms tightened about her, drawing her close to him again.

'Why move yet, Sioned, when this is so comfortable?' he said softly against her cheek.

'Some—someone might come. Dawn is not far off.' She tried to force her suddenly trembling limbs to strengthen. His breath was warm on her cheek ... her nose ... her mouth.

It was a long kiss. His lips moved over her shivering mouth with a persuasion that she could not resist when that kiss ended and another was shared. Then another, before his lips lifted from hers and began to caress her chin, her throat, the hollow between her breasts.

'You must not!' she cried involuntarily as he sought to ease the neck of her gown lower. The hay whispered as she attempted to move away from him.

'Must not?' Cadfael murmured, forcing her close to him again. 'If I cannot eat, I would just as soon spend the time in such a pleasurable way!'

Sioned made to speak again, but he silenced her with an exploratory, probing kiss. She was suddenly frightened—frightened so much that she wondered if she would be able to stop him from possessing her utterly if he attempted such an act. The remembrance of all she had been told of the Norman and English raiders was instantly sharp and cutting in her mind. She reached for the knife she remembered seeing in Cadfael's girdle. With an unsteady hand she pressed the blade against his side, and he stirred uneasily, lifting his head.

'Release me!' Sioned's voice was taut.

'Release you?' He half smiled, and kissed her again.

She dug the knife harder into his side.

'God's blood!' Cadfael drew back abruptly. 'What the ...'

'I am not yours for the taking, Edward's man! Now let me go, or I will thrust this knife into you,' she said in a determined voice.

'You wouldn't!' She heard the slightest hint of amusement as he leaned up on one elbow, causing her hand to be jammed against his side.

Sioned gasped as he squeezed the hand holding the knife. 'You are hurting me,' she hissed, through clenched teeth.

'Did you not intend hurting me?' he mocked.

'Only if you took no heed of me! You gave me your word that I would be returned safely ... to ... to ...'

'Govan?' A derisive smile twisted his

mouth and the hazel eyes were suddenly cool. 'The rich suitor who is to pay your bride price?'

'I should not have come with you!' Sioned sought to wrench her hand from its imprisonment.

'But you did—and I am grateful for that. Drop the knife, and I will let you go. Just for a while I did not think you so unwilling.'

'You gave me little choice.' Her cheeks flushed, and she glanced away from him, letting the knife slip from her fingers. The pressure on her arm and hand eased as he released her, but the next moment he put a hand over her mouth. She struggled, and her eyelids flew wide above his hand.

'Hush! Someone is coming.' Cadfael slid with her from the hay, taking her with him behind the door. Just in time, as the door was pushed wide, letting in the pale light of early morning.

Cadfael held a finger to his lips and pulled her back against his chest as the door nearly hit them. A girl came through, humming softly to herself. She could not have been more than twelve years old, having the soft bloom of youth in her sharp, curiously spiky, thin-cheeked face. They watched as she padded over to the cow, speaking gently in sing-song Welsh. The cow turned and looked at her with placid eyes. She stroked its flank, and then turned and looked down at the calf.

Cadfael eased himself slowly round the door, taking Sioned with him. They were through and out into the open air before the girl turned round. She gave a cry, but already they were running across the clearing and into the hollow where they had hidden the night before.

Sioned drew in a great breath, and for a moment they stood there hand in hand until their breathing steadied. It was cold and grey, and several of the peaks were wreathed in thick blankets of cloud. Then she slid her hand from Cadfael's and stepped away from him. They stared at one another appraisingly.

'Well?' he said softly. 'Where do we go from here?' He began to brush stalks of grass and flecks of chaff from his arms and tunic, while all the time his eyes were on her face.

'It will be best if we move swiftly. We will be warmer, and there is no sense in delaying.' She plucked a stalk from her hair, glancing over to the bracken and grass on the slopes that were beaded with moisture. Already her gown was wet at the hem.

'But where?' Cadfael repeated quietly. 'You could lose me in these mountains, as you said. If that is your intent, best we part now.'

'Part? And where would you go to seek Megan, Edward's man?' she taunted, feeling her power now that she was out in the open in her mountains again.

'I have a tongue in my head—a blade—and some money,' he answered. 'I grant that it would take me longer without you, Sioned.'

Sioned turned her head and looked at him. She could leave him now and go to seek out Dafydd. He seemed willing to let her go. Yet now she could go, something perversely held her back. She could still take him to Megan's and go on to seek Dafydd afterwards. There was his mother to think of, she told herself.

'You would need to trust me if I lead you—and how will you know if I will not still lead you astray?' she asked in a derisive voice.

'I will take your word on it—if you give it.' His glance held hers steadily.

She gave a low laugh, flushing slightly under his eyes. 'So be it. I will take you to Megan, Sir Cadfael Poole. But after that ...?' She shrugged her shoulders, leaving their future together in question.

Cadfael nodded. 'You lead and I will follow, but if you betray me I will come after you, never fear.' He grasped her arm and brought her close to him. 'Do not forget that it was foretold that you would help me in my search, Sioned. Even—believe it or not—that you would save my life,' he added mockingly.

Sioned looked up at him, her expression half angry, half puzzled. Then she wrenched her arm from his grasp.

'This way; and let us pray that the rain does not come too soon.'

They travelled a steady pace all morning, and grew hungry, but were not so cold, once they were on the move. The sun hid beyond the grey roof of cloud which stretched as far as the eye could see. High above a valley, they paused for a while to rest.

'It is not much further,' murmured Sioned, watching Cadfael cast a stone from his sandal. 'And you can be certain that Megan will make us welcome. Her hospitality may be sparse, but she will share it with us.'

'Even a bowl of pottage would be welcome! You look tired—and your feet are bleeding,' he said in an exasperated voice.

'It is of no matter,' muttered Sioned, trying to hide her toes beneath the hem of her skirts. 'You have blood on your toes.'

'I did not think. I forgot you had no shoes.'

She was surprised at the concern in his voice, and not wanting it. 'Do not worry yourself, Sir Cadfael. Megan will give me some salve. Let us go on.' She uncurled abruptly.

'Be that as it may, have my stick to lean on.' He pressed his stick into her hand before she could gainsay him, folding her fingers about the wood.

She wanted to refuse it, but it seemed churlish, and already he had turned away, looking down the slope towards the river, which was just a thin grey ribbon flashing white now and then, far below. Sioned felt irritated by his actions. But soon—soon they would be parting, and his actions would be no concern of hers any longer.

As they began to move down the hillside, Cadfael suddenly felt a tingle at the back of his neck, and realised that he had been hearing the soft pad of feet behind them for some time, but had not heeded it. He did not turn round, but only glanced about him. There was little cover on the slope, and what there was consisted of heather, bramble and gorse bushes. He carried on walking, listening hard. It might only be children from a small cot they had passed earlier. Children with nothing else to do but play games of tracking strangers.

'We are nearly there.' Sioned glanced at him. 'Are you going to tell Megan the truth?' She frowned, realising instantly that he had not heard her. 'What is it?' Instinctively she drew closer to him.

'We are being followed.' His voice was barely audible. 'It might only be children, but I think not. When we reach that clump of brambles ahead—the ones where the hill seems to come to an end before dipping again—I want you to walk on alone.'

'But what ...' she began, forcing herself not to look round.

'Do not argue with me! Just do as I bid, and go on to Megan's with all speed.' He took the knife from his girdle and slid it into the palm of his hand.

Sioned frowned but nodded, keeping her thoughts to herself. It was not far to the place he had indicated, and now she was aware of their presence, she too caught the sound of the stealthy footsteps.

'Go now!' Cadfael pushed her, as the hill dipped. Briefly, they were hidden from whoever followed them, and he melted into the cover of a bramble bush while she passed on. He watched her for a moment before turning to confront whoever followed.

There came a slither of quickening footsteps, and with a hasty breath he stepped out from the cover of the bramble. The taller of the men facing him thrust his friend back and growled as he swung a blow at Cadfael's head with his staff. Cadfael sidestepped and kicked the man's feet from beneath him, so that he toppled and rolled over the top of the hill. Cadfael wasted no time in seeing where he landed, but spun swiftly to meet the other man's attack. The spear descended as he flung up his left arm to guard his chest, and the shaft caught him a cracking blow on his lower arm. He gave a hiss of agony, and his arm dropped uselessly to his side. Giving the man no time to bring back his spear arm, he flung himself on to his assailant. When his knife went into the man's shoulder, he let out a groan and stumbled into the heather, his spear dropping from nerveless fingers.

Cadfael swayed and took a steadying breath, his arm dangling at his side. He pressed his lips tightly together and bent to wipe his blade on the grass. Unexpectedly there came a crushing blow to the side of his head and his knees gave and he sank into the heather.

Sioned had only gone a short way down the hill before she turned back, to see the man bend over Cadfael. He snapped off the pouch hanging from Cadfael's girdle, opened it and flung it aside. Then he reached for the knife Cadfael had dropped, and stared down at him. She began to run as she saw the blade flash down towards

Cadfael's throat. She hit back a scream, then saw the man held a leather pouch in his hand on a thong. She leapt the last few feet, just as the man brought down his knife again. Swinging Cadfael's staff, she caught him a whack across the shoulders, and he spat out a curse as he fell forward on to Cadfael, the knife still in his hand.

Sioned gave him no time to recover. She hit him again, cracking him across the knuckles with one end of the staff, swinging it and catching him under his bearded chin as he turned and stared at her with furious eyes. She hit him again, so that he tottered and spun before falling on the grass beside Cadfael. She dropped the stick, and with her heart knocking her ribs so hard that she felt dizzy, she bent over Cadfael. Blood oozed from the cut on his head. She pressed her ear against his chest, and at first she could hear nothing but the beating of her own heart. Then at last she caught the flurry of his breathing.

She gave a great sigh of relief, without realising the strength of her thankfulness, before looking once again into the face that had become strangely familiar in the last few days.

Cadfael looked unlike himself. His pallid face was smoothed of all teasing, arrogance, concern or pain. Her gaze flickered over his quiescent form, noticing the way in which his left arm lay. So had Owain's once looked when he fell from a tree. She would have to leave him and go for help. Megan's cottage was only a short distance away, for all it was out of sight.

Sioned glanced swiftly at the other man, and as she did so, she felt a few drops of rain fall chillingly on her face. Slowly and with much difficulty she dragged Cadfael by the shoulders into the shelter of the bramble. The rain pattered on leaves and grass, dampening her gown, wetting her hair. She stepped back from the bushes and, catching sight of the leather pouch that the man had taken from about Cadfael's neck, she picked it up and slipped it down the front of her gown, where it lay heavy between her breasts. Then with a last glance at Cadfael's pale face, she turned away and hurried down the hill to find Megan.

'It will not be easy, Sioned, my girl,' panted Megan, shuffling along at the other side of the makeshift litter.

'I know it,' Sioned replied somewhat distractedly, as she peered through the rain to where the brambles grew on the rise. The litter bumped the last few yards as their feet slithered on the wet grass. She looked about her for the man she had hit, but he was gone. With a tightness in her throat, she went over to the bramble and lifted a dripping branch with hasty fingers. 'He is here,' she cried over her shoulder.

Megan ambled over with a seemingly unhurried gait before bending and looking into Cadfael's drawn face. She drew in a hiss of surprise as she scrutinised him from beneath a fringe of pure white hair.

'Raven-thatched, I see,' she muttered.

Sioned nodded, not speaking. She twisted her hands together as she knelt on the grass, not heeding the wetness. Megan touched gently the swelling on Cadfael's head and lifted an eyelid, letting it drop back. She felt his arm carefully, then spoke softly.

'Let us get him on to the litter, child. All is not lost yet, although certain I am that it will be some time before the man is on his feet again.'

A frown tightened Sioned's brow, and she rose stiffly and brought over the litter. Somehow, by means of gentle tugging, pushing and easing, she and Megan managed to lift Cadfael on to it, his feet hanging awkwardly over the end.

Megan stared down at his length. 'Longshanks, isn't he?' she muttered. Then without another word she took the rope the other side of Sioned and began to pull the litter down the sodden hillside.

CHAPTER EIGHT

The journey was more arduous than Sioned had imagined it would be. By the time they had reached the tiny wooden hut and set the litter upon the earthen floor, she thought she would never be able to straighten her back again. But need set her walking again—lifting, bending, fetching water from the pail outside the door to pour into the blackened pot set over the fire. All the time her eyes darted to Cadfael's pale angular face as Megan bent over him and slit the damp sleeve with a knife.

Sioned knelt on the floor, watching Megan straighten Cadfael's arm with what seemed to be only a quick push, pull and twist, but which set him groaning. His eyelids flickered, and he peered up through the dim light in the room.

She leaned forward swiftly, her bronze braids swinging. The end of one brushed his cheek, and he tried to wipe away the dampness.

'Cadfael!' Sioned took his right hand between her own as the dazed hazel eyes attempted to focus on her face.

‘Sioned?’ he muttered, before his eyelids drooped again.

Megan’s wise old eyes went to Sioned’s face. ‘Come, child, help me with this,’ she ordered in a brisk voice.

Sioned took the sticks, holding them firm while Megan bound them with linen strips to Cadfael’s broken limb. When she had finished, Sioned placed the splinted arm carefully by Cadfael’s side before rising to her feet. She watched Megan shuffle over to the huddle of utensils in the corner of the room. From a pot, she took a handful of herbs and flung them into the steaming pot on the fire, adding some liquid from a small flask. She stirred the concoction with a wooden spoon, muttering an incantation as she did so.

‘Now, Sioned, while this infuses, you must make up a bed of rushes for you both. I have some cut and stored in the lean-to at the back. By the time you do that, I will have this man out of his wet clothes, and this liniment ready for him.’

Sioned stared blankly at Megan, hearing her words, but not quite understanding them.

‘Come, child, make haste,’ chivvied the old woman. ‘He is not going to die just because you leave his side.’

Sioned blinked drowsily. She felt strange,

her head ached, and her limbs seemed unwilling to obey her. Slowly, stiffly she moved across the room as if in a dream and opened the door to go out to the lean-to. She had to make several journeys before she had enough rushes to form some semblance of a bed. Megan gave her a pile of blankets, which she had taken from a beautifully carved chest. Rubbing her cheek against the soft wood, Sioned found a strange comfort.

'This man will need to be kept warm, Sioned. For I doubt not that he will take a fever after lying in the rain after such a blow. He will need you, child ... Make haste ... Make haste.'

Megan turned away, muttering to herself, while Sioned made up the bed with the homespun blankets. As soon as she had finished, Megan called her, holding out a wooden bowl and a cloth. Sioned took them from the narrow, wrinkled hand, murmuring her thanks.

Sioned did as Megan bade, and kneeling on the floor, she parted the hair sticky with blood and began to bathe the wound with the herbal infusion. Cadfael muttered uneasily, wincing as she pressed the cloth on to the injury. His head moved restlessly against the litter, and for a moment she stopped, but after a few moments, when he had quietened, she started to clean him again. Slowly, unwillingly it seemed, his eyes opened.

He gazed up at her in bewilderment. He no longer wore his tunic, but a white linen shirt, old and darned, open at the throat. Gripping her wrist tightly, he drew a great breath. 'You will not—not betray me, will you? You ... will ... not betray me?' he demanded.

'No!' Sioned's voice was only a harsh whisper.

He half smiled, and then his eyes closed and his hand slid to the ground.

Sioned got to her feet and went over to where Megan had another larger pot swinging over the fire. Two bowls had been set on a small table, and the savoury smell of rabbit stew rose in the smoky air. Her mind felt numb.

Megan's old wrinkled face softened, and a smile sent fresh wrinkles dancing. 'Sit down, child. We will eat, and afterwards I will find you one of my old cottes. Like I found your man one of my husband's shirts. A fine shirt, which he had from his mother for our wedding.'

'He is not my man.' Sioned sank wearily on to a stool. Her face was drawn, and there were dark smudges beneath her eyes. 'He is one of Edward's men.'

'If that is so—tell me what you and this man are doing, visiting old Megan?' She stared at Sioned. 'You were coming here before you were set upon?'

Sioned nodded. It was a moment she had foreseen, but now she was unsure what to say. She was silent for a while.

'It is Cadfael who seeks you. He says he is looking for his half-brother. A monk—brother Thomas—said that you might be able to help him.'

Megan nodded her head thoughtfully. 'He is a good holy man. We have healed many a body and soul together. But, tell me. This half-brother who is sought—could he be called Rhys ap Glyder?'

Sioned lifted startled eyes to Megan's face. 'How did you know?'

Megan chuckled. 'It is not by spells or magic, child! But if you feared that this man might have lied to you, fear not. There is a Rhys ap Glyder, but it is best we wait until this—Cadfael—comes to his senses. Then we will talk. Although what you are doing with him is another tale, I think?'

Megan's eyes flickered over Sioned's face. Sioned made no answer, wondering how much to tell Megan about her plans. Megan stayed a moment, then pushed back a strand of hair and rose, setting a pot under a drip splashing on the floor through a hole in the roof.

'Now we shall eat. Afterwards we will

move the man from the litter, and I will make a mixture. Vervain would be best, I think, when he starts to burn and wander in his mind, as surely he will.' Megan took up a bowl and filled it from the steaming pot, placing it before Sioned, and handing her a spoon.

'Some call vervain the wizard's herb, using it in their spells, for only God knows what purpose,' she continued conversationally. 'But I consider it one of God's healing herbs and, with a little prayer, it will surely do the man some good.'

Sioned nodded. She had faith in Megan —and God—although she wondered now what his plan for her was. She had meant to leave Cadfael once she reached Megan's, and to go on. On to Dafydd, whom she was certain would help her. He had told her that he loved her, and if it had not been for Hywel, he would have married her. They could wed while Hywel was still at Govan's. Her only fear was that her brother might return earlier than he had planned ... unless he waited at Govan's keep. Maybe it might occur to both of them that she had been carried off by the English.

Slowly at first she began to sup the stew. It was thick with barley, leeks, peas, and chunks of rabbit meat. Then her hunger asserted itself, and she ate more greedily. As soon as her bowl was empty, Megan filled it again. Sioned could not help thinking how much Cadfael would have enjoyed the food.

When she had finished, Sioned exchanged her damp gown for a woollen homespun of green, old, and much darned like the shirt Cadfael wore, but it was warm, and that was what mattered to her.

It was difficult to lift Cadfael from the litter on to the bed of rushes, and their handling set him groaning. Several times he opened his eyes to stare unseeingly into their faces before muttering incomprehensibly and lapsing into an uneasy slumber again. Sioned removed only his sandals, before covering him carefully with all the blankets.

Although it was only mid-evening, it was dark in the cottage. Megan had put a shutter over the window to keep out the rain, and the fire gave only a little light now that it burned low. Sioned set down the medicine that Megan had made on a stool, and slid, fully clothed, under the blankets. She lay, listening to Cadfael's breathing and the flurry of rain blown by the wind which made the shutter creak. The draught sent a creeping curl of smoke up to the darkened roof. Exhaustion, and a niggling worry over what she should do, seemed to press her aching body into the rushes. Her eyelids closed, and in moments, all the physical and mental stress of the day sent her into a dreamless sleep.

She woke with a jump. Something heavy was lying across her breast. It was hard and clumsily flailing about, saturating her with fear. She could not remember where she was and what she was doing there as she climbed up through a maze of sleep. Then she heard a man's voice speaking huskily, gasping out words with shunted breaths. Easing herself up on the bed, she carefully removed Cadfael's broken arm from across her. She slid to the floor, waiting a moment before moving and her eyes became accustomed to the darkness. Then she felt for the medicine, wondering now how she was to get him to take it.

'He is restless, child? Do you wish me to help you?'

'Oh, please!' Sioned saw a shadow rise and come near to her.

'You clasp him strongly now, Sioned. Lift him, and when he struggles, be firm with him. He must have some of the mixture down him.'

Megan took the spoon from Sioned's hand, and somehow the girl managed to lift him, bracing himself so that his head rested against her shoulder. He muttered, and told them in no uncertain manner to leave him be. But Megan forced his mouth open, singing as she did so. It seemed to quieten him, so that he swallowed the vervain obediently. Sioned eased him back on to the bed, and drew a quivering breath.

'What did you sing to him?' she whispered.

'Do you not know it, child? It is a lullaby.' Megan chuckled, and patted Sioned's arm. 'But rest while you can. I doubt you will get many hours' sleep in the next few days.'

It was to be as Megan said. The fever rose, making Cadfael burn and wander in his mind.

'Isabella?' he called out one night, peering into Sioned's face. He reached out and touched her cheek, then shook his head. 'No ... not Isabella. She—she never came when I—I called her.' He closed his eyes again, still muttering, 'Isabella's dead ... Both dead ... I'm cold ... So cold.'

Sioned felt an unexpected pity and compassion for him and, reaching out, she drew his head on to her breast, holding him in her arms. Cadfael let out a long sigh and, still muttering, he dozed again.

She lost count of the days. During the nights she rested little as the fever mounted and Cadfael tossed and turned and she sought to keep the blankets on him. Why did she feel that she could not leave him until she was sure he would live? She only knew that she had to stay until that moment. So she watched, cared for him, and waited.

A day came when Megan scolded her and told her to go and walk outside. 'Do you think that I cannot care for him as well as you?' She shooed her outside.

Sioned went. The air outside, though fresh with the scent of grass and trees, seemed to have little substance in it. She was tired, more tired than she could have believed possible and still remain on her feet. The mountains seemed distant and unfriendly, the river's chattering voice sounded unsympathetic and cold. She did not stay out long before going back inside.

It was quiet in the room, and as she watched Megan smoothing the blanket covering Cadfael, she realised just how quiet it was now that his hurried breathing and mutterings could not be heard. Her heart jerked in her breast as she leaned against the doorway. 'Is he ...?' Sioned's voice faltered.

'Nay, child.' Megan's voice was filled with satisfaction. 'The fever has broken at last, and he is sleeping the sleep that heals.'

Sioned sank on to a stool, and for a long

time she did not move or speak. ‘Now I can go,’ she said at last.

Megan looked towards her. ‘Go where, child?’

‘To Dafydd,’ she replied in a low voice. She had not spoken to Megan about how she came to be with Cadfael. Now she did.

Megan did not interrupt her, only now and then did she frown over Sioned’s words—or perhaps it was what Sioned did not say that caused her to think more deeply.

‘And what of him—this Cadfael?’ Megan asked at the tale’s end. ‘You will leave him to find his own way back through the mountains?’

Sioned hesitated, glancing towards where he slept. She nodded. ‘You could guide him to the drovers’ path, Megan. There are tinkers and drovers who could help him.’ Her voice was hard.

Megan spoke slowly. ‘What of this Dafydd? You are sure of him? Angharad’s cousin, you say ... There is something about ...’ She gave a tut. ‘Ah! it is gone—but it will come back.’ She rose to her feet. ‘Let us have a bite to eat, though. When do you plan to leave, child?’

Sioned rubbed a hand across her forehead wearily. ‘When he is on his feet. Then ... Then I will go.’

Megan nodded and went over to the fire. For a moment she stared into its embers before placing the cooking-pot on to them.

Cadfael slept all evening, but Sioned had little appetite for the pottage Megan put before her. As she slid beneath the blankets that night, she experienced a sense of relief that he would no longer wake her with his mutterings and wandering words. She was asleep in moments.

Cadfael moved his head uneasily, wincing as he did so, before opening his eyes. He gazed into the darkness, wondering where he was. It was warm and muggy, and not in the least like his home. He turned his head slowly and caught the gleam of a fire. Gradually, as his eyes swept round, he began to make out shapes. The outline of a pot, then a stool, next the humped bulk of someone sleeping. He could hear breathing—a high-pitched snoring kind of breathing. Old and female, he hazarded, attempting to raise himself on his elbow. He gave a smothered curse as he did so. With his right hand, he felt his left arm touching the linen and hard wood. Broken! What had happened to him, and where was he? He could not think. His head, like his body, felt strangely airy. He suppressed the twinge of unease that surged in his mind and lay flat on the warm blanket. Unexpectedly, he heard the rustling of bedding as someone near him moved. With some difficulty he turned, and this set his head spinning. He clutched the blanket, gritting his teeth until the whizzing void settled down.

There came an abrupt catch in the breathing next to him, and he saw the shape move and then turn hurriedly towards him. The face was just a ghostly blur until she moved closer to him, her brown hair rippling over her shoulders. A hand reached out and touched his face. It seemed the most natural thing for him to take her hand, turn it palm upwards and kiss it.

'So!' said the voice in a throaty whisper. 'You are awake at last!' She tried to pull her hand away, but he held it tightly.

He had heard her voice before—often in his dreams, it seemed. Calling him, holding on to him when the pain had been great. He tried to remember who she was. There was something ... 'Where am I?'

'Megan's hafod.' She had thought he might not remember anything. 'She helped me fetch you down from the hill when the men attacked you.'

'Men?' Cadfael's voice held a vexed, puzzled note.

‘You do not remember?’

He thought she frowned.

‘They followed us, and you fought them. One broke your arm, then the other returned and hit you over the head.’

‘I don’t remember.’ His hand twitched about Sioned’s wrist.

‘Perhaps it is not so surprising!’ she replied. ‘You were out in the rain and caught a fever, and have been out of your senses for days.’

‘I have?’ He gripped her hand tightly. ‘What am I doing here? There is something, but ...’ He peered at her through the darkness, seeing her clearer now. She was comely. Suddenly he knew her. They had been going somewhere together ... to find someone. ‘Rhys,’ he murmured slowly. ‘We were looking for Rhys, you and I.’ He raised himself in the bed, and instantly his face was close to Sioned’s.

When she attempted to push him back, he did not budge. ‘You must rest. In the morning, you can talk and have some food. A light broth, perhaps.’

‘I must have been ill.’ The firm mouth eased into a smile. ‘I could eat a whole boar, I think, Sioned! It is Si-o-ned?’ His voice was suddenly serious.

‘Ay, but you must rest.’ She felt she had no breath for her voice. To hear him speak her name for the first time in days gave her a strange feeling.

'By the sound of it, I have been resting for days,' he murmured drowsily. 'Have you been here all the time, taking care of me?'

'Not—not all the time. Only—only when Megan could not watch over you. I must have fallen asleep this night. You were so much better, Megan said.' Her voice trailed away.

'Have you slept beside me all the time?' Cadfael's voice was expressionless as he caressed the back of her hand with his thumb. 'I seem to remember in my dreams ...'

'No! You dreamed ... so many dreams—of a woman—Isabella. Was she the wife you mentioned who died?' Sioned could feel heat flooding her face as he gazed at her.

'Ay, Isabella was my wife. But it was not she who came when I called—whose breast I laid my head on.' He sounded as if he were falling asleep again.

'You dreamed it.' Sioned did not want his gratitude. She did not want to have to answer the why—to the reason she had fought so hard to keep him alive—even to sleeping with him!

'I dreamed it? You are sure?'

She could hardly hear the words. Relief

flooded her. He was falling asleep. 'You dreamed it,' she said softly, taking her hand from his grasp. He let her go, and there was silence between them. She moved away and lay on her back. It was some time before she slept.

Voices woke her, and she sat up, startled, rubbing slumber from her eyes. The room was empty except for a ginger and white cat which sat washing itself where the sun painted a golden line on the floor through the open doorway. She heard Megan's throaty chuckle and Cadfael's protesting male tones. She flung back the covers and slid from the bed, and in that moment she wondered if he had remembered their conversation of the night and believed her words. She had meant to get up and leave him alone in the bed.

'Now, what is it you wish to know concerning Rhys ap Glyder?' said Megan, as Sioned emerged slowly into the sun-splashed day.

'You know of him?' Cadfael's eyes were bright and alert, despite the dark shadows under them and the hollows in his cheeks. The spoon he held was stilled halfway to his mouth as Sioned slid on to the bench besides him. For a moment his glance held hers before he faced Megan again.

Sioned watched him as he listened to Megan, idly taking in every detail of his thin, unshaven face. It could be the last time she was seeing it.

CHAPTER NINE

'Who are you, Master Cadfael?' Megan began to shell the pods in the basket on her lap. 'And who is Rhys ap Glyder to you, and what do you want with him?'

'I think you know.' Cadfael's gaze challenged hers.

'Ay, I do! Sioned told me he is your half-brother. But I would have known it anyway,' Megan chuckled. 'He has the hair, Sioned, my girl. And the eyes, and there is a likeness in his face when it is in repose.'

'I am not like Rhys.' Cadfael swallowed a spoonful of the broth. 'I take after my mother—perhaps you knew her? I fancy you did?'

'Perhaps.' Megan's mouth quivered. 'Perhaps a long time ago ... more than thirty years ago, at least. A sweet girl she was, and a beauty. Dark-haired with fine eyes, the same golden green as yours.' She stilled her eyes and hands. 'They deemed me old, even then. Most soon forgot I was widowed and had lost a child. But not Elin. She was kind, and oft brought me a gift from her husband's store, unbeknown to him.' She smiled at the memory, and shook her head. 'But this is not helping you. Tell me your full name.'

'Sir Cadfael Poole—son of Elin ap Glyder, who was your friend, I think. I am here to find Rhys for her.' He took another spoonful of the broth, and there was a silence except for the low mooing of a cow somewhere and the clucking of hens.

Megan began to pod the peas swiftly, her mouth working as she did so. 'Your mother wishes to see him, I suppose. Why she had to marry an Englishman, I do not know!' she muttered. 'But she would have him, after she found him wandering lost on the mountain. He had charm—I'll give him that.' She gave Cadfael a darting glance. 'You have it, too, and I vow you could charm a maid if you put your mind to it!'

Cadfael half smiled but made no answer, only taking another slow spoonful of the broth, waiting for Megan to reveal the information he wanted in her own way.

'He is no longer here in the mountains,' she said abruptly, popping a pea into her mouth and chewing it with her six remaining teeth.

'He is not dead?' Cadfael's head shot up.

'I said that he is no longer in the mountains. Hasn't been for a long time. He went to Ynys Mon with his grandmother.' Megan's hands busied with the pods again. 'Where exactly they are I do not know. After his grandsire—and yours—was killed ... her heart was almost broken. She had lost two sons, and determined that Rhys would not suffer the same fate. These senseless blood-feuds!'

Cadfael let out a breath, and a strand of curling hair fluttered. 'You have no idea where on Anglesey?' He toyed with the spoon, stirring the half empty bowl of broth.

Megan was silent, and only the sound of popping pods could be heard. Sioned wondered what Cadfael would do now.

'There is a small parcel of land that was left to Rhys, but I only know that it lies where the mountains of Gwynedd can be seen from it. I doubt not that your mother will know where it is ... What is wrong that she wishes to see her firstborn, Sir Cadfael?'

'She is dying.' He placed the bowl on the bench, and cradled his broken arm against his chest. 'My thanks to you, Mistress Megan, not only for the information, but also for the shelter you have given me, and all you have spent in time and goods to speed my recovery.' He leaned forward, and lifting Megan's wrinkled hand, he kissed it.

The faintest of blushes darkened the withered cheeks as she scowled at him and snatched away her hand. 'I do it for Elin, my fine knight! As for speeding your recovery and saving your life, you have Sioned to thank for that. She saved you from the robbers, and kept you warm when you would have died for want of such warmth, and cooled your brow when you burned.' Megan's mouth worked and her eyes darted to Sioned's averted profile, then to Cadfael's enigmatic face. She began to shell the peas again. 'Just you give your mother my love, and tell her she is constantly in my prayers. Why she had to marry an Englishman! But there, I suppose she knew what she was doing. She had the sight.' Megan chuckled suddenly.

'Ay, she foretold Sioned saving my life, and that she would act as my guide.' Cadfael's voice was low and stiff. He rose abruptly to his feet. 'I think I would stretch my legs, if that is allowed.'

'If you think you will not overtax your strength.' Megan's tone was mild now. 'Sioned, you had best go with the man. The cow is in need of milking, and that journey will be far enough for him this morn, as he will discover.'

'But ...' Sioned's eyes pleaded with Megan. Why had she had to speak so of her saving Cadfael's life!

‘Go, child.’ Megan smiled.

With a sigh, Sioned rose, not giving Cadfael a glance, and in silence they walked the short distance to where the cow waited. The river lay shimmering only a short distance from them. On its far bank, some miles back, several roofs could be seen. It was a beautiful morning.

Sioned approached the cow, setting down the stool and pail she had brought, and speaking gently to the beast. She was glad to press her cheek against its flank, away from Cadfael’s eyes, for she had been aware that he watched her all the time they walked. She had found it unnerving, and did not wish to talk to or look at him.

‘I am grateful, Sioned.’

She jumped when Cadfael spoke, and milk squirted into the pail in a shaky stream.

‘How did you save my life?’ There was a friendly warmth in his voice.

‘There were two of them. One you had already vanquished. I just hit the other man several times with your stick when he knocked you out and stole your money.’

‘My money?’ Cadfael sat down on the grass a few feet from her.

‘It was round your neck—in a pouch. I have it here.’ She put a hand to her breast.

'I will give it to you when I have finished milking the cow.'

'Thank you.' He smiled. A soft breeze lifted his hair from his brow. He still looked terribly pale, she thought irritably. 'I wish I could have seen you—but I do not doubt you. Tell me, will you be ready to leave on the morrow?'

'On the morrow?' she said in surprise. 'You are not fit!'

'Am I not? But I have been away far too long.' Cadfael stretched himself out on the grass and shut his eyes against the sun. 'Now that I know Rhys is not here, I must return as soon as possible. Take time to see my mother, and find out where he is exactly.' He yawned.

Sioned could not think how to answer him. The silence stretched between them as the warm stillness of the morning enfolded him, bringing its peace. There were only the gushing of the milk in the pail and the sound of Cadfael's low steady breathing to disturb the silence.

Having finished the milking with a pat on its rump she left the cow, taking the pail with her. She glanced at Cadfael. Was he asleep? She put down the pail and walked slowly over to where he lay slumbering. Soon she must leave.

His eyes were firmly shut, the dark lashes fanned out. His hair had grown, curling about his ears and thin cheeks. Sioned's throat ached unexpectedly and she turned away, only to be stopped by a hand closing on her ankle.

'Where are you going?' The lashes lifted, and Cadfael stared up at her. 'You did not answer my question.'

'You will not be fit on the morrow—and as for where I am going now, I am taking the milk to Megan.' She had no intention of telling him more. 'Now will you let me go!' She attempted to walk out of his grasp, but he held on tightly.

'Stay with me and talk awhile? Have I not been so sick that you thought I would die—do I not now need a little comforting, Sioned?' His eyes wore a teasing expression.

She steeled herself to resist his sudden charm. 'You will recover better if you rest here in the open air. I have tasks to perform.' She was trying to excuse herself.

'The tasks could wait—have pity on me, Sioned,' he coaxed. 'I have been out of the world for more days than I can remember, and you talk of tasks. Let us instead talk of each other. I could tell you tales of far lands—of camels, and white-walled forts and towns, and of strange peoples!'

'Camels?' Sioned's guard slipped a moment.

'Camels.' He eased his hold on her ankle and elbowed himself into a sitting position. 'They are beasts with long necks and a hump on their backs.' He took hold of a fold of her skirts and tugged hard, almost making her lose her balance. 'That was when I was on crusade. I almost died, then. We were ambushed, but a seer assured me that I would live to a ripe old age and die peacefully in bed. An unlikely fate for a knight in Edward's host, don't you think? Do sit down!'

'Perhaps. I would not know.' Sioned sank on to her knees. His words, so quickly spoken, bemused her. 'Was it then that you called for your wife and she did not come?' She wished the words back as soon as she had said them. He would think she was interested in his past—and she was not!

'Ay! She was not like you,' he said casually. 'Why did you not let me die? I—one of Edward's men?'

Sioned felt trapped, and sensed that he had arranged it so. 'It ... it was foretold that I would save your life. God only knows for what purpose! I was fulfilling your mother's prophecy, and perhaps caring a little about how she would feel to lose you and never find Rhys.' She was surprised at how controlled her voice sounded. 'So, if you do not mind, I will ...' She made to rise, but he grabbed her by the waist and pulled her close.

'You mean all that went through your mind when you hit that man with my stick?' he murmured, his mouth suddenly seeming very close to hers.

'I would have done it for any creature left defenceless!' she said vehemently. She really was trapped.

'I believe you would.' Cadfael pulled her down on top of him and kissed her, gently at first. 'I am grateful,' he said softly. 'Very grateful.' He kissed her again, despite her murmur of protest and struggles. And again.

Somehow, without her realising how he did it, they were lying on the grass. Her head was pillowed on his shoulder, and he held her captive with his unbroken arm.

'Do you know you have the most beautiful ears?' Cadfael nibbled gently at the lobe with his teeth. His fingers curled comfortably about her breast. 'And neck.' He kissed the curve beneath her chin. 'And throat,' he whispered, pressing gentle kisses down the side of her neck and throat where the pulse beat rapidly.

'You must not,' she said in a shaky voice. Her body felt so right and comfortable curved against his, but her mind would not let it rest so. 'I have tasks ...'

He covered her mouth with his again

in a kiss that this time was not so gentle and that coaxed so insistently that when he drew his mouth from hers, their lips clung. He felt slightly lightheaded, but could not resist kissing her again with a fervent starving passion that evoked such an answering response in her that she could no sooner have withdrawn at that moment than touched a star.

It was some time before they drew apart, and whether they both felt as if they floated because of the instant passion between them, or because of the tensions and fever of the preceding days, they did not ask themselves. Something had changed between them. Cadfael was shaken to the limits of his weakened strength, and Sioned felt an overwhelming sense of panic. She could not stay—she must not stay! She scrambled to her feet, and Cadfael let her go. He could not have stopped her—in that moment, her strength was greater than his. She reached for the pail of milk, not speaking, and was gone.

Sioned's quickened feet took her to the cottage and Megan.

'What is it, child?' Megan put aside the peas, staring at Sioned's flushed face and into the wild frightened eyes.

'I must go.' Sioned set the pail down by the door and clasped her trembling hands together. 'He—he is resting down by the river. I must go to Dafydd now, before he comes back here.'

'Must, child? Why, what is it?' Megan got to her feet and put a wrinkled hand on Sioned's arm.

'It is Dafydd I love. I must go to him!' Sioned lifted her eyes to the mountains. 'My life is here—here in these mountains.'

'You must do as you think right, child,' said Megan soothingly, and if she noted the uncertainty and panic in Sioned's voice, she did not think it right to interfere. People must decide their own paths in life, and she was not a woman for meddling in others' lives without their asking. She only wished she could remember what that gossip, Aranrhod, had told her about Sioned's Dafydd.

'I will go, then—now!' Sioned's body seemed to sag, and her voice sounded tired. She and Megan exchanged glances.

'I will get you some bread and cheese to take with you.' Megan patted Sioned's hand. 'Sit a moment and have a horn of ale. It will not take long.'

Sioned's whole body seemed to ache, and she stared unseeingly down towards the river, trying not to think. Megan was back in a few minutes, pressing the horn into her hand and bidding her drink. She did, and felt better. Then she went into the cottage, which was dark—very dark inside after the bright sunlight.

'I have not thanked you. Thanked you for asking no questions and doing all that you have, Megan.' Sioned stood at the old woman's shoulder and dropped a kiss on her cheek.

Megan turned and looked up, and there was a hint of a sparkle in her eyes. 'If my daughter had lived, child, I would she had been like you.' Her voice was a husky whisper as she pressed the napkin containing the food into Sioned's hand. 'God go with you, child. Go now.'

Sioned stared at the bowed head and bent shoulders, and with a sob jammed in her throat, she went from the cottage.

Sioned went up. Up the mountain slope above the cottage, past the place where the men and Cadfael had fought, and by a small path slanting about the curve of the slope.

It was just a weakness of the flesh that she had wanted him to kiss her and hold her, and go on kissing and touching her. And if she had let him go on, as her senses had demanded, he would have taken her sooner or later, and that would have been that.

What were the alternatives? A whore to one of Edward's men—there was no future there. Or love? It was Dafydd she loved, and she would thrill to his kisses again.

It was hot beneath the sun, and her skirts seemed heavy and cumbersome about her bare legs. The way became tedious and arduous, the path never-ending. She felt lonely, her ears constantly reaching out for the flap of Cadfael's sandals that had accompanied the gentle tread of her bare feet before they had reached Megan's hafod. There was no sense in thinking of him: their ways had parted. She had helped him to find Megan, and he had enabled her to escape Govan. He was part of her past, and she must let it go like a leaf in the wind. She concentrated on Dafydd—on the way his fair hair fell in heavy locks on his broad brow, the blue of his eyes and the full sensuousness of his mouth. Except when she thought like that, it was Cadfael's mouth she could feel pressing against her lips. His gold-green eyes lazily smiling into hers. Sioned increased her pace angrily. He had bewitched her, and she was not having it! She would soon forget him once she was with Dafydd.

She stopped only once, to eat the bread and cheese Megan had given her. Then on again. She had never come to Dafydd's hafod this way, and the way seemed long, keeping as she did a landmark of a peak and river in her eye. Perhaps there was a quicker way that she did not know and dared not risk. So her journey went on and on, until the sun's heat began to cool and she neared her destination, hoping that Dafydd was at home and not on a raid with his father and older brothers.

Cattle grazed in the meads not far from the wooden walls of the hafod, but all seemed quiet. Trepidation began to quiver in her nerves. What would she do if he was not there? She was weary now, and mostly the thought of lying down and sleeping was uppermost in her mind. Her eyelids kept drooping, but she kept on putting one foot in front of the other. The sun was sinking fast, and as she grew closer to the house she could hear voices. Singing and laughing they were, and their vitality and raucousness seemed to mock her weariness. Her heart plummeted. She was in no mood to make an appearance in a crowd of drunken men and any women they might have with them. Her footsteps slowed, and she looked about her. The byre was to the left of the hafod, and she began to move in that direction.

The door of the house opened suddenly, and immediately the noise of merriment increased in intensity. Sioned backed against the byre wall hurriedly as a man and woman came outside.

The man swiftly slipped his arm about the woman, and he bent his head and kissed her. They were in darkness now that the door of the house had shut behind them, and Sioned could not see their faces. They kissed for a long time before beginning to move towards her. Quickly she slid round the byre wall and through the door that was partly open. Surely they would pass and go on their way home? But they did not; they came into the byre.

She stayed motionless behind the partition to which she had moved when their footsteps came nearer. She heard the rustle of straw and a low laugh, light and musical. Shock ran through her. Angharad! Sioned had thought some unflattering thoughts about her brother's wife—but not that she would be unfaithful to Hywel!

Sioned put up her hands to shut out the whispering voices and the sound of their coupling. Her face was hot, and she sank to her knees on the earthen floor. If only she could escape from the byre—but she would have to stay until they left. Still she could hear them, and she did not know what to do. They were talking now. At least the worst was over, and they would go soon. She took her hands from her ears, and immediately she recognised the other voice, which had been muffled and distorted until then.

'This will have to be the last time,

dearest cousin. We go on a raid tonight, and soon Hywel will return.' The deep familiar tones were amused, lazily satisfied. 'He would kill us if he knew.'

'There will be other times,' murmured Angharad, her voice a caress. 'And who is to know whether the child I bear will be yours or Hywel's, little cousin? As long as he does not! If there is talk, he is too arrogant to believe that I would need another man to keep me satisfied.'

'You're a greedy bitch! I wish I could do without you, but you're in my blood.' He kissed her. 'I presume he will return without Sioned. A pity! I found her innocence curiously appealing.'

'That is why she had to go. I will have no rivals!'

Angharad's voice had hardened, and suddenly Sioned realised that she was biting her lip so hard that there was blood in her mouth. A furious anger surged through her body, but caution kept her still.

'I will find you a wife—do not fear,' Angharad laughed softly.

Sioned heard them get to their feet and walk together to the door. She waited a while before she went over to the door. It did not yield beneath her hand. She lifted the latch and pushed, but it shifted only slightly. Panic mingled with her anger as she hurled herself at it with all her strength, but the bar on the outside held. Tears of fury sparkled on her cheeks, and a sob escaped her. Slowly she went over to the hump of hay in a far corner and sank on to it to give way to her tears. She was trapped until morning, at least.

CHAPTER TEN

Cadfael lay a long time in the grass, the sun warm on his face. He was unreasonably angry with himself and his weakness. He wished he could have followed Sioned, but his body felt curiously heavy and as if it did not belong to him. He had frightened her. Yet she had responded to his kisses in such a way that he could still feel her soft warm body moving against his length. His eyelids drooped; he was so tired. The sun seemed to be pressing him into the ground. He wanted her. The heat relaxed his body, lifting him so that he floated—floated in an unearthly world with Sioned in his arms. He slept.

It was Megan who woke him. Her wrinkled face wavered above him, all the lines gathered together in a great frowning mass. 'She has gone,' she said. 'And I am anxious about her.'

'Gone?' Cadfael blinked, forcing his eyes open. He could not think. 'Who's gone?'

'Sioned! She has gone to Dafydd, and I have remembered what it was that Aranrhod told me about him.'

He stared at Megan stupidly, trying to

take in her words. 'Who's Dafydd?' he said at last, sitting up and running a hand through his unruly hair.

'Sioned fancies herself in love with him, but he is not worthy of her. We must go after her.' Megan's mouth worked.

'Wait, Megan!' Cadfael had a strange chill in his stomach as if a great hand had hit him.

'He is not worthy of her, sir knight!' Megan hissed angrily. 'You are to blame for her going to him, so you must bring her back.'

He dropped his hand and stared at her. 'You said she is in love with him?' His voice was taut. 'Why should I bring her back, if that is so? I thought she wished to wed Govan, but it ...'

'Oh, will you stop blabbering, man! I will go alone if you do not care what happens to Sioned. I thought ... But then I am an old woman, and it is a long time since a man looked on me in that way.'

She glared at him, and he felt the colour run up under his skin, flushing his cheekbones. He laughed suddenly.

'You have greater confidence in my strength than I do, Megan!' Cadfael rose to his feet stiffly.

'I will give you something that will keep you awake and on your feet. The way is not so far if you know the secret paths across the marsh.'

'You are determined that Sioned needs rescuing from this lover?' His voice held the lightest hint of bitter derisiveness.

Megan did not bother to answer him, but led the way back to her hafod, glad that there would be a moon that night.

Sioned did not know how long she had slept, but suddenly she woke. Light came beneath a slit under the door. Was it dawn already? She blinked her bleary eyes. Rising slowly from the hay, she went over to the door. It was the moon. She squinted through the gap between the outer edge of the door and the jamb, hearing the murmur of voices. Men's voices! She stepped back quickly, and went back to her mound of hay and burrowed deep within it as the door was opened.

What had Dafydd said to Angharad? A raid—they were going on a raid—and what better time to go than on a moonlit night when your neighbours would not expect such a visit? Chaff tickled her nose, and she held back a sneeze as footsteps came closer and some of the hay was lifted from above her.

'Is Dafydd bringing that new calf in here with its mother before we go? It seems somewhat weak on its legs.'

Sioned pressed herself to the ground, praying that Dafydd's brother would not come back for more hay.

'Maybe. He's been told to. Will you be long here?'

'I'm coming now. Have you my spear?'

The footsteps retreated, and Sioned sneezed. She must get out of here! She had not heard them locking the door, and it was likely they had left it open for Dafydd.

The door opened, and within seconds she was through it and sliding along the side of the byre into the shadows. Dafydd was coming! The shadows hid her well, and he did not see her as her eyes washed over him in cold disillusionment. Then she waited until he had disappeared inside the byre before moving along the wall again, her fingers scraping the wood lightly in her nervous haste. Once she reached the corner, she could be off and up into the hills. She worked her way slowly round to it.

'So! I thought I heard something!'

Sioned's head spun round, and she bit back a cry as she looked up at Dafydd.

'By all the saints—is it really you, Sioned!' He reached out and held her by the shoulders. His disbelief was real. 'What are you doing here? I thought ...'

'I know what you thought!' Sioned's

voice was hard as she wrenched herself out of his grasp.

'But where have you come from?'

Her eyes flickered involuntarily towards the byre, and in that moment she realised her own danger if Dafydd guessed that she knew of his relationship with Angharad.

'Has Hywel returned also?' Dafydd grabbed her arm again. He was scared of her brother—she had known that when he had spoken of him to Angharad. She nodded her head and sagged against Dafydd's chest.

'You cannot know what it was like—I ran from him this day, but he is behind me somewhere. He wants me to marry Govan—who is gross, and ... and I could not bear it. He is furious with me.'

Dafydd put his arms about her. 'You ran from him—to me?'

'Ay. I thought you would help me.' Her strained voice was muffled.

'I see.' Dafydd's fingers caressed the back of Sioned's neck.

'You said that you loved me.' Despite the control she had over her feelings, she could not help a note of rebuke creeping into her tone.

'You doubt me?' Dafydd's voice was gentle. He was remembering the direction she had been going in when he had seen her, and how she had pulled away from him at first. His hands rested about her throat as he turned her face up to his kiss. It would be over with quickly, and be better for her than any plans Angharad might have for getting rid of her if she knew Sioned might have overheard them and told Hywel. But how he would enjoy coupling with Sioned first! Angharad would never need to know—and it would not take long!

Cadfael was tired and angry, despite Megan's words. He had left her behind at the curve of the hill and Dafydd's hafod was in his sights. What the old crone expected him to do at this time of night he had no idea. But Megan's anxiety had infected, even as it had irritated and infuriated him. If Sioned wanted to go off to an old lover it did not concern him. Except that Megan thought it did. Women!

His feet slithered on the grass as he descended, and now he caught the sound of ponies moving about. Then he saw them—and the warriors gathering beyond the huddle of buildings below him. They must be going raiding, and all Megan's fears were for naught. Another flicker of movement held his gaze steady, and faint—faint as a whisper—there came a sound, a voice that was abruptly cut off.

He skidded the last hundred feet, erupting almost on top of Dafydd. His hand shot out and grasped Dafydd by the neck of his tunic, heaving him backwards and off Sioned.

It had been a scream. He barely glanced at Sioned before spinning Dafydd round and smashing his fist into his face. The fair-haired man went down without a sound. He turned, and only for the briefest of moments did he look at Sioned before he pulled her to her feet.

'Megan's waiting,' he said in a low, harsh voice. 'Come on.' He gave her no chance to recover her wits or voice, but dragged her up the hill with the strength of his arm, not heeding when she almost tripped over her skirts and whispered to him to slow down. He did not stop until they reached Megan.

'There!' he said in a hard voice to Megan, whirling the girl round. 'I have brought her to you from the arms of her lover!' He released Sioned's hand and swayed. For several seconds he swayed, before he toppled to the ground.

'He is strong. Stronger than many men I have met.' Megan nodded her head several times before dropping the chopped leek into the pot. 'But he will need help.'

Sioned made no answer, but sat listlessly.

It was two days since Cadfael had dragged her from Dafydd's arms. They had waited on the hillside until morning, and then Megan had gone off to a lady who owed her a favour and borrowed a donkey to carry the still slumbering man back to Megan's hafod.

Now he was on his feet again, sitting outside on the bench in the sun. He and Sioned had barely exchanged a word. She could think of nothing to say, not wanting to explain. Let him think what he liked about her! They had agreed to part, and if she had erred in her judgment that was her affair, not Sir Cadfael's. Only she could not forget how he had collapsed at her feet after rescuing her—or how her heart had leapt in her breast when she had seen him in the moonlight. What was she to do? She had suggested to Megan that she stay with her and share the work, and learn from her—but Megan had refused, saying she was far too young to live such a solitary life with an old woman. Now, it seemed, Megan thought she should go with Cadfael and guide him back to his camp. What was she to do?

'I will see to the food, child. You go outside and see if Elin's son needs aught.' Megan shooed her out, and she went reluctantly.

Cadfael sat motionless, his broken arm

cradled in his other one, staring down at the river. He did not look up until Sioned spoke.

'Is there anything you wish for? Ale? Some bread?'

'Ale,' he responded curtly. 'If you would be so kind.' His gold-green eyes washed over her slowly. 'You still have my pouch with you, Mistress Sioned?'

'Ay!' She flushed, reaching up quickly and lifting the leather thong from about her neck. She dropped the pouch into his outstretched palm, before going back inside to fetch him his ale.

'I will pay you!' Cadfael raised his voice slightly, causing Sioned's hand to waver as she reached out for the pitcher of ale.

She came out slowly, a pitcher and horn in her hands. 'Pay me for what, Sir Cadfael?'

He looked not at her, but up at the clear sky. 'To guide me back through the mountains and to the camp.'

She stared at his uptilted profile, noting the sharp line of his jaw and the pallor of his skin. 'I do not want your money.' Her voice was low and determined.

He turned then and looked at her, his eyes narrowing. 'You mean you do not want to go with me, I think, Mistress Sioned?'

She nodded.

'You would rather stay here and await Dafydd's coming for you?' He flung the words at her with vehemence.

She looked startled. 'He will not come here! He does not know where I am!'

'He will sooner or later, if you stay. You say that many people come to Megan to seek for a cure for this and that! The news will out that she has a young pretty maid staying with her—who is Hywel ap Rowan's sister.'

'I will not stay here, then. I—I will go somewhere else.' She did not want him to see how he had disconcerted her, so she poured the ale into a horn and handed it to him, her face averted.

'If you come with me, Sioned, I will pay you—then you will have your amobr. You can then choose your own man.'

Sioned lifted her head and looked at him. 'I do not want your money—but surely I will come with you. I owe you that!'

Cadfael took a gulp of the ale. 'You owe me nothing, Sioned,' he said crisply.

She gave a curious small laugh. 'It is thanks to you that I do not carry in my head a stupid dream! A dream of a man who never, never cared, after all. I am not so foolish now. Now I know that men, Normans or Cymri, take what they want without asking—or paying the price that such caring would demand!' Tears sparkled in her eyes. 'But do not talk about owing, Sir Cadfael—shall we say rather that we are equal? You rescued me from Dafydd, and I will guide you to your own people. Then my life will be my own affair.'

Cadfael stared at her and took another drink of ale. 'So be it, Mistress, if that is what you wish.'

'It is.' She gave a brisk nod and walked away and down to the river, where she stood for a long time, looking at its tranquil surface.

They left two days later, and the parting from Megan was not without its sorrow.

'If you come once more to these mountains in peace, do not fail to come and visit me, Elin's son.' Megan's voice shook slightly.

'I won't.' Cadfael bent and kissed the wrinkled cheek, pressing several coins into Megan's palm. 'Do not return them to me. It is the least I can do for your help and wisdom.'

'You will take care of Sioned?' Megan's face was stiff and stern. 'Deal with her not so roughly or gently that she does not know what you are about.'

He frowned down at her, his eyes dark, but Megan just stared back at him. He turned away and left the hafod. Sometimes she reminded him greatly of his mother!

Sioned was already outside, waiting. She had said her farewells, but now as Megan followed Cadfael out, she turned and kissed Megan again.

'The saint go with you.' Megan's voice was fierce as she shut the door firmly on them. They exchanged brief glances, but did not speak, and soon Megan's hut could be seen no longer.

Sioned was glad of the silence. Her own grandmother she had never known, and her mother had died at a time when she had had most need of a mother's guiding hand. Yet she was sure that if Owain, her older brother, had not gone away, she would not be in her present predicament. She must think and pray, remembering the first day she had seen Cadfael and the English camp, and the ships that had lain at anchor in the Dee estuary. So many ships. It was curious that the king could find a use for them all. But ships meant men—mariners. Her heart lifted.

'The ships that keep your king supplied—where do they come from?'

'The ships?' Cadfael glanced at her swiftly, then looked away. 'Why do you ask?' He eased on his shoulder the pack that Megan had given him, containing food and blankets.

Sioned shrugged her shoulders. 'I am

curious. Do any come from Ireland?'

'Ireland?'

'Ay, Ireland!' It seemed to her that he was repeating everything she said. 'The land across the sea.'

'I know where it is,' he retorted. 'And if you do—I wonder at your asking if my king would recruit Irish pirates.'

'Pirates?' Now she was at it. Their conversation seemed to be going nowhere!

He grinned unexpectedly. 'My brother-in-law would call some of them pirates. He deals with many a master mariner from across the sea.'

'Oh! So none of the king's ships comes from Ireland?'

'Unlikely.' Cadfael was wondering just what was behind her questions. Could it be just curiosity? 'Most come from the Cinque Ports in the south of my country. Some from Chester, where my brother-in-law lives with my sister and mother.' His voice had stiffened, so that it almost made Sioned refrain from further questioning.

'That is where you will go to ask your mother about Rhys, your half-brother?'

'That is where I will go,' he replied with obvious patience.

She nodded, and fell silent for a long time.

Later, they fell in with a pedlar, who was talkative, and his chatter eased the constraint that seemed to be growing as they approached their destination. As the weather was good, they slept in the open. They parted from him at the Clywd, and after that the silences between them seemed more noticeable.

Cadfael was tired. The journey had wearied him more than he thought it would, but now there was a lightness in his steps with the camp only a short distance ahead, beyond the well of St Winifrid.

'Let us take some time to visit the well,' he said unexpectedly. 'I would get some water for my mother. Do you know the tale of the saint and her spring?'

Sioned nodded.

'Tell it to me, then.' Cadfael murmured. 'It will help to pass the time.'

When she glanced at him, he seemed serious enough.

'A pagan prince fell in love with Winifrid, who was beautiful, but had made a vow to God never to wed. The prince tried ... tried to force her into doing what he so desired ... but she managed to trick him ... and escape through a window.' Sioned paused and glanced sidelong at Cadfael. 'You have heard the story, perhaps?' she said stiffly.

'Not the whole. Go on.' There was a cool gleam in his eyes.

'He caught her in front of the church, and when she still refused him, he chopped her head off.' Her voice had risen. 'St Beuro saw what had happened, and he uttered a curse that melted the prince into the ground.' She saw that Cadfael's lips twitched. 'You do not believe it? Then I will not continue.'

'Did I say that? Carry on.' His voice was smooth.

Her brow puckered. 'St Beuro picked up St Winifrid's head ... and restored it to her. Instantly she came to life again—and a holy spring came into being on the spot where her blood was spilt,' she finished, with a slightly dramatic air.

'A little gruesome,' Cadfael said with a shudder.

'You do not believe it!' she snapped. 'Yet great miracles are said to have taken place on the spot.'

'That must be the greatest!' Cadfael smiled suddenly. 'Yet I do not deride your tale. But what a punishment to an unwelcome suitor!'

Sioned's eyes sparkled. 'He did chop her head off, Sir Cadfael!'

'Of course. I had forgotten!' The slightest of smiles eased his mouth. 'What happened to the lady?'

'She took the veil.' Her voice was subdued.

'Why do we go to the well if you do not believe the tale?'

'Perhaps I want to believe. Life would be hopeless without some faith and—and trust.' He fell silent.

Sioned gave a sigh. There was something she would have liked to ask him, but she did not know how to disturb his sudden mood of abstraction. Nor, in truth, did she know how to ask what she had on her mind, now that the time had almost come for parting.

They stopped only briefly at the well, speaking with a monk who gave them a small phial of water. In exchange, Cadfael donated a small gift of money, placing the phial carefully in his pack.

It was as they were leaving the well that Cadfael spoke. 'I must get in touch with your brother, Sioned. You understand that?' His voice seemed emotionless. 'I gave you my word that I would return you to him and Govan—and I always keep my word.'

'What?' Sioned stared at Cadfael incredulously, and her heart began to thud. 'What do you mean?' She backed away from him. 'You are going to ransom me ... as you said in the beginning?' Her voice contained a note of horror.

Cadfael pulled her roughly to him. She tried to get away, but his fingers were hard as steel. She was furious with herself for having come so far with him.

'You do not want to wed Govan? Have you changed your mind about all his wealth, Sioned?' His voice was harsh.

'You must know I don't!' She tossed her braids back with an angry shake of her head. 'It was Hywel, my brother, and his demanding an amobr.'

'Of course.' Cadfael gave a tight smile. 'It was Dafydd you really wished to marry.'

'I don't wish to marry either of them—or any man!' Her voice was now as harsh as his.

'So that is the way of it!' He shrugged. 'Still, I must see your brother ... and talk money.' So saying, he kept a tight hold on her arm as he forced her to walk on with him to the English camp.

CHAPTER ELEVEN

'Eat and drink up, missy,' muttered John, scratching his head.

'I'm not hungry,' said Sioned, her mouth set mutinously.

'Of course you are! Sir Cadfael said that you had not broken your fast this day. Don't be foolish, missy,' he added in a coaxing voice. 'He will soon have matters arranged.'

Sioned looked at John's homely face. 'Money matters! Why cannot he set me free?' She picked up the horn cup and took a gulp.

'Matters cannot be arranged any which way. Sir Cadfael's an honourable man, so don't you be worrying.'

'Worrying!' Sioned took another gulp of the wine. 'Your master pretended that he was going to set me free. He even offered me money to guide him, and I refused—fool that I was!' Her eyes gleamed. She took another gulp of the wine, then reached out for a slice of bread. It was wheaten, and tasted very different from the barley bread they had eaten at Megan's. 'I saved his life.' She took another large gulp of the wine.

John shifted uncomfortably from one foot to the other. 'Ay, and very grateful his mother and sisters will be. But do not fear.' He patted her shoulder comfortingly and shot out of the tent, wishing he knew just what his master was up to this time. Why couldn't he just have bedded the wench and got her out of his blood? But all this talk about money—never mind the danger! Well, he just hoped naught would go amiss.

Sioned frowned at John's retreating back and had an urge to fling the cup after him, but thought better of it and finished the wine. Her eyes smouldered. How dare Cadfael treat her so! She had trusted him, and this was the way he repaid her trust. She realised that she had drunk all her wine, but noticing that John had left the pitcher on the table, she filled her cup again defiantly. She had no idea how long she might have to wait before Cadfael returned, but she would tell him just what she thought of him! What did she care if she never saw him again after she left this place! She gulped the wine swiftly.

Hywel would beat her! A trickle of fear chilled her, despite the wine. He would blame her for being captured by the English, and beat her. She had never told even Megan about his cruelty. He would be furious about losing the amobr from Govan. For surely it was in doubt that he would pay it, once he knew she had been in the English camp.

Sioned gave a bitter laugh. Cadfael might find he had bitten off more than he could chew. Tears suddenly cluttered her throat. She had begun to hope that he was ... different. He had been kind at times. She hugged herself, remembering—remembering many things.

Footsteps sounded outside the tent, but Sioned did not look up—not until Cadfael stood before her.

'A meeting has been arranged for tomorrow at noon.'

Sioned gazed into Cadfael's face, unable to read any hope or regret there. 'Why, you have ... have worked quickly! But then you know the way, don't you, Cadfael ... to Govan's keep?'

'I want matters settled swiftly. I have to go to Chester,' he retorted impatiently. 'Surely you understand that, Sioned?'

'Of course! My ... help is no longer needed. Best be rid of me, and gone!' She swayed slightly and clutched the edge of the table. 'Why should it matter to—to you if my brother beats me!'

'He won't beat you.' Cadfael's voice was soft as he picked up the pitcher and poured himself some wine, using Sioned's cup.

Sioned laughed. 'Why? Because you will swear that I am still chaste? Dear Sir Cadfael! He—he will not believe you!'

'You think not?' He smiled at Sioned over the rim of the cup. 'I must confess that the temptation has been great!' He took a sip before placing the cup on the table and coming closer to her.

She did not move away, but gazed defiantly at him. 'You will not get your money if you touch me!' She was suddenly trembling. Her limbs felt like water, and whether it was the effects of the wine or Cadfael's closeness, she did not want to know. He was one of Edward's men. An enemy—who had used her for his own ends. She hated him!

Even as Sioned thought the words, his arms slid about her waist and he was lowering his head to kiss her. She did not want him to kiss her ... She did not want ...

Her lips yielded to his mouth's gentle caress. Yielded and shared—gave back kiss for kiss. He had shaved, and bathed in the river, and his skin was smooth and smelt of salt and sun, and she wanted to slide her fingers down his cheek and throat, to touch the flesh beneath his linen tunic. She wanted him to hold her. She shivered in Cadfael's hold. He was her enemy, and after tomorrow she would never see him again. She told herself she was glad, yet there was a great ache in her breast as he pressed her body against his length and kissed her with increasing passion. They seemed to cling together, although her mind told her to fight him. He pressed hard, savage kisses down her throat, and moving aside the neck of her cotte, kissed the upper curve of her breast.

Cadfael cursed his broken arm. She was warm and yielding, slightly tipsy, and he wanted her! His hold on her tightened, and he arched her body back over his arm and buried his head in the valley between her breasts, letting out a groan.

There was something in the sound that half excited, half frightened her. Warmth flooded her being as she felt the hard wood of his splint pressing her side, and she was aware that he was trembling. Her senses seemed heightened. Each kiss pressed against her bare skin sent pleasure throbbing along her nerves. The strength in his arm made her feel captive, and she did not want such bondage. Yet her body wanted to respond to his touch, to give and give of herself and to go on giving. She moaned softly, and whispered his name.

Abruptly Cadfael released her. She would have fallen, had he not gripped her wrist hard. They stood staring at each other. Sioned's eyes were wide and dazed;

Cadfael's a smouldering gold. She saw his throat move, and his fingers hurt her wrist. He dropped her hand as if it burnt him, and she heard the swift grinding of his heel as he turned and left the tent.

She could not believe ... could not think! She could still only feel the strength of her yearning as she stared after him. Her head whirled, and she felt as if her stomach curled with an icy chill. Carefully she lowered herself on to the pallet on the ground. How could she—Sioned ap Rowan—have allowed herself almost to offer herself to him? One of the enemy—Edward's man! What madness had seized her? Her blood still tingled from his mouth's contact with her skin.

Sioned sat staring at the billowing tent wall, hearing the calls of the English army as they went about their affairs. He had not wanted her—and yet ... He had touched and held her in such a way that had it been Govan, she would have been terrified. She closed her eyes. Money? Or honour? Which was it that drove Sir Cadfael Poole? Suddenly she was angry. How dared he treat her so! Furious tears started in her eyes, then she buried her head in her arms and wept for herself.

Sioned was ready just before noon the next day. Her braids were neatly plaited and her face washed clean of the tears she had been unable to prevent. She held herself proudly, despite her bare feet, and met Cadfael's appraising look with calmness.

The sun shone and the birds sang as they walked amid the trees. She hardly noticed the bowmen slipping away one by one. She felt frozen inside, and Cadfael seemed distant. She wondered if she had imagined her feelings when he had kissed and held her.

He was silent, carrying his long sword, alert for any sudden movement. John followed just behind.

At last they came to a clearing, and halted. Govan and Hywel were there, sitting on a fallen tree. Hywel, his dark hair long and straggly about his thin face, rose, flashing his sister a black look. Govan stayed sitting, his plump face dragged down by his irritation. He thrust the knife with which he had been paring his nails inside his belt, and looked into Sioned's expressionless face, scrutinising it carefully.

'You want a ransom?' snapped Hywel, stopping a few feet from Cadfael and Sioned. His legs were a little apart and his hands clenched in his girdle.

'You would pay it?' Cadfael's voice was lightly amused. 'How much would you suggest?'

Hywel shrugged, and glanced at Govan. 'If my sister is still chaste, it would be more—but we have heard much concerning what your kind do to our women. So I would say ...' He looked thoughtful for a moment, then glanced again at Govan before naming a sum.

'Too high,' grunted Govan. He stared at Sioned moodily.

Sioned stared back, standing straight as a lance, not showing her fear.

'You think so, Master Govan?' Cadfael's voice was cool. 'You would pay so little for a bride?'

'No woman is worth that sum, once she has been with the English!'

'You think not? I consider the price fair.'

'I would not pay it,' growled Govan, going scarlet.

'You are not being asked,' said Cadfael softly. 'This is between the lady's brother and myself.'

Govan stared at him and kicked the ground. His eyes were dark as he gazed at Sioned and Cadfael. The sun slanted down through the trees behind them, casting on them a mottled shifting light, bonding them in some strange way.

'I leave your sister in your hands, Hywel.' Govan exchanged one brief angry glance with Hywel before nodding and stamping out of the clearing.

Cadfael was looking at Hywel, who was running a spear through his fingers with some force. He tapped it against the palms of his hands, returning Cadfael's gaze. Then he threw back his head and laughed.

'I deem that my sister has shared your bed, and so I demand for her virginity the amobr that is rightly mine—shall we say the same price you are ransoming her for?'

Sioned gave a gasp, but Cadfael hushed her and bade John hold her. With some awkwardness he took the money pouch from his neck and flung it on the ground in front of Hywel. 'Take it! There is sufficient there for your sister. She is mine now, so do not try to reclaim her.'

As she stared and stared at the money on the ground, her heart began to thud. But she had no time to think. Cadfael threw his sword to John and grabbed her, hurrying her from the clearing. He dragged her along at breakneck speed, soon leaving her brother behind. She bit back a scream as a man dropped from a tree in front of them. Cadfael's face set grim as he spoke with him, then he turned to John and took his sword.

Govan and his men attacked just as they rounded a bend. They approached like wolves, howling and whistling, spears in their hands as they charged forward. Cadfael flung Sioned to the ground, and ducked as a spear went whistling over his head. It landed with a thud in a tree behind them. There came the swish, swish of arrows from Cadfael's bowmen. Sioned rubbed a hand across her damp and dirty face, spitting out crumbled leaves. She watched as Cadfael rose to his feet. Govan lumbered forward, a knife held high, and made a slashing sweep with the blade at him. There was barely time for him to fling up his left arm, and the knife dug deep into his splint, and stuck. Pain flashed in Cadfael's face as the blow jarred his arm, but without hesitating he drew back his sword-arm and drove his blade into Govan's body.

Sioned stayed on her knees, trembling, as Govan's face twisted in pained surprise. His plodgy fingers slid from the hilt of his knife as Cadfael dragged out his sword. Govan sank to the ground a foot away from her.

Cadfael grabbed her by the arm and pulled her to her feet, his sword slipped through his sling. 'Come!' His face glistened with sweat, and his mouth was tight with pain, but he pulled her away from the scene of carnage.

Already the raiders were fleeing, their

spears spent. Several men from both sides lay dead or dying in the tangled undergrowth. Then Sioned was running with Cadfael, running and running. At last they reached the edge of the forest, and there they halted a moment on the road the axemen had widened.

'You—you killed him!' Sioned muttered to Cadfael, her face still blank with the shock of seeing death at such close quarters. She pulled her hand out of his and held her palms against her cheeks, hot with exertion.

'He would have killed me first! Kill or be killed, Sioned. This is war, and there is not much beauty in it.' His breathing was hurried, and his eyes pain-filled. 'He could have fought for you in the clearing. I thought he might.' Cadfael took her arm and began to drag her along the road. 'But don't you see that leaving your brother behind was a ruse to keep me talking and to give Govan time to call his men to him?'

'That is why you paid the amobr Hywel asked? You never trusted them to play fair?' Her voice shook.

'Trust a Cymri warrior on his own ground?' Cadfael cast her a sardonic glance. 'I might be some sort of fool, but not that one! Your brother does not lack nerve.' His stride slackened, and they looked at one another, the sun hot on their heads. 'I wonder if you will be worth the price I paid? Only time will tell, I think,' he murmured thoughtfully.

Sioned's heart had barely settled down to a steady beat when it began to quicken again. 'What are you going to do with me?'

'Do?' Cadfael let out a long breath. 'I must sleep on it, I think.'

'But ...' Her throat tightened.

'In the morning, Sioned.' Cadfael's voice was soft. 'I have matters to arrange, and John must reset my splints. I only pray that Govan's blow has not shattered all Megan's good work.'

Sioned hardly slept that night. What would Cadfael do with her. Maybe—maybe he would set her free? Where would she go, when she had almost made up her mind to ask him to take her to Chester? It was a port, and many ships came there. Maybe—maybe even Owain's!

She shifted on the pallet. No! He would not let her free, not having paid money for her. What had he said? She was his, and her brother was not to claim her? Her nerves jumped. He would make her his mistress, as Govan had Annest. Annest—would she be grieved over Govan's death? Or would she accept his death with the same placid patience that she had accepted being his mistress? What would happen to her? Mistresses did not have the same standing as wives ... or widows. She turned over restlessly. If Cadfael took her for his mistress, how long would it be before he tired of her and cast her off? She wanted to believe that he was not that kind of man, but common sense and her recent treatment at Dafydd's and Govan's hands made it unlikely that he could take any other course. Heat suffused her face as she realised she was accepting the inevitability of becoming Cadfael's mistress—and that she did not find the idea utterly unacceptable. At last she slept, tired out by emotions that warred within her, and even when dawn lightened the tent walls, she still slept on undisturbed.

Cadfael narrowed his eyes against the morning sun. 'There is a ship returning to Chester this morning, you say, John?'

John nodded his grizzled head.

Cadfael tapped his fingernail thoughtfully against his teeth. 'You will come with us, of course. I will need you. There is not much doing here until the road is opened fully to Rhuddlan. Besides, Master de Grey thinks I will be of more use if I go and rest awhile—let my bone knit, and return in time for the final stratagem of this campaign. Such a plan would suit me well, and I can carry on with my search for Rhys then.'

'Ay, you need to rest, Sir Cadfael.' John looked anxiously at his master. He was still pale, and thinner than he should be. 'Have you told the young lady yet?' Not by a flicker of an eyelash did he reveal just what he thought of his master's latest coil.

'Not yet.' Cadfael toyed with the seal ring on his finger, and rose to his feet. 'You will tell the ship's master that we will come within the hour. I will go and fetch Sioned now.'

John picked up his master's pack, and went towards the river.

Sioned's elbow touched Cadfael's as she gazed down at the silky green-grey waters. The ship skipped before the wind, her sail billowing out. Delight stirred within her, and for a moment she concentrated all her thoughts on Owain, her brother. Was he still alive? Or was it as Hywel had said, and he might have lost his life on the sea between Ireland and Wales?

'You like being aboard ship, Sioned?'

She lifted her head and looked at Cadfael. 'It is pleasant,' she responded in a stilted voice. 'I—I was not sure if I would find it so. I have heard that the motion can make one sick.' She gripped the darkened oak tightly as a wave surged high against the prow.

The sun danced on the water, burnishing the surface into a sheet of splintered silver, dazzling her eyes. She was aware that Cadfael's eyes were on her face, and shifted her gaze, attempting to pierce the heat-haze that screened the far shore, catching glimpses of low hills clad in shapes of misty greens, golds and browns. It gave her a strange feeling to see the land she had been reared to despise taking on reality. It was England she was going to—England! A nightmare land occupied by a cruel and overbearing race of people, whose king sought to conquer her country.

If only she had the courage to ask Cadfael outright what he intended doing with her! He would surely go and visit his mother? Perhaps he would leave her in John's care, and she would have a chance to walk along the riverside, gazing at the ships and the mariners. Maybe John would take her to his manor. It was over there, somewhere on that far bank. It would be so different from her own soaring mountain peaks—a much gentler country when it came to landscape. His sister lived there, she remembered. What would she think of him bringing home a woman from the mountains? She glanced down at her bare toes peeping from beneath the hem of her gown. The deck was warm beneath her feet. A barefoot maid, who did not speak their language, and he had bought her. Perhaps he would give her to his sister as a servant? What was he going to do with her?

'We shall soon catch our first glimpse of the city.' There was pride in Cadfael's voice.

'Already?' Sioned moistened her lips. She was scared all of a sudden. Her fingers twisted together on the wood.

'I think you will enjoy Chester. We will be staying there for some days. I wish you to meet my sister Matilda, and my mother.'

Sioned's eyes flew to Cadfael's face. 'You are taking me to visit your mother?' Her voice rose in amazement.

'You object?' His eyes narrowed. 'Where else do you think I would take the woman I intend to make my wife?'

CHAPTER TWELVE

The banks slid by, and suddenly on the left-hand side a short distance ahead appeared the pink sandstone walls of the city of Chester, washed rosy orange in the afternoon sun. Still Sioned stared up at Cadfael, not speaking, her brown eyes dilated.

'You do not wish to become my wife? Perhaps you would rather be my mistress?' Cadfael's voice was rough.

Her throat moved slowly, 'I ... I did not expect ...' She lowered her voice. 'Why? Why? You could marry a woman of your own race, not I!'

'I have paid your price—so why should you not be my bride?' he mocked, putting his hand over her trembling fingers. 'I have need of a wife, Sioned. More than I need a mistress.'

'But we are enemies! Our lords are in conflict. I have been reared to hate your land!' Her thoughts were in confusion.

'You are no enemy of mine, Sioned ... And how can you hate a land that you have never set foot on?' He pressed her hand. 'You saved my life. Conflicts come to an end, and it will not need to concern us much then.'

Gratitude! He was marrying her because she had saved his life. Her heart beat wildly. She had thought she did not want to marry any man, and had almost come to accept the thought of becoming his mistress. Yet she could not deny his attraction or the effect his words had upon her. She had thought to look for Owain here in Chester and somehow find safety with him. But how did she know she would find him—or even that he would want her? Where could she find rest from the tumult inside her ... a tumult caused by this man?

'What of your family? Your brother, your sisters—and your mother? What will they think?' There was tension in her low musical voice, and she would have pulled her hand free so that she could think the better away from him, but his grip tightened.

'You are anxious about meeting them?' He sounded thoughtful. 'There is no need. My mother will welcome you. Matilda is alway wanting me to marry. As for Kate,' he hesitated, 'she will come round.' He smiled and squeezed her fingers. 'All my family speak Welsh, and understand more than they can speak. You will need perhaps to learn French and English, but do not worry about being understood—you will be.'

'That will make matters less difficult,' she said, a little breathlessly. He was sweeping away all obstacles, it seemed.

'Well?' Cadfael's eyes searched her face.

Sioned knew she had no choice. Yet still, it seemed, he was asking her—not demanding from her. What if she refused—would he make her his mistress? Why had he paid her amobr?

'I will do my best to give you value for the money you have paid for me.' She sounded almost unhappy.

'I am sure you will!' His voice was hard. 'Then it is settled.'

Sioned glanced at him swiftly. He looked tired, and she was aware that it was not so long since she thought he would die. Suddenly she realised that it was likely he thought he was doing her great honour by marrying her. 'I ... I thank you for asking me, Sir Cadfael,' she stammered.

'The pleasure, I hope, will not be all mine, dear Sioned. I hope you will enjoy being my wife.' He lowered his head and kissed her lightly, before tucking her hand into his arm. 'We are almost there. I hope you will like our city.'

Her face flushed by his words, she looked towards the city walls. There were towers on each side of the gateway, and she felt bewildered.

'This is the Water Gate, and the tide comes and goes daily across the Roodeye,' he said.

'I ... I have never seen such a city,' said Sioned in a stilted voice, her eyes lighting with interest despite the tumult in her heart. 'It is like a place out of a tale!'

Cadfael smiled. 'Yet it has its thieves and pickpockets—its destitute and lepers. The abbey is magnificent, and the castle walls are strong. The riverside is fascinating with ships coming from many lands. There is wine from Gascony, corn from Ireland, cloth from Flanders. Even furs and skins are brought from the cold lands far north, and spices from the east.'

Sioned gazed enthralled at the ships and small boats passing to and fro, thinking of Owain. For a moment she forgot her fears.

They left the ship and entered the city. The lanes were noisy with the sounds of men and women chattering and calling to one another. It was a fine afternoon, and the river bank was thronged with folk. Children, some as barefooted as Sioned, darted between the jostling crowds, playing games with a ball.

'It is forbidden to play in the lanes with a ball,' whispered Cadfael in her ear. 'But nobody enforces the law unless someone suffers a blow to the head, or is brought down by treading on the ball.'

'There are so many people!' She clung to Cadfael's arm as her eyes darted hither and thither.

'It is market-day,' he replied. 'You will be able to see what wares are for sale. However, I have little money with me.'

She thought that was so because he had given all he had to pay her bride price, and she wondered at him doing so.

They came to the market-place, where booths and trestles were set up. On the right side of the square rose the imposing abbey of St Werburgh.

'Look at the clothes!' murmured Sioned. 'So bright and gay—so richly made. By St Winifrid! ...' She came to a sudden halt, a smile on her mouth.

Cadfael's gaze followed her, and he grinned as he took in the latest fashion. 'It is a cote-hardie,' he whispered in her ear, urging her on again, somehow making the crowd part before them. 'The two colours are popular. Yellow and red do not clash too much, I think? But did you note the liripipe on his head?'

Sioned twisted round and stared back at the young man, then twinkled up at Cadfael. ' 'Tis a wonder he does not trip over it!'

'One could always fold it over one's arm!' Cadfael's lips twitched. 'Should I have such a hood made, Sioned? Long enough to hang down my back to my feet? Do you think I would look fine as a peacock?'

She flushed at the teasing note in his voice. 'But—but what would I wear, if you are to be dressed so fine?' she responded pensively.

'Ahhh!' His eyes scanned the crowd. 'What think you of that cote-hardie? It is of cloth of lake, a fine linen, and the sides are cut away to show the underskirt beneath. Matilda, my sister, knows all the latest fashions. You must ask her advice.'

Sioned smiled hesitantly. Perhaps his sister would not wish to give her advice? She gazed with pleasure at a woman whose auburn hair was caught up in a net of gold, over which was draped a gossamer-fine veil. Her cote-hardie was of a dark green silk.

'There, Cadfael!' Sioned pressed his arm. 'Is that not a pretty gown, and she so lovely?'

He gazed intently. 'It is Matilda! Come, Sioned, I must make you known to her.'

'Your sister?' Nerves tightened her stomach.

'Ay.' He stroked her hand reassuringly.

'There is no need to be anxious. Everyone likes Matilda.'

Sioned was not so sure if Cadfael's sister would like her! She appeared so lovely and self-assured. What would she think of Sioned dressed as she was—and shoeless?

Cadfael thrust his way through the crowd, dragging Sioned in his wake, until they caught up with his sister in front of a stall laden with lengths of cloth. He released Sioned's hand and took hold of his sister's arm, as she assessed the roll of woollen fabric held up by the effusive vendor.

She spun round, surprise on her delicately rounded face, only to let out a delighted cry when she saw Cadfael. 'Cadfael!' She made to fling her arms about her brother, but was brought up short by the sling on his arm. 'What has happened to you?' Her voice was deep and pleasant. 'We did not expect to see you so soon, brother.'

'A slight altercation with some robbers.' Cadfael grinned, and allowed his sister to kiss him. 'It might have been much worse, had it not been for Sioned.'

'Sioned!' Matilda waved a slender white hand dismissively at the stall-holder as he flourished another bolt of cloth before her.

'Sioned—the bronze-haired maiden, who

would save my life.' Cadfael's eyes gleamed with a droll amusement as he met his sister's incredulous stare. He put an arm about Sioned's blue-clad shoulders.

'You mean ...?' Matilda's green eyes grew round as she stared at Cadfael and Sioned.

'Mother has not lost her disturbing habit,' said Cadfael drily.

Matilda paled, and clutched at the front of Cadfael's surcoat. 'Were you in terrible danger? I would not have sent Ned, but Mother was so ill—and so insistent!' she cried.

'Danger?' Cadfael quirked a brow, and his mouth twisted. 'What—with the reassurance that my rescuer was at hand?'

Matilda was silent as she smoothed the scarlet fabric she had creased on Cadfael's chest. She faced Sioned, a smile lighting her face as she held forth both her hands. 'My mother did not say his rescuer would be both brave and beautiful!' She seized Sioned's hands and pressed them in gratitude.

Sioned was puzzled, but she smiled in response to Matilda's warmth of manner. She had been unable to understand a word of the swiftly-spoken French.

'Sioned speaks only Welsh, Matilda. You must help her as much as you can before I take her to my manor.'

'Your manor?' Matilda looked at her brother, and her expression showed her uncertainty. 'What do you mean?'

'I am going to marry Sioned as soon as it can be arranged.' He spoke in Welsh. Matilda stared at him, and her astonishment was apparent to Sioned.

Sioned's cheeks flushed, and without realising she did so, she squared her shoulders and lifted her chin. She was extremely conscious of her bare feet and that her gown had dust smeared across the front where she had brushed against a sack on the ship.

'Where is our half-brother?' Matilda licked her lips nervously. 'We thought it might take you much longer to find him.' She spoke in Welsh.

'I did not find him,' he responded with a frown. 'Rhys is no longer in the mountains, but has gone to Anglesey. His whereabouts, Mother will know. I found that out only through Sioned.'

'I see.' Matilda slipped one hand through her brother's arm. 'The search will have to wait, then. I am certain Mother will understand. But let us go to my house, and Mistress Sioned will be able to refresh herself there and change her gown.'

'I do not have another gown. And it is your brother who wishes to wed me, Mistress Matilda.' Sioned's steady brown eyes met Matilda's discomforted ones. 'He has paid my bride price.'

'Your bride price?' Matilda's glance shifted from Sioned to her brother's face, sensing some mystery. Why was it the girl had no clothes and what did she mean by 'bride price'? She gave a small smile. 'I am delighted that my brother is to marry. He has remained unwed too long since Isabella's death.' She gave a sigh, but her brother said nothing. 'But we will not talk about that. As for Kate, I presume she will still live with you, Cadfael?' She held her head a little to the side.

'Of course Kate will still live with me. Where is Ned, 'Tilda?' he asked, sensing Sioned's uneasiness, and wishing his sister had not spoken yet of his dead wife and Kate. 'Is he at home or away?' They had left the market-place and were walking down a lane.

'He is at the waterfront, waiting for a shipment of spices. It is a wonder you did not see him. But he is sure to be home for supper.' Matilda's face softened, and there was a bloom about her that made Sioned feel a little easier somehow. 'You can meet him then, Mistress Sioned.'

'I shall take Sioned with me to see Mother as soon as we have tidied up, Matilda,' said Cadfael firmly. 'She has a gift for Mother—some holy water from

St Winifrid's well. It will augur well for our meeting, if she is with me. Without Sioned, I would not be here, and as Mother foretold, she saved my life. She and Mother have much they can talk about. They are both from the mountains, and have a mutual friend.'

'If that is what you wish.' Matilda glanced at her brother. Why was he marrying the girl? Was it gratitude because she saved his life? Not that she was not a beauty. With dressing, she would look superb. She changed the subject and began to talk about Chester, the market, clothes, and her mother. Then eventually, to Sioned's surprise, what sort of gown she should have made for the wedding.

Sioned listened, her heart beating uncomfortably fast as they came to Matilda's house. It seemed there was to be no escape. Cadfael really meant to marry her. Could it really be true? And that she was, in reality, in England? She only wished that she did not feel so frightened about going into the house. Somehow, it made the reality even more real that she would meet Cadfael's mother.

'Si-o-ned! It is a pretty name,' said the lady Elin Poole in a voice that was weary, but did not conceal the lilt that had never disappeared in all her years in the

Palatinate. She gazed across at Sioned, one thin hand plucking restlessly at the coverlet over her knees. 'Come, child, sit next to me and tell me a little about yourself. Cadfael has explained how you saved his life, and took him to Megan. I thank you for that. You are just as pretty and good for him as I thought you would be when first I saw you.'

'Saw me, my lady?' Sioned sat up straight on the three-legged stool near the wide bed. She wondered what to say, and how to begin.

'I saw you in a dream.' Amusement lit Elin's face, which was the colour of vellum. 'Now that Cadfael has gone to visit the priest, I shall tell you.'

Matilda stood silently listening, and she smiled reassuringly. 'We are all ears, Mother. Go on!'

'I knew that you were the one for Cadfael. But if I had spoken such words, he would have closed his mind to the thought of marriage.' Cadfael's mother frowned, and one thin hand plucked the coverlet again. 'He was greatly hurt after Isabella.' She sighed. 'But I will not talk about that. It is in the past, and it is to the future we must look—or you must look, Sioned. There is not much time for me.'

'Perhaps the holy water ...' began Sioned, stretching out a hand and covering the sick woman's hand with her own. Already she found herself caring for her, despite her former feelings.

'Holy water or no, child, I will die. I have lived long enough, and I do not fear death.' She chuckled. 'I have well endowed several orders that will pray for my soul, and I will be united with my man. Life has been tedious without him.'

Sioned could think of nothing to say. Her sympathy was not needed, it seemed. 'I shall do my uttermost to make ... Cadfael ... happy,' she murmured, flushing.

'I think you mean that, child—even though you are not so sure about marrying my son.' The lady Elin's fingers twitched beneath Sioned's firm young grip. 'I recall the same fear on leaving my mountains and marrying my Englishman.' Then her face grew serious. 'But I see pictures that disturb me ... fire ... men running ... and ships, many ships. There will be pain for you, Sioned. But you will overcome. You and Cadfael together.' Her voice dwindled.

As the lady's eyes closed, wonder and fear chilled Sioned's mind. How could she see so much, or was it all in a mind overwrought with the images of the past, perhaps, and—despite the lady's words—fear for the future? She glanced at Matilda, thinking that the lady had fallen asleep. Matilda nodded, and Sioned made to pull her hand free, but it was held fast as the lady Elin's eyes fluttered open.

'So many dreams,' she murmured drowsily, 'and in the midst, I see Rhys. I am certain he is Rhys.' She sighed. 'If only he would turn round so that I could see his face ... His is tall and dark, with broad shoulders. His hair curls crisply like my first-born's. He was a fine boy.' Her lids drooped, and after a few moments Sioned eased her fingers gently from her grasp, and rose to her feet.

'I did not tire her too much?' Sioned's voice was concerned as she followed Matilda from the chamber.

Matilda shook her head, giving her a reassuring smile. 'It has done her good to see you. And, as you must have guessed, she is glad that Cadfael is to wed again.' She lifted her skirts, carefully watching where she trod on the stairs. 'It seems, in truth, that Mother knew Cadfael would marry you.' She paused. 'Though she would not own to it, Cadfael is Mother's favourite, and he is also the most like her. That is why I cannot really understand why she wishes to see Rhys so much after so many years.' Her eyes softened. 'But then, I am a mother myself, and perhaps it is that our first-born holds a special place in our hearts. I would not know yet about that, having only one child.' She opened the door that led to the hall.

Sioned admired the blue-washed walls, upon which hung many richly coloured tapestries. Instead of rushes covering the floor, there was at the far end of the room a patterned scarlet covering, where a small boy played.

Matilda rushed forward and scooped him up, blowing into his ear. He giggled and rubbed his sandy head against his mother's chin. Sioned approached more slowly, and he stared at her out of great wide hazel eyes.

'This is our son, Edward.' Matilda's voice was filled with loving pride.

'He is a fine boy.' Sioned put out a hand, and the boy reached out and took two of her fingers. He jerked them vigorously, laughing as he did so. Her face broke into a smile.

'He is a little boisterous at times,' said Matilda, leading Sioned over to a cushioned settle against a wall. 'But it is a fine thing to have a son, and, God willing, you and Cadfael will be so blessed. You know that Isabella and her child died?'

Sioned's hands stilled in the act of smoothing her skirts as she sat down next to Matilda. Was Cadfael marrying her for breeding, as Govan had wished to?

Her throat tightened. 'Cadfael has hardly spoken of Isabella.'

Matilda absently stroked back a curl from her son's brow, as he rested his head against her. 'I think it an episode in his life he would like to forget. He was on crusade when it happened. Isabella had Kate staying with her in Gascony.' She met Sioned's wide-eyed gaze. 'You do not need to fear that there will be ghosts at the manor on the Wirral, Sioned! Isabella did not set foot in England. Cadfael married her in Gascony. It was arranged between her father and mine. Mother did not want Cadfael to wed Isabella, but my father overruled her wishes. I think he was jealous of her fondness for Cadfael, and regarded her "seeing" as foolishness. Anything that he could not understand, my father did not like.'

'It is disconcerting,' murmured Sioned, giving a small smile. There were several questions she would have liked to ask, but lacked the courage.

'You are thinking of what Mother said to you?'

Sioned wasn't, but she did not say so. Matilda wrinkled her dainty nose. 'Ships! Fire! Men running! It could be just a fire down on the waterfront that Mother has seen in the past and that now recurs in her mind. You must not let her words worry you. She is not always right in her predictions.'

'Yet it is because of your mother's words that Cadfael sought me out.' Sioned's voice was low as she gazed at the embroidered leather slippers that Matilda had given her. 'You must think it strange that he brought home a barefoot bride with no baggage.'

Matilda shrugged, and smiled. 'I presume he met you first, to think of you when I sent word. Where did you meet?' Her curiosity was well concealed.

Sioned hesitated but a moment. 'He came to spy on the man I was going to marry! He played the part of a Cymri raider and minstrel, but I knew he was not, for I had seen him when I spied on the English army.'

'How strange!' murmured Matilda. 'This man you were to marry—what happened to him? How was it you went with Cadfael?'

Sioned's eyes were suddenly dark. 'I did not wish to marry the man in the first place! It was arranged by my brother, Hywel. Govan was to pay my bride price. Cadfael persuaded me that it was foretold that I would guide him to find Rhys ... I wanted to escape, to return to ... to the mountains, so I went with him.' Sioned paused. It sounded mad and reckless!

'I see.' Matilda let her son slide off her

knee on to the floor. 'Did you ever see this Govan again?'

'Ay!' Sioned remembered the moment, unaware that Matilda was hanging onto her words. 'Cadfael killed him, and paid the amobr my brother demanded.'

'Goodness!' Matilda stared at Sioned in surprise. Here was a side to her brother that she had never known or seen!

Sioned returned Matilda's gaze, and shrugged. 'I could not go back for my clothes. There was a fight, you see. That is why I have but one gown.'

'I see.' Matilda saw far more than Sioned did, yet some aspects of the story had been left untold. She wondered what had happened between her brother and Sioned while they had been seeking Rhys. It seemed that her brother was at last putting Isabella out of his mind.

Matilda rose to her feet, calling the serving-maid who had been setting the table, and she handed Edward into her keeping.

'If you would like, Sioned, we could look at some material I already have in my chest. You can choose whichever one you desire, and it will be a gift from Ned and me for your wedding. I will wield my needle alongside yours, so that with all speed the gown will be ready in time. Cadfael does not intend to wait, and I think the priest at St Peter's will not gainsay him!'

'Thank you.' Sioned was relieved that the questions were finished with for the moment. She went over with Matilda to one of the large oaken chests that stood in the hall, and Matilda unlocked it with a key that hung with many others from her girdle.

Once again Sioned was conscious of a sense of unreality. Was this really happening to her? The ease with which she had been accepted by Cadfael's sister and mother made it possible to believe that she could be happy here in England. Could she really? Would the obstacles that were bound to rise prove as painful as the lady Elin had foretold? Suddenly she was frightened, and needing reassurance. Reassurance that only Cadfael could give. She wished he would come, so that she could rid herself of a sudden sense of foreboding.

CHAPTER THIRTEEN

Material covered the far end of the trestle table. Sioned's head shot up as the door opened and Cadfael entered. Her heart lifted as he smiled, and then her glance went to the man who accompanied him. His rather serious countenance lightened as Matilda moved forward.

'Ned! Come and meet Sioned, who is to wed Cadfael.'

Matilda held out her hand, and Sioned took it and went forward with her. 'Just say "Croesawu", Ned, and shake Sioned's hand.'

Matilda's husband took her hand firmly, and she looked into steady grey eyes.

'Croesawu, Mistress Sioned,' he greeted her obediently, and added some words in English to Cadfael, who smiled.

'He is complimenting Cadfael on his good fortune,' Matilda told Sioned with a smile, before moving to Ned's side. She began to speak to him in rapid English.

Cadfael said, 'Well, Sioned, have you passed your time pleasantly while I have been arranging our wedding?' He walked with her over to a settle and they sat down a little apart.

'Your sister is kind, and your mother has expressed her gladness that we are to wed. When is the ceremony to be, Sir Cadfael?' Sioned moistened her mouth, not looking directly into his face.

'In a week's time. Will that ...'

'A week? So soon!' She could not prevent the words slipping out.

'You think it too soon?' Cadfael's face was taut.

Sioned raised her head. 'It—it is just that your sister has such plans ... for finery ... that I never dreamed about all my days.' She thought that her answer satisfied him, for he grinned.

'I told you that Matilda knows all about what is fashionable! She will enlist more help to sew, if that is what is needed. Do not fear on that score.' He adjusted the sling about his neck, and she noticed that the splints had been changed to shorter ones of a smoother wood.

'You have seen a physician? What did he say about your arm?'

He grimaced. 'Nothing that I did not already know! I must keep the splints on for several more weeks.'

'But you are more comfortable now? It is not so painful?' Sioned's brown eyes were concerned as she looked into his face.

'Not so painful,' Cadfael echoed softly. 'Sioned ...' He paused. 'I make haste to wed you, knowing that I will have to go away in a short time. I wish you to have security just in case anything befalls me.'

There was a short silence while she turned over his words. They were a reminder of his being one of Edward's men, who would go and fight against her people. Her stomach twisted uncomfortably. She did not want to think of him fighting—of being hurt. 'You—you forget what the seer said, Cadfael,' she murmured, staring down at her fingers. 'And you will bring Rhys home, won't you? But—but I would that you did not speak of going yet.'

'I must—but it is not the parting that I meant just now.' Cadfael seemed pleased with her words. 'I have matters to see to, and arrangements to make for your coming to my manor. John will accompany me.'

'You will leave me here?' Sioned cried. Was this her chance to seek her brother?

'It is best that you stay here.' He puckered his brow. 'I hope to bring Kate back with me. Maybe Matilda will be able to persuade her to stay in Chester, so that you may have a better chance to settle at my manor before I have to go to Wales again.'

'I see.' Fleetingly, she wondered why Kate shunned company, but she had no chance to ask, for Matilda and Ned came over and the conversation took a different turn.

Cadfael left the next day, and Sioned waved him farewell with a strange confusion of feelings. She had been in his company each day—most of each day. Yet she saw his going as the perfect chance to look for her brother with no questions being asked. She soon discovered, however, that Matilda would not let her roam the lanes or the waterfront alone. Was that at Cadfael's command, she wondered with an angry spurt of rebellious emotion. Yet, otherwise, Matilda was helpful and kind.

Sioned had much with which to occupy herself. She went marketing with Matilda who had, it seemed, since her mother's words, accepted Sioned's marriage to her brother as inevitable. She attempted to teach her some French and English words, and discovered that she was a quick learner. Still, it was difficult for them both. Some part of each day Sioned spent with Cadfael's mother, listening to Elin talk of the far-off days when she was young.

Once she spoke of Isabella. 'She would not go with Cadfael on crusade, even though the lady Eleanor went with the prince. Isabella said that she would be in terror of her life, and that the only truly civilised lands were France and Italy.' Elin sighed. 'That was the only time I saw Cadfael displeased with Isabella. They had been married for such a short time, and he naturally wished her to go with him. He wanted her to come to England with Kate and myself, but she said she saw no reason to, if he were not there. So he gave in to her, and even allowed Kate to stay in Gascony until his return. It was a mistake. I should not have left her, knowing the visions I had seen.' Her greying head tossed restlessly against the piled-up pillows.

'What happened?' Sioned's question dropped into the sudden silence, but there was no reply, and she realised that Elin had fallen into a doze. So she rose, and went down to the hall.

Matilda was there, playing with her child. She looked up guiltily when Sioned appeared, and gripped her bottom lip between her teeth before letting out a laugh.

'I know I should be sewing your gown, but Margaret is carrying on with it while I spend some time with Edward. I thought, if you were willing, I would have Margaret's cousin to help her with the sewing. She plies a skilful needle. The weather is so fine that perhaps we could go for a walk down to the river, and take Edward with us.'

'I would like that!' Sioned thankfully placed the saffron silk undergown she had started to sew upon the settle. 'My eyes ache after setting such tiny stitches in my cote-hardie last night.'

'I know what you mean!' Matilda rolled her eyes expressively. 'But it is easier to sew the linen than the silk.' She called Margaret over to her, and gave her some orders in English before addressing Sioned.

'Shall we go now? You will be warm enough in that gown?'

Sioned nodded. 'I am very grateful to you for giving it to me.'

Matilda looked appraisingly at her. 'You are fortunate in being able to wear that crimson. It never became me, I'm sorry to say, but I did not like to discard it once I had paid such a large sum for the fabric.' She put a hand through Sioned's arm, and with her son's small chubby fist held firmly in her other hand, they went out of doors.

The sun shone from a hard brilliant sky of purest blue, and the walk would have been delightful but for the stench of the filth in the lanes, which had not been cleared away that day. Sioned wrinkled her nose, wondering how Matilda, who was so fastidious, could bear to live in the city all the time.

At the river bank, Sioned's eyes shone

with pleasure. The sights and sounds of the mariners and merchants, as well as other city folk, made her forget the dirty lanes. The ships were interesting, and she was glad that they had come a different route from that which Cadfael had brought her that first day. She gazed at the busy traffic on the bridge, noting the mill on her left, and the weir that stretched across towards a huddle of buildings on the far bank.

'The weir was built by Hugh Lupus to supply power for the Dee mills. There is a gate named after him—the Wolf Gate.'

'Are there many gates leading into the city?'

'Several, and a toll is levied by the sergeant who keeps the gate. Ned knows all about tolls.' Matilda pulled a face. 'We export, of course, as well as import. Our cheeses are famed far abroad, and have been ever since the city was a Roman port.'

Matilda gave a sudden cry, as Edward pulled himself free of her restraining grasp and darted towards the water's edge, and she swiftly flew after him.

Sioned watched, a smile on her face, then she followed them, pushing her way through the bustling crowds. She chuckled as she saw Matilda catch her son and tuck him firmly under her arm, posterior upwards, his short stubby legs kicking frantically at the air.

'Well caught!' The voice came faintly to Sioned's ears, and she turned her head towards the direction whence it came.

A man stood in the stern of a ship that was already sailing. He grinned and blew a kiss in Matilda's direction. His weather-darkened face was bright with laughter, and his brilliant blue eyes stared out from beneath a mop of almost black hair that curled in tight springs about his ears and forehead.

Sioned stared and stared across the gap that was widening between the ship and the bank, and moved forward at last. The wind was filling the sail, and the man turned away as she ran alongside the riverside.

'Owain!' The wind took the name away and scattered its sound. Sioned waved frantically as the ship took her brother further and further away. But it was too late, and she gave up her chase. Her feet slowed and she came to a halt, the breath burning in her throat. For a long moment she stood gazing after the ship until it disappeared from her sight. Then she turned, hearing Matilda's footsteps and Edward's pattering feet.

'You are acquainted with Owain, Sioned?'

Sioned nodded. To be so close to her brother, and not hold proper speech with him—not to be able to touch him or to reassure herself that all was well with him. She had hoped and prayed that she might see him again—someone of her own kin who was dear to her.

'He comes here often. Ned says he's a pirate, but that does not prevent him buying from him.' Matilda made a droll face. 'I did hear that he came from the mountains. He had speech once with Mother, when she was well.'

'It is a long time since I have seen him.' Sioned's spirits soared. He would be returning!

'Ned told Cadfael about him, and my brother it seems was suspicious about his motives. The success of the king's plans in Wales is dependent on secrecy.' Matilda's eyes were pensive. 'Not that I know what they are, but Ned just told me what Cadfael said to him when he complained of the king requisitioning one of our ships, and he asked what they were all needed for.'

'I see.' Sioned had been about to tell Matilda about her brother, but changed her mind. She would wait and see what would happen, if Owain returned to Chester and she had a chance to see him again. Cadfael might not be pleased about her having kin of her own here while the war went on. He might think

Owain was like Hywel, and forbid her to see him.

'Did you know Owain well?' Matilda was curious.

Sioned considered her reply. 'When—when I was a child. It is a long time, as I say, since we have met.'

Matilda realised that Sioned was not going to tell her any more. It could be that Owain belonged to a part of Sioned's past that it would be better not to tell Cadfael about. She herself had had an infatuation that Ned knew nothing about: a first love that she had almost forgotten. It was unlikely that Sioned would see Owain again once she was living in Cadfael's manor, and her brother would be back tomorrow.

Matilda, too, resolved not to speak of Owain to her brother, yet he was much on Sioned's mind for the rest of the day. She looked forward to Cadfael's return with an excitement that surprised her.

Cadfael had spent several exhausting days with his steward and bailiff discussing the coming harvest and several other matters. His steward would visit his small manor in France, while he was at home. Cadfael also spoke with Gwenllian, John's wife, who really kept house for himself, helped by Kate when she felt like it, concerning the preparations he desired in the house.

For the first time in his life Cadfael found himself giving thought to relinquishing his place in King Edward's train and settling down to a life of domesticity. Could he give it up? His life had been exciting, fascinating—yet also arduous and lonely, despite his companions in arms. He would have to see the campaign in Wales through, and find Rhys. He had such a short time to settle Sioned into life on his manor; only three weeks, perhaps. He frowned as he thought of his younger sister and her determination not to come with him to Chester. Should he warn Sioned what to expect when she met Kate?

Cadfael tossed off his wine, thinking deeply. He could see some disruptions ahead, but nothing that he thought he would be unable to handle. But he would not speak with Kate again about going with him to Chester. He would not have her upsetting Sioned and spoiling their wedding. Kate should really see their mother before it was too late—but that, like finding Rhys, would have to wait.

The next day, he arrived at Matilda's home at noon. The awkwardness caused by his broken arm made him feel weary as he slid from the horse. He climbed the steps with an eagerness that he could not control, realising with a shock how much he had missed the sight of Sioned and the lilting music of her voice.

The hall was filled with activity: a couple of serving-maids were preparing the table for dinner; Ned was talking to a customer in a secluded corner over a cup of ale; Matilda was sitting on a settle instructing Margaret on how she wished the neck of Sioned's cote-hardie to be embroidered in gold. Sioned herself knelt on the floor-covering playing with Edward, showing him how to work the wooden joints of the soldier that his father had brought him that morning.

Hearing the sound of his feet, Sioned lifted her head, and a tinge of rose flushed her cheeks. A smile trembled on her mouth as she uncurled herself. Such a rush of melting happiness seemed to dissolve her heart as she gazed into his face, that for a moment she could not speak to Cadfael, who gripped her fingers.

'You have missed me?' he said lightly in a mocking voice.

'Hardly at all!' she smiled shyly at him. 'I—I have been far too busy. You have not brought your sister with you?'

Cadfael shook his head, hearing the warmth in her voice. 'She would not come.' He frowned. 'I am hoping you can help me with Kate. If anything, my sister seems to have become more strange.' He hesitated. 'Has Matilda or my mother spoken of her?'

'Not really. I gather there is some—disagreement between Kate and your mother. That she was in Gascony for a while when you were on crusade.' Sioned was conscious of the warmth of his fingers on hers, but suddenly she sensed that his thoughts had gone far away from her. 'What happened?' She could not prevent the question.

'It—it was because of Jean, really, that it all happened,' he began slowly.

'Jean?' Sioned queried. There had been something odd in his voice.

'He was Isabella's cousin, and Kate was utterly besotted with him. She wanted to marry him, despite her already being betrothed to a man here in England. Mother refused to countenance the idea. But, to make up for her decision, she allowed Kate to stay on in Gascony after I left on crusade.' He paused, and stared across the hall.

'What happened?'

'There was an accident. Kate tripped over a stool and dropped a candle. It set fire to the hangings in the bedchamber where my wife and the child lay. Kate tried to drag the hangings down with her bare hands, but she could not stop the fire.

She went for help, but when they returned, Isabella and the child were dead.' There was a blankness in his face that caused Sioned to let go of his hand.

'You still care, don't you? It hurts you to think of it?' she said in a husky voice.

'Hurts?' Cadfael's eyes flickered. 'Kate has never forgiven herself. I think she blames my mother, thinking that if she had been allowed to marry Jean, she would not have been staying with Isabella to cause the fire. She is wrong, of course. The die had been cast long before she or I went to Gascony—but Kate will not believe me.' There was a gruffness in Cadfael's voice that caused Sioned's heart to twist inside her. He shrugged his shoulders. 'But we all believe what we want to believe, perhaps. Kate came home to England with me, and Mother let a year pass before arranging a meeting with the man she was betrothed to. He refused to marry her. If he had not, I think there was a chance that Kate would have long cast off all remembrance of Jean, and lived again, despite ...' he hesitated, 'despite what happened to her in the fire.' He took a quick breath. 'But you will see, when you come to my manor. Then you will understand why I wish you to befriend Kate. You will be company for each other, I hope, when I have to leave you and go in search of Rhys.'

‘I shall do my best.’ There was a tightness in Sioned’s throat. She was remembering the anguish in Cadfael’s voice when he was in fever at Megan’s hafod. Perhaps it was not only Kate who had not forgotten the past? But Sioned had no more time to dwell on the thought, for Matilda came over at that moment to greet her brother and talk to him about the wedding in two days’ time.

Thoughts of Kate, Isabella and the shadowy past that was Cadfael’s were buried but not forgotten by Sioned.

CHAPTER FOURTEEN

'Here! Let me twist this into your garland. It is rosemary, a plant brought from Gascony for my herb garden. They call it the herb of remembrance.'

Sioned handed the garland of roses and gillyflowers to Matilda, so that she could twist the narrow-leaved spray of leaves among the flowers and yellow ribands. As she watched, she remembered—remembered all that Cadfael had told her two days ago concerning his sister, and the death of his wife and child.

' 'Tis said to clear the head and make one merry,' smiled Matilda, bidding Sioned stand still while she fixed the garland over her hair, loosened so that the rich bronze silk waves rippled past her waist.

She stepped back and gazed at Sioned appraisingly. Her face broke into a smile and she clapped her hands in delight, before leading her over to the polished metal mirror that hung on the wall of the bedchamber.

The cote-hardie of palest lemon linen was fastened up the front from the waist, which fitted snugly, held as it was about her slenderness with a girdle of silver leaves of leather. From the elbows of the tight sleeves trailed fine pieces of white gauze. The skirts were full, and set in their fronts were two perpendicular openings so that Sioned could lift them from the ground and also reveal the rich saffron silk undergown beneath.

Despite her inner trepidation, Sioned smiled at her reflection. She looked unlike herself. Her brown eyes seemed larger than normal, and her face was pale beneath its dusting of freckles. She scrubbed at her cheeks until they glowed, and then slipping her hands into the openings of her whispering skirts, she lifted them and followed Matilda out of the doorway and down the steep stairs.

The early morning sunlight washed out the shadows, brightening the porch of St Peter's church. Sioned's pulses quickened as she cast a glance at Cadfael standing next to her. His expression was stern, and her anxiety deepened.

What did this ceremony mean to Cadfael? He had paid her bride price, but was he like Govan in wanting a wife merely to provide a son? To wed her and bed her, get her with child and then go off to war? Panic, and an overwhelming yearning that he desired from her more than that, mingled, twisting her heart.

She noted the whiteness of his linen sling; the one she had made for him, washed and rewashed. It was bright against his cote-hardie of light and dark green, which emphasised his height, the hem of the skirts coming to below his knees. His hose were green also, one leg clad in pale green, the other in a deeper shade.

'Note—no liripipe,' he whispered unexpectedly.

Sioned met his gleaming eyes, and smiled, as he had intended. Suddenly she was not afraid, remembering the first day in Chester.

The ceremony was swiftly over, and if it had not been for the weight of the heavy gold ring on her finger, Sioned would have thought she had imagined she was now Cadfael's wife. They walked back to Matilda's house in procession, rose-petals and heads of cornflowers and poppies scattered beneath their feet as they wended their way. Sioned felt as if in a dream. Only Cadfael's fingers were warm and real entwined with hers.

Matilda, hand in hand with her son and husband, talked cheerfully of the breakfast awaiting them. She looked breathtakingly lovely in a green linen cote-hardie with a red cotton underskirt showing through slits in the side of her skirts.

The trestles bore their burden of food

well. There was salmon, fresh from the Dee, in a rich creamy herb sauce; woodfowl roasted over the fire; pasties of mutton and leeks. Freshly baked bread with honey stood next to round white cheeses made in the palatinate. There were gooseberry tarts, and bowls of raspberries and cream. All to be accompanied by some of the finest wines from Bordeaux.

Before breaking their fast, Sioned and Cadfael went to visit the lady Elin in her bedchamber. Her hair had been dressed, her braids entwined with blue silk ribands. She wore an undergown of lavender, and despite her frailness and pallor, Sioned considered she must have been one of the loveliest women from Snowdonia.

'You will try and make each other content,' ordered Elin in her soft lilting voice, taking a hand of each in hers. 'Happiness and bliss comes and goes. So does sorrow and anger. But contentment is a much unappreciated state—and I wish it for you, my children.'

Sioned was not sure what she murmured in reply, for her mind was busy turning over the thought behind the words. Contentment! Could she be content, knowing that Cadfael could not forget his first wife? Again she recalled the anguish in his voice. She supposed that she could only try to attain such a state of contentment.

'You will not be too long, my son, before you go in search of Rhys?' Elin turned to Sioned. 'I would that I did not need to take him away from you so soon, my daughter—but I know you understand.'

Sioned nodded, seeing the pain behind her words, but Cadfael made no reply to his mother's question, only thanking her for her words of wisdom. They talked a while longer before she bade them leave her and join their guests.

'I have never seen so much food,' murmured Sioned as Cadfael led her to her place at the high table between himself and Ned.

'It is somewhat different from the fish we caught and cooked, but I doubt it will taste any better.' Cadfael's eyes were warm as they rested on her face.

Sioned nodded, remembering the battle her heart had fought against caring for him then.

He could have taken her—but he had not. Would she have succumbed to his will if he had? Would she now love or hate him—this enemy of her people who had stolen her heart?

Ned spoke to her in his slow, laborious Welsh, and she attempted to answer him in English. She wondered what he really thought of Cadfael marrying her, this so English Englishman.

The conversation rose and fell, almost unheeded, about her. She ate with pleasure of the good food before her, and thought of Cadfael's sister Kate. If only it were Matilda with whom she was to share a home, she would not have such apprehension about going to Cadfael's manor. Well, not too much, anyway. She quivered inwardly when she thought that tonight he would make her his wife in deed as well as in word.

The sun had disappeared when they emerged from the hall, and it was cool for August.

'You do not mind travelling pillion?' called Cadfael as Sioned turned to accept Matilda's kiss.

She shook her head, suddenly shy.

'Do not forget us now,' said Ned, lifting her into the pillion seat. 'Come and stay with us when Cadfael goes back to Wales, if you are tired of Kate's company.'

Matilda gave her husband a nudge and translated swiftly into Welsh some of what he had said. Even Ned was tactless at times!

They made their farewells, and Cadfael's and John's horses, with some baggage, were trotting towards the North Gate. Soon they had passed beyond the pink walls of the city and were riding amid the cultivated fields that for most part belonged to the abbey of St Werburgh. Ahead, beyond where their road forked, the land was thickly forested.

Sioned yawned, for her head was light with wine. During several miles, the desire to see as much of the countryside as possible kept her from dozing. They travelled beneath the dark shadows of oak and beech for what seemed an age on a road busy at that time of day with carters, merchants, and monks travelling to the priory at Birkenhead. Most of the travellers stayed close together, wary of the outlaws who were known to roam the forest.

Despite her determination to stay awake and the discomfort of being jolted on a road often rutted, Sioned's eyes began to close. Her head slid down against Cadfael's back and she fell into an uneasy doze. It was not until the horses came to a halt and Cadfael dismounted that she woke.

'We have arrived, Sioned!'

Even in her drowsy state, she heard the pride and affection in his voice. She took his hand and slid from the horse, her heart jumping nervously.

Her first sight of her new home was disappointing. She had not known what to expect—a castle, perhaps? The house was founded on red sandstone, of which the ground floor was built, with only arrow-slits showing here and there. The first floor was constructed of wood and was pierced by several lancet windows. A flight of stone steps led up to it. The trees had been cut well back from the house, but to its rear the woods lurked dark and gloomy on this day that had changed from sunshine to cloud. The whole effect was to create a picture of strength and gloom on that first sighting.

A door set at the top of the stone steps was flung open suddenly as John called to Cadfael. Sioned looked up swiftly expecting to see Kate, but instead a tiny figure was standing there, who in the next moment came running down the steps.

'Croesawu, my lady!' she called in a sing-song voice as she came to a standstill in front of Sioned. She was clad in a brown surcoat over a grey undergown, and a cream kerchief was wrapped about her neck and greying hair.

'You are Cymri!' Sioned's eyes were dazed as she looked down at the sprightly figure of the old woman.

'Ay, my lady, Gwenllian I am. I was maid to my lord's mother until I wed John.' She smiled happily up. 'But you must come in out of the chill air. I have a good fire burning.'

Sioned turned to speak to Cadfael, but

he had already gone with John to the stables.

'They will not be long, your man and mine.' Gwenllian beamed at Sioned. 'Mistress Kate is another matter! You might not see her this day until bed-time. But come in—come in!'

Sioned followed Gwenllian up the steps, gazing about her as she did so. Beyond the huddle of outer buildings stretched cultivated fields to the side and front of the house. Gwenllian nudged her arm and pushed the door wider, causing Sioned to give her attention to the house once more.

The hall was larger than she thought it would be, soaring high to where broad wooden beams supported the roof. The smoke rose from a fire blazing in the middle of the floor to lose itself among the rafters before finding its way out of a louvred opening.

On wooden walls that glowed warmly in the firelight hung brightly coloured tapestries depicting battle and the chase, and a rug that Cadfael had brought back from the crusade, so Matilda had informed her. There were two cushion-scattered settles, one near the fire, the other near the lancet window at the far end. A trestle table of polished dark oak was set with bowls and platters, goblets and pitchers. The smell of roasting boar penetrated the hall.

Sioned walked slowly further into the room, removing her cloak from her shoulders.

'Do you like it?'

She turned at the sound of Cadfael's voice, aware of the eagerness in his face and the slightest tinge of anxiety.

'Well, wife, answer!' He laughed, seizing her hands in his sound one. 'Do you approve of your new home?'

'Approve? Of course I do! I would be hard to please if I did not!'

'I am glad.' Cadfael's arm slid about her shoulders. 'I like the place, but I was not sure how a woman would see it. It is home to Kate now.' He hesitated. 'Isabella, though, never wished to come to England.'

'Isabella had been at the court of France!' The voice was coldly petulant.

Sioned and Cadfael turned as one.

'Isabella had dined with princes and earls, and would never have settled in this place.' Kate sat down in the middle of the settle near the fire, presenting her profile. She wore a drab grey cotte and only a few wisps of gold-red hair escaped her grey veil. Her neck was concealed completely by folds of white linen. 'Perhaps you have forgotten that Isabella was a courtly lady, brother?'

'I have not forgotten, sister.' Cadfael's voice was low, his fingers crushed Sioned's shoulder. 'But she is dead. Let her rest in peace.'

'That is what you would like, brother?'

Kate stared at Cadfael a moment longer, her mouth thin and set. Then she turned her attention to Sioned.

'So this is your little savage from the mountains?' She rose and came closer to her, her eyes raking her tall, proud figure.

'You forget yourself, Kate.' Cadfael sounded furious. 'Where are your manners? Welcome your new sister!'

Kate flicked him a glance. 'I have no need of a sister! But I see Matilda's touch in the savage's apparel. I suppose she is dressed so finely to please you, brother? So richly, too. How is our dear sister? Still living in wedded bliss with that dull merchant of hers?'

'Matilda is well.' Sioned shrugged Cadfael's hand from her shoulder and stepped forward, holding out her hand to Kate. There was a flush on her cheeks, but she was remembering how she had resented Angharad's coming to the mountain hafod to usurp her position in Hywel's household. 'Could we not be friends, Kate? I am pleased to meet Cadfael's sister.'

For a second there was surprise in Kate's

hazel eyes, then she gave a sneering laugh. 'I see my brother and sister have been talking to you about me! You feel pity for me. They have told you, I suppose, about the fire?' She rubbed suddenly at her gloved right hand, and whipping off the glove, held it out to Sioned. It was discoloured and badly scarred.

Sioned barely gasped before taking it.

'You are mistaken, Kate. I did not know.'

Kate looked at her in disbelief, snatching it away. 'You are not repulsed? Then how about this!' Kate's eyes flashed, and her hands went to the linen at her throat, unfolding it swiftly, baring her neck and turning her face slightly.

Sioned bit back a shudder. The skin was snatched, pulled tight, puckering, in a long snaking scar down the lower curve of her cheek and neck.

'Not so pretty, is it?' demanded Kate. Her tone was half mocking, half angry.

Sioned gained her composure. 'But did you not come by your scars because of your bravery? Did you not try to put the fire out?'

'But I started it, you fool!' Kate wrapped the linen about her throat again, pulled her veil forward and dragged on her glove. 'Next you will be saying that God forgives my sin in starting the fire, and that my deformity is not as bad as I think.'

'And if Sioned did say such words, Kate, could they not be true?' Cadfael took his sister's hand. 'If you dressed more brightly, and did not fast so much, you could still be beautiful, little sister.' He touched Kate's cheek lightly with his lips.

For a moment she was still, letting her cheek rest beneath her brother's kiss. Then she dragged herself away from him.

'I do not want to be beautiful! It is she, I suppose—your new bride—she would have you find a husband for me, wishing to be rid of me already!' There was malice and a hint of panic in her voice. 'Does she want all your riches spent on her, perhaps? Does she begrudge me the food I will eat at your table?'

'Of course not!' The meeting was worse than Sioned had imagined.

'Kate, you forget your manners again! You will be polite to Sioned.'

'I do not wish to be polite! I was happy here, before you brought her. Why could we have not gone on in the old way, comforting each other in our grief?'

'There is a time when one has to live again, Kate. To forget what once hurt,' he said sharply.

'At least I do not seek to escape into another's arms, as you do hers this night!' Kate flung back her head, and her veil slipped from her hair. In that moment she looked extremely young, and strangely noble. 'Does she know how madly in love with Isabella you were? This one is pretty, but she is not beautiful like Isabella—and she will never replace her in my heart, whatever you say. Nor yours, I think however hard you try!' She tossed the blaze of gold-red hair back over her shoulders, and raced out of the hall before Cadfael could reach her.

Sioned was trembling; trembling so much that she sank on to a settle before her knees gave way. How could she stay? How could she continue with this marriage, knowing Cadfael still loved his first wife?

'You should not have married me,' she whispered as he turned towards her.

'Don't be foolish!' He barely had his voice under control. Sioned had only once seen him like this, white with fury, when he had plucked Dafydd from her.

'If you take notice of all my sister says, you will go mad! Perhaps I should not be away so often, and Gwenllian should not spoil her so much, always coaxing and petting her when she gets in one of her moods. I will not tolerate such behaviour. How dare she insult you, my wife!' He began to pace the floor. 'If only she and Matilda were close ... But they are not—their ways are too different for them to bear with each other for long.' He said regretfully. 'I hoped that you and she could be friends.'

When the door suddenly opened, they both turned, but it was Gwenllian. She came bustling over, and ushered them to the table.

'You must not mind Mistress Kate,' she murmured to Sioned. 'I have given her some spiced wine, and she will sleep. Tomorrow she might be different. Give her time, my lady Sioned, she will come round.'

'She needs a spanking!' said Cadfael in a stiff voice. 'You spoil her too much, Gwenllian. I should never have let her stay here. She would have been better with Mother or Matilda. They would not have let her sulk, have her own way!'

'And if I do, Master Cadfael, is the poor wee lamb not in need of it? Maybe she should be going into society more, but you men don't know the half of it, I tell you! If only she had heeded your mother—but there, she has your father's stubborn ways.'

Gwenllian flashed him a rebuking glance before filling their goblets with wine. 'Not that you haven't suffered yourself, Master Cadfael. And glad I am that you have brought home a wife. Who knows—perhaps within the year there will be an heir to brighten up this old hall?'

Sioned's fingers tightened on her goblet, and Cadfael, noticing her embarrassment, bade Gwenllian be silent and to leave. The silence seemed to stretch after the door closed behind her. Sioned took a sip of the wine. What should she do? What could she say? After what had gone before, she was at a loss how to behave at this wedding supper. Should she pretend that none of it had happened? That she was not affected, or hurt, by Kate's words? Was Cadfael thinking of his dead wife and child?

She took another sip, staring at Cadfael over the rim of her goblet. His eyes were hard and gold-flecked, his face stern. Then suddenly he caught her glance, and saw her. He smiled, and hesitantly she smiled back. Her heart lifted with unexpected hope.

CHAPTER FIFTEEN

Cadfael began to talk and to eat. To talk about the people who had attended their wedding feast; to talk about his manor; to talk about the river and fishing, mountains and cattle. He asked Sioned if she wished to go with him on the morrow about his manor, and where would she like him to take her. She managed to laugh, protesting that he knew his own lands better than she did.

Sioned grew sleepy with wine. Her goblet never seemed empty, and she wondered if her husband was filling it deliberately. Did Cadfael sense her nervousness and seek to abate it by dulling her wits? At last Gwenllian came into the hall and cleared the table, and he bade Sioned go to bed, that he would be along soon. So she went, guided by Gwenllian, to her bridal chamber.

Flames flickered in a brazier, casting a shifting light upon a chest carved with heraldic emblems. Opposite loomed a large bed, spread with an embroidered red woollen coverlet. There was a washstand and a chair, a rod on the wall, and that was all.

Sioned walked carefully across the oaken floor, her skirts making a muted rustle as she pressed herself against the wall and peered out of the window. Rippling fingers of crisp air cooled her flushed cheeks as she held up her face. She caught sight of the river beyond the shifting treetops. Then she turned and began to undo her cote-hardie with an enforced calm deliberation. She kept on her yellow silk undergown and got into bed, a comb in her hand.

She sat combing her hair, waiting for Cadfael to come. At last, when her arm ached so much that she could hold it up no longer, she slid down the bed and pulled up the covers. There was an ache in her throat and chest that matched the ache in her arm. She shut her eyes—she would wait no more. If he would rather brood over his dead wife while in his cups, let him! She would not let herself care.

So Sioned lay when Cadfael came in. He stood looking down at Sioned, at the bronze hair spread about the pillow. He nursed his broken arm against his chest, feeling with impatient fingers the constricting splint. He had waited too long, it seemed, giving her time to prepare, talking to John as he helped him to undress. He sat down on the side of the bed, feeling it give beneath his weight. Slowly Sioned's eyelids flickered, and she stared up at him with a drowsy bemusement.

'I thought you were not coming,' she muttered in a sleepy voice.

'What? Not come to claim my bride? Did I not pay the price your brother asked?' replied Cadfael mockingly, letting his fingers slide gently down her cheek.

Sioned moved her head from side to side on the feather pillow. 'He—he would have sold me ... to Govan. He hurt me ... Tried to force me!' she shuddered.

Cadfael's fingers stilled against her mouth, and a strange twisting anger surged through him. Govan ... Dafydd ... Had he come in time? Did she still care about her Cymri lover?

Sioned pouted. Why was he frowning at her? Was—was he thinking of Isabella, wishing it was her in his bed? Well, she would make him forget Isabella. She—Sioned ap Rowan, who was alive! Isabella dead could not warm his bed or fill his arms now! Sioned looped her hands round his neck, pulling his head unresisting down to hers. She kissed him; pressing her warm, moist mouth against his lips. There was no response.

But in the smouldering gold-green eyes was a curious, questing expression that made her tingle. It was as if he sought to strip her soul, and she was frightened.

Cadfael, having felt her cheek against his

chin, her lips against his and her bare arm against his naked chest, would be governed by his sudden doubt no longer. There was only one way to find out. His arm went round her and he was kissing her lips with a fervency that caused the breath to catch in her throat. She struggled, but he forced her down against the pillows, and somehow, amid kissing her and stroking her, he managed with one hand to rid her of the saffron silk that he was determined to be rid of quickly.

Sioned trembled with a fearful excitement. She had never been completely naked with a man before. 'No, please,' she cried, trying to cover herself.

Cadfael dragged her hands away. 'You are beautiful,' he said in a husky voice, touching the rosy tip of a breast with a gentle finger, seeming not to hear her voice.

'No!' It was a bare whisper of sound this time as she caught her breath, uncertain now why she protested.

'Don't start arguing with me!' There was a shake in his voice as he caught her to him. Then his mouth was on hers again, and despite her confused and warring senses, her lips parted beneath his. He held her so tightly that she thought her bones would crack, and fleetingly she remembered that night in the tent when he had begun to make love to her. Then all thought faded.

She was in a world that contained him and her alone, caught up in a vortex of rising passion that threatened to overwhelm her in its intensity. The burning passion took her unawares, but even as she would have shrunk away, his mouth held hers captive, smothering the momentary gasping pain of his possession.

Sioned submitted, thinking that was all he wanted of her, despite the urges he roused in her to respond. She did not want him to think her wanton! He groaned, and she thought she had displeased him; then he was kissing her with a gentleness that surprised her, as did the tears on her cheeks when he turned from her, leaving her wanting still, and slept.

She woke to her name being called somewhere beyond the border of the warm cream of her dream. Her body felt heavy, and her eyes refused to open. Still the voice went on, until she blinked and her blurred gaze washed over the sunlit bedchamber.

'You have slept well, my lady?' Gwenllian's voice was cheerful and caring.

'What o'clock is it?' she murmured, realising that she was alone in the large bed.

'It is almost noon,' responded Gwenllian, setting a pitcher of warm water on the stand. 'The master said to let you lie.'

'The master!' Her husband!

Gwenllian hung the scarlet gown that Matilda had given her on the rod on the wall. 'Will you wish me to help you to dress, my lady?'

Sioned shook her head shyly, waiting until Gwenllian had left the room before slipping from bed. Her bare toes curled on something that scratched in a tickly way, and she picked it up. It was the sprig of rosemary. She sat on the edge of the bed, remembering Matilda calling it the herb of remembrance, and that it had come from Gascony. Gascony—the country where Isabella had married Cadfael, and died there with their child. Had she loved Cadfael as much as he must have loved her?

Sioned rose, and stood by the window for a moment, thinking how strange it was that Cadfael should take another wife beyond the borders of his own country. Had Cadfael thought of Isabella when he had made love to her last night? Remembrance set her trembling with longing for him. She had not wanted to feel like this towards her husband. There had been no words of love from Edward's man, words that she needed to hear if she was to be happy in this country, but his passion had devoured any resistance she might have thought to put up. They were one flesh, and she was glad.

The rosemary fell from her fingers and fluttered down to the garden. She turned to face the room, and her spirits rose when her eyes fell on the scarlet gown. Somewhere she had ribands to match. If she played her part of wife well, she could become such an intricate facet of her husband's life that he would perhaps cast away all memory of Isabella. He desired her much. She began to hum a Welsh air that Megan had sung. Come what may, there was no going back to what had gone before!

Sioned looked about her as they came out of the cool shade of the trees. Reeds rustled in the slight breeze, and the sun glistened on the rolling expanse of the River Dee.

'You are certain you are not weary?' Cadfael turned to her. 'We have been on horseback all afternoon, and I hazard that you are not accustomed to long rides.'

'That is true, but I am not tired.' The breeze had whipped bright colour into her cheeks, and her eyes were alight with interest. 'I want to have a picture in my head of the extent of your manner and all that happens in it, now that it is to be my home.'

'You already feel like that, Sioned?'

Cadfael's eyes creased at the corners, and pure pleasure lit his angular face. 'I am glad!' He put out a hand to cover hers where it lay on the palfrey's mane. 'I admit that this country does not have the grandeur of your mountains, but it has a beauty just as pleasurable to the senses, as I am sure you will discover.'

Sioned smiled. 'Already I find delight in watching the changing moods of the river.'

'Then I must take you out in my boat again, if you would like that?' Cadfael raised her hand and kissed it. 'It is to the river we look for some of our living. I have a fishery, and also interests in Ned's business, having visited many of the places that the ships sail to from Chester.'

Sioned wondered if this was the time to mention that she had seen her brother Owain in Chester, but already Cadfael was turning his horse homeward. The moment passed, and she thought again how uncertain were the chances of her seeing Owain again. She would wait. It was only a week since she had been wed.

Kate was sitting at the table when they came into the hall. She still wore the grey cotte and grey veil that was her customary garb about the manor.

Sioned forced a smile as she pulled off

her gloves and dropped them on the settle near the fire. 'Have you had an enjoyable day?' she said, determined to be friendly. She sat opposite Kate, wincing as she did so after an afternoon in the saddle.

'Je ne comprehends pas.' Kate gave her a cold stare as Gwenllian placed before her a bowl of chicken broth. She darted a glance at her brother's back as he talked with his bailiff in the doorway.

'You do not understand me?' Sioned frowned. 'But you understood and spoke my tongue last night. In truth, I think you are used to speaking it much with Gwenllian.' She tapped with the spoon set by her bowl. 'Or is this some game to improve my French? Your brother and Matilda have already begun my lessons, Kate.'

Kate made no reply, but began to eat her broth. It seemed that she was still antagonistic.

Cadfael sat down and began to eat his meal. 'Nathaniel's wife will give birth soon, so he tells me,' he said after a few moments. 'Sioned, could you see that she has extra milk when the child comes? And, if you so desire, you could buy some new linen and give her some of our old linen from the chest.'

'I would like that. Some of the linen is much darned, and we could do with some new. Do you think I should go and visit Maud?'

'It would be a kindly gesture, even if she cannot understand what you say. I am sure she would appreciate your concern.' He turned to his sister. 'Perhaps Kate could go with you, to act as interpreter?'

'I do not wish to go with her,' said Kate sullenly. 'She is the lady of the manor now. Let her get on with it.'

'She? Her? My wife's name is Sioned, Kate.'

Sioned almost felt the sparks. It was not the first time they had had this argument. Kate just refused to speak to her, and on several occasions she had countermanded her orders to Gwenllian.

'May we go out in the boat tomorrow, Cadfael?' Sioned asked swiftly before either of them could speak again.

He turned to her with an air of relief. 'If the weather is suitable. We could take some bread and cold meat with us—fruit and wine.'

'Will you give me another lesson in handling the boat?'

'Ay, if you wish.'

Sioned lowered her eyes swiftly, feeling trembling excitement as she remembered the last lesson. She was learning to respond.

'I suppose I can't come with you! I have

not been on the river since you went away, brother. You always used to take me.' Kate's tone was petulant, her hazel eyes angry. She knew they did not want her, and why, for she had followed the boat's progress last time. It had stayed quite close to the shore for a while, and she had ridden among the trees, watching them.

Cadfael shook his head. 'I will take you another time. You are quite capable of using the boat without me, and well you know it!'

Kate pouted. 'It is not the same alone.' She turned to Sioned. 'You would like me to come—wouldn't you? You said you wanted us to be friends—perhaps you did not mean it?'

Sioned hesitated, wondering if Kate was serious, or was she just being awkward. 'Of course I meant it!' she said in a stiff voice. 'Cadfael—I do not mind if Kate comes with us.'

Cadfael quirked one eyebrow. He knew that his wife did, and why. He did not speak for a long minute as he took a deep draught of his ale. In less than two weeks maybe, she would be left alone with Kate. Perhaps it would be best to placate his sister for now.

'If that is what you wish, Sioned,' he said drily.

Kate clapped her hands and laughed,

delighted to have got her own way. 'It will be good! Perhaps we can fish.'

'Oh, don't worry, little sister! I will make you work for the doubtful pleasure of your company.' He grinned.

Kate stuck out her tongue at him, then gave her attention to the food on her platter, forgetting that she had decided to go without red meat that week.

The afternoon was fine. Small white clouds moved across the blue sky, blown by a breeze that was not too boisterous. Kate watched her brother help Sioned into the dipping boat, hating the way she clung tightly to his arm and gazed laughingly into his face. Painful jealousy twisted inside her. How she hated Sioned, and the way her brother looked at her!

They were soon under sail, and Kate took the tiller as Cadfael explained again to Sioned the simple workings of the boat. She listened, nodding now and again. Her eyes were bright as she gazed towards the far hills on the other side of the river. Then she suppressed the memory and looked into her husband's sun-darkened face. She was filled with a glorious sense of wellbeing as he slipped his arm about her shoulders.

The wind whipped the tops of the waves, sending the boat swishing through the water, tugging at Sioned's hair, fluffing out her braids. She suddenly laughed, pressing close to Cadfael as the boat skipped over the waves. They were not the only craft on the river that day; many boats and ships passed them *en route* for the estuary.

'You are happy?' Cadfael whispered in Sioned's ear.

'I am happy,' she murmured, rubbing her cheek against his chin. They kissed, forgetting Kate.

The tiller was suddenly pushed hard over, causing Sioned and Cadfael to be flung to the other side of the boat. Spray spurted up and drenched them both, and Sioned let out a gasp of pain as the edge of the boat caught her side.

'Are you hurt?'

Sioned shook her head. 'Not really. What happened? Was it a sudden wave?'

Cadfael shrugged. 'Maybe—but perhaps I had better take the tiller. We'll head home. I think you had better get out of those wet clothes,' he added grimly, gazing at Kate.

Sioned was about to protest, when she caught sight of Kate's face. 'Perhaps you are right,' she murmured.

In part, Sioned was glad to return. The sea air had made her sleepy as well as hungry. She ate fully of the beef, vegetables and barley that Gwenllian set before them.

Afterwards, Cadfael had to go out to talk to one of the abbey of St Werburgh's tenants from the next manor. It was as Sioned and Kate were eating some fruit that there came another knock at the door. John crossed the hall and opened it.

'May I speak with Gwenllian?'

'What is it, Peter?' called Sioned in hesitant English.

Peter entered, coif cap in hand, revealing a thatch of unruly fair hair. ' 'Tis Maud, my lady. Her pains have started before her time. I wonder if Mistress Gwenllian could come and aid her? My brother is fair worried.'

Gwenllian had been tidying the table, and Sioned had not understood all the words, but could grasp Peter's message.

'Can you help this woman? You have knowledge of such matters?' Sioned asked her.

'I have had children of my own, and assisted at many births, my lady. But this is Maud's first, and firsts can be tricky.' Gwenllian frowned, and rapped out a question to Peter.

'What of Constance?'

'She has gone to the next village.'

'You need help?' Sioned rose to her feet, interpreting Gwenllian's worried frown. 'You would have me come with you?'

'You?' Kate suddenly decided to take

part in the conversation. 'What could you do?'

'She could bring the linen,' said Gwenllian abruptly. 'Unless you wish to bring it, Mistress Kate.'

'I?' Kate's eyes flickered. She took a drink of her ale. 'Help a serf to give birth? No—I would rather not. Let her go if she wishes. She is the lady of the manor now.'

'I will go on ahead,' Gwenllian muttered. 'You follow me with the linen, my lady Sioned.'

'I will also keep my eyes open for raspberry leaves.' She smiled at Gwenllian.

'Ay!' Gwenllian's eyes twinkled. 'It is worth a try.' She went out of the hall quickly, despite her plumpness.

Sioned went to one of the chests and took out the linen she had put aside.

'Raspberry leaves?' Kate scratched her gloved hand and glared scornfully. 'What is this?'

Sioned turned round. 'My mother used to say they helped with the birth-pangs.'

'How knowledgeable you are,' sneered Kate. 'Next, you will have the ordering of the manor court in Cadfael's absence.'

Sioned frowned with puzzlement, not understanding all the words, only the disdain in Kate's manner and voice. 'I will go now,' she said quietly, her spirits suddenly low. Kate's disapprobation of all she did was irritating her at that moment. She closed the door firmly behind her, wishing Cadfael were there.

The sun had already begun its plunge towards the horizon as Sioned made her way through the trees, keeping her eyes open for wild raspberries. She had never seen a child born, but had listened outside several times when her mother had helped at births. The shrieks and groans from the women had been enough to chill her own blood on occasions. She darted over to a bush and pulled several handfuls of leaves from it, praying that they would be of some use to Maud.

When she entered the bedroom in the back half of the low house, Gwenllian was muttering some words in Welsh as she rubbed herbs on each corner of the bed. The woman in it gave a groan, and Sioned moved swiftly to the opposite side of the bed to Gwenllian. As she took Maud's hand, she only hoped that her presence would be of some help.

'Give her some of your leaves, mistress Sioned.' There was encouragement in Gwenllian's voice. 'Who knows? I have known them to work. But I think we are in for a long night. You do not have to stay, my lady.'

'I'll stay for a while.' She smiled down at Maud, thinking only to stay a short time, but it did turn out to be a long night.

Maud's daughter was born just before dawn, after a not too arduous birth. Sioned smiled into the baby's tiny petal-like face, wrapping her in a long strip of linen, and tiny hands scrabbled and grabbed at her sleeve.

'There now,' hushed Sioned, kissing the tiny fingers before tucking the baby's hands into the linen and placing her in the wooden cradle her father had carved with leaves and birds. An unexpected longing clutched Sioned's heart as she turned to leave.

The sun was already brightening the gloom beneath the trees as the women went up to the house. They were tired, and Sioned's hip ached where it had been banged against the side of the boat. She wondered if Cadfael would be angry with her for being out all night. Yet surely he would understand, if he was serious in wanting her to settle down on his manor and undertake her responsibilities as his wife?

CHAPTER SIXTEEN

Unexpectedly, Kate was up when Sioned and Gwenllian entered the hall.

'Well?' she said sharply, coming forward, her hands on her hips. 'You managed without me, then? Does the child live?'

Sioned nodded wearily. 'A daughter—a beautiful daughter. Both mother and child are well.' She yawned. 'Surely you have not waited up all night, Kate?'

'Of course not!' she snapped, folding her arms across her breast. 'I woke early. I have been waiting for Gwenllian to dress my hair and get me some food.' She gave her old nurse an angry look.

'Gwenllian is tired. Surely you can get yourself something to eat, and do your own hair?'

'Gwenllian always does it for me.' Kate rocked on her heels. 'Gwenllian!'

The old woman, who had sunk on to a stool, her eyes drooping, made to rise.

'Gwenllian—go to bed for a few hours. I order you!' said Sioned, her eyes softening momentarily.

'Ay, my lady Sioned.' Gwenllian bobbed

slightly and began to walk towards the door.

'You dare to countermand my orders to Gwenllian?' seethed Kate. 'Who do you think you are?' Her eyes flashed.

'I am the lady of the manor—as you keep telling me, Kate,' murmured Sioned gently. Her eyelids were drooping.

Kate's lips thinned. 'You? A lady? A savage from the mountains, whom my brother bought for whelping, no doubt.'

Sioned's fingers curled and her hands clenched tightly at the insult. 'I am the daughter of a chieftain, and the blood of an Irish prince runs in my veins!' she blazed.

'Irish prince ... Pirate, more like! My father was descended from a Norman knight. He came over with William,' declared Kate in a haughty voice.

'And you are proud of that?' replied Sioned derisively, forcing her voice to stay steady. 'I am tired, Kate, and I am going to bed.' She began to walk towards the door at the far end of the hall.

'Do not think that you will rest easy there!' cried Kate, her cheeks red. 'My brother is furious with you for going down to the village without his permission.'

Sioned's feet barely faltered. With a jerky movement she opened the door of the bedchamber. She could see only the top of his untidy dark hair as she dragged off her gown. Her face burned, and her heart was beating uncomfortably fast. Tears of fury pricked the back of her eyes, and she heard the bed creak suddenly. Cadfael's eyes met hers.

'I am sorry if you are angry with me, but I thought it would be what you wished,' she said in a seething voice, her eyes sparkling. 'But I did not know that you owned me to the extent that I would need your permission to go to help Gwenllian with Maud! Am I a slave, that I cannot move without your say?'

Cadfael frowned and scrubbed at his chin. 'Come here, Sioned,' he answered.

'I do not want to come!' Her tone was defiant, and she turned away from Cadfael to gaze out of the window. She heard him move in the bed, but still she did not turn round.

'Sioned!' His voice was quiet in her ear. 'Come to bed.'

'No! I am tired—and I have the headache,' she muttered, pressing closer to the wall, and concentrating her gaze on an oak tree taller and wider than any other.

'You will do as I tell you!' Cadfael took her arm, and kissed the spot just beneath her right ear. She wriggled, and moved away from him. 'You should not have married me,' she said sadly. 'Your ways are not my ways ... and I miss my own land.'

'Do you? I'm sorry about that.' Sioned looked at him and then down at her feet. 'I had begun to think my ways were becoming very much your ways—but perhaps I was wrong,' he added softly.

'You are part Norman—you were not brought up Cymri,' she said in a muffled voice. She did not want to think how comfortably she had begun to fit into this new life with Cadfael as her husband. 'How do you know how I feel? This is your home and Kate's—not mine.'

'I see. You still feel like that. But I thought ... I had hoped ... You are mistaken, you know. This is your home more than Kate's.' He moved away. 'You were wrong, by the way. I am not angry with you. How are Maud and the child?'

'They—they are well.' Sioned's anger was slipping from her. 'Kate said that you ... were ... furious with me.'

'Kate said—Kate said!' Cadfael gave an exasperated sigh, rubbing his broken arm absently. 'Kate says a lot of things that are not true! What else did she say that has caused you to be so angry?'

'It is of no matter,' she replied in a low voice. 'As you say, Kate says a lot of things that are not true.' She turned away from him and went over to the bed. She slid beneath the covers and lay down, expecting him to come to bed also. But he stayed to look out of the window. Then he left the room.

Sioned sat on the grass. Another week had gone by. She glanced down at Cadfael slumbering by her side. There was a dull ache in her chest. Soon he would be leaving—he had told her so that morning. She lifted her head as she heard the soft thud of the arrow hit the target, and watched Kate. Again she wondered just what Cadfael had said to his sister a week ago. Ever since then, she had been polite in a cool distant way that did not hide her resentment from Sioned, but which satisfied him, it seemed.

'It is a pity I have no competition!' Kate unstrung her bow and came over to them. 'Why did you break your arm, brother?' She kicked Cadfael with the side of her foot.

Cadfael grabbed Kate's ankle, twisted it and brought his sister down flat on the ground. 'I did not break my arm deliberately, Kate—and it does not mean I lack strength! Although I admit I find it frustrating.' He glance at Sioned, and she found herself flushing. She had noticed no lack of strength on account of his broken limb—although his lovemaking had lacked its former passion the last week. There had been a coolness between them. Yet, as their eyes met now, she felt that simmering sexual excitement that his nearness often aroused in her.

'You are a beast, brother! I wish you would leave and go in search of Rhys—and Llewelyn's men. Then it will be peaceful here again,' muttered Kate, smoothing down her skirts with a violent sweep of her gloved hand.

'I will be leaving soon enough!' Cadfael sat up. His face had hardened. 'In a day or so I will go and see Mother. I will take Sioned with me. You can come or stay. I no longer ask you to show a little kindness.' He leaned his arm on his hunched knees, and looked towards Sioned. 'Would you like to sit in on the manor court in the morning, wife?' His tone was careless.

'The manor court?' Sioned was interested. She remembered Kate speaking of it.

'Ay, I shall preside. It is a sore trial to me, and I do not take it on lightly. I have to mete out judgment, unless the crimes are of a more serious nature—such as murder.'

'What kinds of punishments—what kinds of crimes?'

Cadfael's voice was serious, but his eyes danced as he told her. 'Tampering with the lord's flour by adding matters that do no improve the loaf. The baker found so doing can have whatever lies to hand thrown at him while he is fastened in the stocks with the loaf tied about his neck! Then there are the goats that wander into a neighbour's garden. The theft of vegetables is a serious matter.'

'You do not put the goat into the stocks, surely?' Sioned's face was straight. Cadfael grinned. Kate looked at the pair of them, and flounced away.

As it was, there was no manor court the next day. Cadfael was called away early to see the sheriff about some taxes, and said he would be gone until the evening. Sioned felt at a loose end and decided to do some sewing, but could not settle to the task.

'Would you like to go riding?' Kate asked Sioned, her eyes bright.

'What?'

'Would you like to—go—riding?' Kate put her hands on her hips. Sioned noticed that she had changed from a grey gown to a green. It was the first time she had seen her wearing a change of colour, and thought she looked quite different.

'Where would we go? I did not think

you so fond of my company, Kate.'

Kate shrugged, and smiled. 'You are better than nobody to go on a hunt. Let us go to the forest.' There was suddenly a suppressed excitement about her. 'We could perhaps catch a hare for the pot, or a pheasant.'

Sioned frowned. 'Will it be safe?'

'Safe?' Kate smiled derisively. 'I have often roamed the forest alone and never seen a sign of outlaws, if that is what you fear.'

'Cadfael said ...' began Sioned.

'Cadfael said,' mimicked Kate. 'He has tamed the savage, it seems!'

Sioned's eyes sparkled. 'I will come. You should not wander about so much alone, Kate.' She rose to her feet, dropping her sewing on the settle.

'I shall do as I wish,' retorted Kate. Before Sioned could speak again, she strolled across the hall and out through the door. Sioned followed more slowly.

It was quiet among the trees, but for the occasional piping of a bird and the rustle of an animal in the undergrowth.

'Don't you ever miss your own country?'

Kate's question took Sioned by surprise. 'Why do you ask? I did not think you would care.'

Kate rubbed her nose. 'I just wondered. It must be so different here.'

'It is, yet there is much that is similar. I chiefly miss the soaring power of the mountain peaks.' Sioned realised that was still true, yet she had to admit that she had become accustomed already to the gentle countryside and the changing face of the Dee. In truth, she loved the river.

'There is no man you miss? You are gloriously, wonderfully happy with my brother, perhaps?' There was a malicious note of mockery in Kate's voice.

Sioned hesitated, but she had no intention of discussing her relationship with Cadfael. 'I am content.'

'I am content!' mimicked Kate. 'Then you will not mind too much when Cadfael goes back to Wales to thrash your pendragon and his savages?'

Sioned could feel her temper rising. 'Cadfael goes to seek Rhys.'

'Ay! But he also goes to join the army to bring Llewelyn to his knees!'

Sioned's eyes were sparkling. 'You are a spoilt, ill-mannered brat, Kate! And I tire of your company.' She tugged on the reins, digging in her heels before galloping off between the trees.

Kate's mouth hung open in astonishment. She had meant to infuriate her brother's wife, but she had planned that it would be she who would gallop off and lose Sioned in the forest. Not utterly, of course! She would have circled round, keeping Sioned in her eye, leaving her lost just long enough to give her a fright. But Cadfael would be furious if she really did lose her! She turned her horse swiftly, and went to follow Sioned.

Sioned came to an abrupt halt. It seemed a long time since she had left Kate, and she had not realised that her precipitate gallop would take her into a part of the forest she did not know. But now the trees seemed to be thinning out, and water gleamed beyond them. If she followed the river bank ... Surely that was the river ahead? She set off again between the trees, until suddenly she heard voices. She slid from her horse and cautiously crept forward.

There were six of them, squatting round a fire over which fish were cooking. Now she could see a ship anchored on the river. Sioned frowned, realising that unless she made a wide detour she would have to walk past the camp to the river bank. The men were passing a jug round, and their weapons lay on the ground, near to hand. They did not particularly look like outlaws—but then how did an outlaw look? She smiled inwardly. None of them was thin, ragged or hungry-looking. Indeed, one was as broad as he was tall, with a bushy black beard that reached his waist. His face was plump, almost cherubic. Only one man had his back to her. His shoulders were covered by fine blue linen and his dark curling hair reached the neck of his surcoat. He spoke suddenly, and there was a lilt to his English.

Sioned began to tremble. If only he would turn round—if only she could see his face! He took the jug, and began to pour ale into a horn. As he did so, he turned slightly, and she could see his profile. Her heart began to beat rapidly. It was he! She pushed her way through the bushes, unaware that Kate had just discovered her horse a little way back.

Hearing the rustle in the bushes, the men grabbed their weapons, and Sioned was quickly seized by two of them. She struggled.

'Owain!' she cried, finding her voice.

Her brother turned and stared at her from beneath frowning dark brows. 'You know me?'

'Brother—do you not know me?' Tears sparkled on her lashes.

'Sioned?' Owain's blue eyes blazed. 'It can't be!' He stepped forward. 'Will—Tom, let her go. It is my sister.'

'Your sister?' rumbled the man with the bushy beard. 'You never made mention, Owain, of having a sister hereabouts.'

'I never knew it myself!' He took Sioned's hand and pulled her into his arms, hugging her tightly. 'By the saints, Sioned, how did you come here?' His voice was muffled. 'It is so good to see you!'

'And you! Long did I look for you from the hill by the hafod. But Hywel said you were dead.' She stood on tiptoe and kissed his cheek. 'I never did believe him!'

'Hywel! Our dear brother,' murmured Owain in a dry voice. 'And how is he? I never did like leaving you with him. I thought I would be back—but ...' He shrugged well-set shoulders, 'the time went, and I was busy making my fortune.'

Sioned released herself from his embrace. 'He was well when last I saw him—and richer! He sold me to a knight in Edward's host.' She half smiled at the disbelief on her brother's face. 'You do not need to fear, Owain.' She spoke in rapid Welsh. Her brother had drawn her a little to one side, away from the other men. 'I was not unwilling, although it was unexpected. He was going to sell me to Govan, a Cymri raider.' Sioned pulled a face. 'But it is a long story. Too long to tell here.'

'This knight must have wanted you badly to pay Hywel's price! Who is he? Besides, what happened to your own amobr?'

'Sir Cadfael Poole.' There was a note in her voice that caused Owain to look closer at her. 'And Hywel spent my money.' She shrugged.

'Cadfael ... Poole?' He glanced swiftly at the bearded man.

'His mother is Cymri,' said Sioned, thinking she interpreted the look aright.

'Does your man know you are here in the forest alone, lady?'

Sioned addressed the bearded man. 'No, I was riding with his sister. We separated—by accident. I will be missed if I do not return soon.' She moved perceptibly closer to Owain. 'I lost my way.'

'I see.' Owain and the bearded man exchanged glances. 'She is my sister,' he said softly, his hand resting on the knife at his girdle.

The man stared at him hard, and then he laughed. 'Sister or no, you had best make sure she stays silent!' He turned away, and picked up the pitcher of ale. Owain drew Sioned even further apart from the men.

'It would best, Sioned, if you made no mention to your husband of seeing me or these men here.'

'Why? I would have liked to have made you known to him.' Sioned's eyes were regretful.

'Let us say, that it could be a matter of life or death. Another time, Sioned. Give me your word on the matter.' Owain's expression was intensely serious. 'I have to sail soon for Chester.'

'Chester?' Sioned's face brightened. 'We are going to Chester on the morrow, I think. I could see you there.'

'That is good!' Owain smiled at her. 'If you come to the riverside, I will be able to see you before I sail for Ireland. Now, give me your word.'

She hesitated before saying, 'You have it. But ... I will see you again, Owain?'

Her brother grinned. 'Of course! Have I not said so. In Chester. Now, where is your horse? I will set you on the right path.'

'Owain?' The bearded man's voice was rough.

'I know her,' Owain said in a hard voice. 'She will not break her word.' He turned to Sioned again. 'Come, let us go.'

They went.

CHAPTER SEVENTEEN

Just as Owain and Sioned finished talking, Kate moved away. She had been unable to hear all that had been said, but it was apparent that Sioned and the tall Welshman with the curling hair knew each other. She must away before they caught her spying. Another man she had recognised, as his description had been circulating about the Wirral and Palatinate for some time as a known outlaw. Cadfael would be interested to know his whereabouts, and might also find it of some importance that his wife seemed at home in the company of such men!

Kate was in the saddle and off before Sioned and Owain had left the clearing, and if they heard her, they took no notice. Owain was telling Sioned the name of his ship—*St Winifrid*—and her whereabouts.

'I will not be sailing for a couple of days, so I will await your coming, Sioned,' said Owain, helping his sister up into the saddle.

She smiled. 'I will count the days, brother! And then perhaps we will be able to exchange all the tales of what has happened to us in the last few years.'

'I look forward to it. You will be staying at your husband's sister's home, I take it?' He stepped back from her horse.

'Matilda's? Ay! You know her, perhaps?'

'A little.' Owain grinned. 'I have dealings with Ned at times.' He lifted a hand in farewell. 'I will have to go before Blackbeard changes his mind about you. Farewell, Sioned, and may the saint go with you. Best not go near the camp again, even though it is quicker—but if you follow that path ...' he pointed, 'you will still find your way home. I will see you soon.' He disappeared among the trees and bushes.

Sioned flicked the reins and urged the palfrey forward. It would take her some time to reach home. She started thinking of her brother, and some of her childhood memories of him. Owain had always treated her more kindly than Hywel, and for that reason if no other she had loved him. But he had wit and charm, and a reckless daredevrilry that she hazarded had never left him.

She had not liked giving her word to Owain, but she had sensed that her appearance on the scene had made it difficult for him. Were the other men outlaws? That her brother was involved in some mischief she was pretty certain. She wondered what excuse she could make for being late home. Getting lost could be part of it—yet she was fairly certain that Cadfael was going to be angry with her for going into the forest in the first place.

The rain came half an hour later, soaking her linen cotte and drenching her hair and veil. She had not thought to put on a cloak, as there had been no sign of rain when they had left the house, but now she regretted its lack. For another half-hour she sat the plodding horse through the slanting rain until at last she caught sight of a familiar landmark. With a sigh of relief, she turned away from the tiny harbour and made her way inland once more.

Gwenllian let out a shriek when she saw Sioned enter the hall. 'By the saints, where have you been, my lady? They did not keep you prisoner, then? Mistress Kate came flying up the steps, telling the master such a tale of outlaws and of your being seen with them! The master went out with her and some of the men in search of them.'

'He did what?' Sioned allowed herself to be led over to the blazing fire. Cadfael would be furious. Kate! What had Kate seen and told him about her? She shivered, watching the steam as it rose from her garments, breathing deeply, closing her eyes in bliss as the fire's warmth penetrated her sodden gown.

Gwenllian, who had bustled away,

returned with a large blanket. Sioned stood still, letting her unfasten her cotte and strip it from her. She stood naked only a moment before Gwenllian wrapped the rough multicoloured blanket about her chilled body.

'It is to bed with you, as soon as you have dried your hair and drunk the mixture I will make you!'

Sioned nodded sleepily while Gwenllian poured hot water into a cup and placed the aromatic drink at her elbow.

'Now you drink that up, while I see to warming your bedchamber. Then I will have to prepare food for the master, and John, Nathaniel, and Miss Kate, not to mention the sheriff's men.' Gwenllian made a clicking noise with her tongue, and took herself off.

Sioned, warming her frozen fingers on the cup, had hardly heard her. Her head was drooping even as she sipped the drink, sweet with honey and tangy with the taste of fruit. She tried to think, but she was weary beyond belief. What could she say to Cadfael without betraying Owain?

Later, Gwenllian took the cup from Sioned, placing it on the table before helping her to her feet. Sioned leaned on the old woman as she took her to bed. Still wrapped in the blanket, she was asleep before the door closed.

The sound of the door opening woke Sioned some hours later—and the sudden weight on her feet. She moved uneasily in the bed, struggling against the blanket tight about her arms and the lump on her feet.

'Good, you are awake!' Cadfael's voice was strained and laboured.

Sioned blinked, forcing her eyes open to behold the shadowy outline of her husband sitting on the bed, his torso bare.

'Where were you? What happened to them? Who was this Welshman you were—oh so friendly with, my oh-so-dear wife?' He fired the questions at her with a barely suppressed fury.

Sioned sat up abruptly, clutching the blanket about her naked shoulders. The colour had drained from her face. 'I was lost—and it took me some time to find my way home.'

'Lost? Liar! You arranged to meet that man, knowing I would be out of the way. Kate told me how you wanted to go into the forest and how you galloped away from her, saying you tired of her company!'

Kate must have followed her! Sioned stared at Cadfael. 'That is only part true, Kate ...' she began in an unsteady voice.

'Kate! So you are going to blame my sister for it all now! Say that the whole matter was a lie! Deny it, then! But I would not believe that even Kate would try to get you into trouble to the extent of having me call out the sheriff's men and search the forest with me in the pouring rain!'

Sioned's eyes blazed. 'So you would believe your sister, but you are not prepared to listen to aught that I would say! I deny that I went into any forest to meet any man. It was your sister who wished to go, not I!' She dragged the slipping blanket about her with an angry movement.

'You say that she lied about the whole matter?' demanded Cadfael in a seething voice.

Sioned lowered her eyes. 'It would not be the first time your sister has lied,' she said in chilly tones.

'She described the man too well. The great black beard to his waist—his cherubic face and great girth! He is known to have slit the throats of at least six men, one of them a friar. And ravished several women.' Cadfael scowled.

Sioned felt unexpectedly weak, and the blanket drooped in her nerveless fingers.

Cadfael saw the shock in her face. 'It was about him and his men that I went to the sheriff; not about taxes. One of the woodsmen thought he caught sight of him two days ago.' He frowned. 'Of course,

Kate might have overheard us talking about him, and ...' He let out a long breath.

Sioned moistened her mouth, and waited.

'What of the Welshman Kate mentioned?' Cadfael bit his thumbnail, gazing at Sioned. He was tired, and angry that he had called out the sheriff to search fruitlessly in the rain. He had realised, when he had not found her, how much she was coming to mean to him. Yet how could she arrange such a meeting? She had never been to his manor before.

Sioned still said nothing, her heart beating fast. She knew that if he chose to believe Kate, she could offer no defence. She could not break her word to Owain. Then as his eyes flicked over her face, she impulsively let the blanket slip from her shoulders. The anger faded slightly from Cadfael's face, and she did not retreat when he put out a hand and brought her roughly against him, squashing her breasts.

With a sense of thankfulness, Sioned's arms went about his neck. She began to kiss him with a grateful fervency. He dragged off the linen cloth about his waist and slid into bed beside her. She winced as he did so, and pulled away.

'What is it?' he muttered.

She touched the dark shadow on her hip-bone. 'It is where I hit the boat last week,' she murmured. 'The day Kate came with us.'

'I remember.' His voice was grim. He pulled her close again with a controlled violence, and bit her neck where the pulse beat jerkily. 'You women!' he muttered, nipping her neck again.

Sioned wrenched herself away, but he caught her quickly to him and kissed her, so that she could scarcely breathe. Even when she lay beneath him in the cocooning softness of the bed, Cadfael gave no time for her senses to adjust to his swift assault. Yet she acquiesced, praying that he would forget Kate's words and all thought of the Welshman—who was her brother—if she submitted. His passion was such that it swept her along, but contained no hint of caring or softness. Here was the man who had bought her, expecting her to do his will with no thought of her needs or desires.

Kate's eyes swept the pleasant, comfortable hall where she had lived for the last four and a half years. Her gaze hardened as it came to rest on Sioned, and she smiled. She would get her revenge yet! Cadfael and John were even now seeing to the horses that were to take them to Chester. Only in the last hour had she asked her brother if she could go with them.

'Why?' Cadfael's voice had been cool. 'Are you scared of the outlaws?'

She had felt strangely at a loss. He did not believe her! What had Sioned told him? 'Of course I'm not scared!' She was, now that she had actually seen Blackbeard. 'I just want to go with you. You are always nagging me to see Mother. Well—I will go and see Mother.' Kate smiled sweetly at him. 'If you can go all the way to Anglesey to please her, I can go as far as Chester.'

'You mean it? This is not some trick of yours?' he had said harshly.

'Of course I mean it!' Kate grinned. 'Unless Sioned does not wish me to go. I know her wishes come above mine.' She had placed a hand on Cadfael's sleeve. 'I understand why you would rather believe her than me.' She had lifted innocent, wide eyes to his face.

'Do you, Kate?' His eyes had flashed gold. 'Then perhaps you are putting old memories behind you, if you can feel for me again.'

Kate frowned as she remembered Cadfael's words. Then she eyed carefully the blue cote-hardie Sioned wore. She lifted a fold of her own grey gown, and suddenly she loathed it.

They set out just before noon. Sioned

was looking forward to seeing Matilda and Cadfael's mother—but most of all she was eager for the moment when she would see her brother again. She would ask him if she could tell Cadfael about seeing him with the outlaws. Sadness darkened her eyes. She had not mistaken the restraint and slight coolness in Cadfael's manner towards her that morning.

They reached Chester early in the afternoon. The wind had torn the clouds apart, and great patches of blue showed above the city lanes. John knocked on the door of Matilda's house as Cadfael dismounted. Kate gripped her hands tightly together. There would be no going back. Cadfael would make her see their mother. The door was flung open to reveal Margaret, who stared at them in surprise, a ladle in her hand.

'Lawks! The master and mistress are not here right now, Sir Cadfael.' She bobbed a curtsy. 'They have gone down to the river, but should be back soon.'

'My mother?' asked Cadfael, pulling off a gauntlet.

'She is still cheerful, but ...' Margaret sighed.

Cadfael frowned, and looked at Kate.

'Perhaps,' began Kate, 'you and ... and Sioned could go up first. To prepare her for me.' She swallowed nervously. 'I was thinking of going down to the river to see if I can find Matilda. To hurry her up.'

'Why not?' Cadfael smiled. 'The walk would do you good. But do not get lost, Kate. It is some time since you were in Chester.'

'I won't!' Kate slipped out of the door without another word. Unlike Sioned on her first visit, she was unaware of the city smells. Her attention was firmly fixed on people, and the signs of life about her. She walked slowly down the lanes towards the river, enjoying the stroll despite the two matters uppermost on her mind. Her thoughts were uncomfortable. Perhaps her mother might not want to see her? Kate shrugged. Why should she care? For the past few years she had hardly seen her mother. She could carry on living still. Yet unexpectedly, now that she was in the city, memories of when she had lived with her after her father's death were sharp in her mind. They had been close then. Her eyes and throat felt curiously sore.

The river was suddenly before her. Bridge—mill—river craft, of all shapes and sizes. The sun dazzled on the water, and excitement seized her. A spring came into her step and a sway to her hips as she began to walk along the river past huddles of gossiping women, playing children and knots of mariners and merchants. She had buried deep the remembrance of how alive and colourful the Dee was at Chester.

The bridge was crowded with carts, horsemen, and travellers on foot. On the other side of the river lay the road that led to Mold, and on deep into Wales. Kate gazed and gazed, enjoying the sights as she went in the direction of the Water Gate. For the moment, she had forgotten the reasoning behind her coming to Chester, and to the river bank.

It was the sudden sight of her sister that reminded her—and the ship. Many ships looked alike from a distance, but the one Kate had caught sight of the day before had a sail of a distinctive yellow and black. She had come to a standstill, but now she moved forward, round a group of men unloading cargo from the ship. When she reached the spot where her sister had stood, there was no sign of Matilda.

Kate glanced about her, exasperation written clear on her face. She pushed back a handful of red-gold hair. Then she looked at the ship.

'Are you looking for someone, lady?' The voice had a lilt to it. Kate found herself looking into eyes of the most startling blue. She felt the heat in her face as he held her gaze longer than was necessary, and he smiled.

'No!' As she turned from him abruptly,

she slipped. Her arms flayed as she tried to keep her balance but her feet skidded in some spilt wine.

She would have fallen if the mariner had not moved swiftly and caught her. He set her on her feet, still keeping an arm about her waist. It was a long time since a man, other than her brother, had touched Kate. Or that a man's face had been so close to hers. His was darkened by wind and sun, and a coif of blue enhanced his good looks. After a moment she averted her face, pulling her hair forward to hide her scar.

'I am all right now. Please let me go!' Kate put a hand on his arm, attempting to move it from her waist.

'Certainly!' He released her with obvious reluctance. 'Are you sure you are quite recovered, Mistress?'

'I do not think I am in any risk of falling again!' She glanced briefly at him as she dusted her skirts. 'I thank you for helping me—and bid you farewell.'

He inclined his head as she straightened, and turned away. Kate stared at his back, slightly puzzled, then she began to make her way back to Matilda's house.

Sioned and Cadfael were sitting on a settle talking to Ned in low undertones. They looked up as Kate entered, and both men rose to their feet.

'I thought you must have got lost, little sister,' said Cadfael with a slight smile. 'Mother is waiting for you.'

'I saw Matilda, but she suddenly vanished.' Kate's voice was unsteady, her stomach twisting and turning in the most unpleasant fashion.

'You must have just missed us, Kate.' Ned explained. 'Matilda is with your mother at the moment. Would you like me to go up with you and show you the way?'

'I would rather Sioned came with me.'

Sioned gave a start. 'You want *me*?' She stood up slowly.

'If you would not mind, Sioned. I feel the need of another woman at the moment.' Kate was surprised at her own words, but she could not really reveal that she did not want Sioned going off unless she could keep an eye on her.

'Of course I do not mind.' Sioned sent Cadfael a swift glance. He nodded, and she took Kate's arm to go upstairs to the finely appointed chamber where the lady Elin Poole spent her days and nights. Sioned noted the tension about Kate's mouth and the apprehension in her eyes, and she pitied Cadfael's sister in that moment. 'I will wait outside.'

Kate nodded, and if anything her face seemed thinner and paler than ever. She knocked on the door, pushed it and went in.

Matilda sat by the bed, her son on her knee, talking with her mother. They both looked at Kate as the door opened, and there was a silence.

'So you have come at last, Kate.' Her mother's voice sounded querulous, and for a full minute Kate could not speak. She wanted to run and run, so shocked was she by the thin bony face and the hazel eyes that stared at her from deep shadowy sockets.

'I'll go, Mother, to leave you and Kate to talk.' Matilda barely glanced at her sister as she passed her to leave the chamber. Her emotions were in utter disarray. She wanted to shake and kiss her sister at the same time—to scold for the delay and thank for the coming at last. But, of course, Matilda did none of those things; she only handed Edward to Sioned when she shut the door behind her and sat on the bed in the other room to cry silently.

'You knew I would come, Mother,' said Kate at last in a husky voice.

'I knew. Knew it when Cadfael brought his bride to me. Knew she would stir you up—make you suffer.'

'You think I need to suffer? You do not think I have suffered enough?' There was a note of anger in Kate's voice.

'Ay, child! That is why it has to end. Only you though, can end your own suffering. Others can help, but you have to forgive yourself.' Elin moved her head restlessly on the pillow. 'Do you understand?'

'You mean my causing the fire that killed Isabella—and Cadfael's son, I suppose,' she gulped.

'Not Cadfael's son.' Her mother stared up at her. 'Stop pretending, Kate. I know! Deep inside, you do also! Even as a small child you could count up to nine.'

Kate stared wide-eyed at her mother. 'I ... I didn't want to believe it. Even when she taunted me with ... with the truth.' She pressed her hand to her head, sinking on to the bed.

Elin's fingers curled about her daughter's gloved wrist. 'You were fourteen; ripe for falling in love with a handsome man who showed you a lot of attention to hide his liaison with Isabella.'

'He ... He loved me! He was prepared to marry me, even with this!' Kate touched her neck and cheek with an unsteady hand. Her eyes swam with tears—tears she should have shed a long time ago.

'Of course he was. You are not without attraction still, Kate. And you have coming to you all my money. Money your grandmother gave to me, which Jean knew about.'

'Your money?' Tears rolled down Kate's cheeks as she stared unbelievingly at her mother.

'Ay. My money. For a dowry—that is the Norman way. In Wales we deal with such matters differently. Isabella told Jean about it.'

'But why? Why would you still give me your money?' Kate's lower lip trembled. 'I do not want it! I—I do not deserve it!' She rose to her feet, pressing her hands against her cheeks.

'You might wish to take a husband?' Elin's eyes were serious, but a small twinkle lurked in their depths.

Kate's throat moved convulsively. 'I am not a ... a virgin, Mother.'

'I know.'

'How do you know? How do you know about all that happened, Mother? I don't want to believe in your sight! It frightens me.'

'Tush, Kate.' Elin shook her head wearily. 'Gwenllian told me after she returned home with you and Cadfael. You were out of your head with the pain of your burns when she nursed you.'

'Cadfael knew, because Gwenllian told him? He was so hurt and bitter. I thought his anger was directed at me. When he spoke of Jean, I thought it was only because he did not like him—not that he knew all.'

'Cadfael was hurt, naturally—but perhaps the hurt was more to his pride than his heart.' Elin smiled painfully. 'Now kiss me. I am tired; but we will talk again. We have delayed too long, perhaps, in talking, but I believe that there is a right time for everything under the sun. And maybe this is the right time for you to leave your brother's charge and think of living a different kind of life.'

Kate stared at her mother hard, and then she lowered her head and kissed her.

CHAPTER EIGHTEEN

Sioned was still holding Edward in her arms as the door of Elin's chamber opened. Pity swelled within her at the sight of Kate's tear-stained, pallid face.

'Kate, love,' she began, only to stop when she felt Matilda press her arm.

'Not yet,' murmured Matilda. 'Let her alone for a while.'

Kate did not seem to see them, but walked past as if in a trance, and down the stairs.

Sioned turned to Matilda. 'She looks so tragic!' Edward wriggled in her arms, and she passed him over to his mother.

'It's the shock, and ... regret. Such a waste of time to cut yourself off from people you love.' Matilda sighed, and rubbed her cheek against Edward's soft downy head. 'Perhaps if Cadfael had never gone on crusade, or had stayed on in Edward's train, he might have brought them together sooner. But only my father could ever handle Kate.'

'She has a strong will!' Sioned's voice was rueful.

'Kate's stubborn.' Matilda gave a twisted

smile. 'Let's go in to Mother and see if she is all right.'

Sioned nodded, and opened the door. They both went in and looked down at Elin's face.

'I think she looks happier,' Matilda frowned pensively. 'Yet I fear that if ...'

'You fear that if Cadfael does not leave soon in search of Rhys, it will be too late,' whispered Sioned. 'I have thought that myself, since coming here.'

The two women exchanged glances, and both crept towards the door, opening it gently and going out.

'I did not want you to think that I would press Cadfael into going, Sioned,' murmured Matilda, her lovely face encouraged. 'But a messenger came the other day with news for him from the army. It could be that it is from the king.'

Sioned paled. 'I knew that he ... he would have to go sooner or later. Better now, if he has to go.' She continued, as they went down the stairs, 'There is no "if", is there? He has to go?'

'I think so. To Cadfael, his duty is clear.' Matilda sighed. 'I only wish that arm of his were better. But then that might prove a godsend. He will not be in the forefront doing any fighting—that's sure!'

A cold chill trickled down Sioned's spine. 'I—I had not thought of that! It will be some comfort to me, I think.'

'You love him!' Matilda's tone was soft and low. 'I knew you did almost from the first time I saw you together. I'm glad! My brother needs as much love that you can give him, Sioned.'

It was almost on Sioned's lips to say that she did not think Cadfael needed her love or wanted it, but they had reached the hall. There was no sign of Kate, and Cadfael came over to Sioned. He was clasping a piece of parchment.

'Where's Kate?' Sioned asked him, remembering again how she had looked when she had come from the lady Elin's bedchamber.

'She went out. I would have gone with her, but she said she wished to be alone.'

'It was a great shock to her to see how your mother is now.' Sioned's brown eyes were concerned as she looked up into Cadfael's face.

He nodded. 'If she does not return soon, perhaps, I will go in search of her, but I deemed it best to let her go for now.'

'That is what Matilda thought—that Kate needed to be alone. And you both know your sister better than I do.'

'Do we? I'm not so sure,' said Cadfael grimly. 'I need to give thought to her future. Especially what to do with her while I am in Wales.'

'You mean when you leave to go to Anglesey?' Sioned's eyes clouded slightly. 'You think the king will let you go in search of Rhys?'

'You know of the message? Matilda mentioned it to you, perhaps?'

'But I thought you would go soon. There is not ... not much time for your mother, I think. I'm sorry, Cadfael.'

'It was expected.' Cadfael's face was hard set, and he toyed with the paper in his hand. 'I must go, you understand.'

'I know. When?' Sioned's voice was taut.

'Tomorrow. One of Ned's ships is sailing, and the master will put me off at Deganwy.'

'I see. So soon!' Sioned's fingers twisted convulsively together. 'You must not concern yourself about Kate and me. Perhaps now she has come to Chester to see your mother, she will be happier.'

'I pray so.' Cadfael's eyes wore an enigmatic expression. 'Do you wish to stay here until I return, Sioned? Or go back home?'

'I will do whatever you wish. It ... It is of no consequence where I am if you are not there,' she said quietly. 'See what Kate wishes to do.'

Cadfael's mouth twisted. 'She will most likely not know what she wants—but I will ask her, none the less. If she has not returned soon, I will go and look for her. She will most likely be down by the river. That was always her favourite place.'

But Kate was not at her favourite place in Chester. Why her feet should lead her into the abbey of St Werburgh, she did not know. She pulled her veil further over her hair as she knelt. Grey smoke rose from tapers and candles creating a haze and a pungency in an atmosphere that was already heavy with incense. She concentrated on the flame of the candle in front of a saint. St Werburgh's own bones rested in this place, but she had forgotten why that lady had been canonised.

Did saints understand the sins and fears of ordinary mortals? Kate's small, tight smile was forced. She badly needed someone to understand her. Seeing her mother, listening to her words, had caused such turmoil in her mind. The horrors of her situation five years ago were fresh, stark, newly bared like the white flesh of an apple when bitten. Thinking that she was with child by Jean, she had gone to Isabella believing that she would help her. Instead, Isabella had been furious. She had flung words at her that had seared, but which had been so hard to understand at the time that Kate had been stunned.

Kate shifted uneasily on her knees. Time to forget! The thought seemed to come from nowhere into her mind. Forget—forget! All the time she had been blaming her mother and herself—why had she not confided in her mother sooner? Why hadn't her mother told her about the money—or Cadfael? He must have told Isabella about it. Isabella! She had been two people. Was her mother right in saying that it was only Cadfael's pride that was hurt? She thought of how he was now with Sioned. He loved her! A quiver raced through her. But Sioned—was she another, like Isabella, showing different faces? Why had she lied to her brother—as she must have for him not to believe herself? A spurt of her old bitterness and anger rose in Kate. She rose, and walked stiffly to the outer door. Her thoughts were still in confusion, but a way was a little clearer to her.

The sun had disappeared once more behind gathering cloud when she came out of the abbey. She crossed the busy square, hurrying now. There came a tug at her girdle, and a hard push in the back sent her flying into a wall. Her knee collided with stone, and all the breath was forced out of her. A woman put her arm about her in a motherly fashion, and there was the sound of hastening feet and the clamour of voices.

'Are you all right, me dear?' asked the woman in a gentle voice. 'You look a mite pale, me dove.'

'I—I am not much hurt, believe me,' murmured Kate, rubbing a knee.

The woman did not seem convinced. 'Where is your direction? My man will see you home.'

'No! I will be fine. What happened?' Kate lifted dazed eyes to the woman's face.

'Here—let me through!'

Kate looked up at the owner of the voice, who wore a blue surcoat. His coif was down, and his black hair curled without restraint about his forehead and ears. He had a man by the throat, and in his other hand he held Kate's pouch.

'I saw him snatch your pouch, lady.' The blue eyes widened as he recognised her. She stared back at him, still unsure whether he was the man whom Sioned had spoken with in the forest.

'Thank you,' Kate's voice shook. 'What will you do with him?'

'I will take him to the constable. It seems that he could be responsible for the spate of violent pickpocketing that has been going on in the town recently, so some of the men round here say.' His eyes were running over Kate in that appraising way they had done when first they met.

This time she did not blush, but tilted her chin. 'Do—do you think I will be needed as a witness, Master ... er?'

'Owain. Owain ap Rowan.' He twisted the man round as he struggled in his grasp. 'You are fit to get home, lady?'

Kate nodded. She was feeling rather shaken, but she was not going to admit that to him.

Owain stared at her. 'I will see you home,' he said unexpectedly. 'One or two of these good citizens can take this fellow in charge.'

Immediately, there was a clamour of voices offering to do so, and within minutes Owain had disposed of the pickpocket. He turned to Kate, who had risen with the aid of the woman at her elbow.

'It is really not necessary!' Kate's voice quivered.

'You think not?' Owain smiled slightly. 'That is the second mishap you have suffered this day, lady. You really need someone to take care of you.'

'I have a brother for that!' She took a deep steadying breath. Really the man was overbearingly arrogant! 'I am really all right. You may go your own way, sir.'

'My way might go the same way as yours, lady. You are well enough to walk? Or would you like my arm?' There was a gleam, deep in the brilliant blue eyes.

'I do not need your assistance.' Kate gave a sigh of exasperation. She needed to think, and she did not want him to go with her if she was wrong about him, however, satisfying it might be to confront Sioned with her proof! 'I can walk perfectly well.' She frowned at Owain.

'You still might be glad of my arm.' A slight pucker had appeared between Owain's dark brows. 'I am perfectly harmless, lady!' He put out a hand and took her gloved one in his grasp. She gasped and snatched back her hand, but left her glove in Owain's grasp.

'Give me my glove!' She reached out, but Owain took her hand instead.

'You seem to make a habit of having mishaps, lady. This is a bad one, but naught to be shamed about. You snatched some morsel from the cooking-fire, perhaps?'

Kate nodded, pulling her hand from his, and he returned her glove. She had never thought that anyone would see such a commonplace explanation behind her claw of a hand. Always she had looked upon it as a symbol of her sin and guilt. She was unexpectedly upset by the gentleness in his voice.

'I thank you, sir, but I must go now or my brother will come looking for me,' she told him stiffly.

'If that is your desire.' Owain inclined his head, turning away. She roused his interest, but he was not a man to push too hard, and he did not doubt he would see her again. Sooner or later she would return to the river.

Kate stared after him for a moment, an inexplicable, confused anger within her. People were dispersing, and she began to walk back to Matilda's house, limping slightly. Her knee still hurt, but fortunately her skirts had cushioned it fairly well. The hall door was ajar, so she went in slowly and quietly.

Sioned and Cadfael were sitting on a bench at the trestle table. Matilda and Ned were on the other side of the table. They were drinking wine, and talking, the four of them, with an intimacy that sent envy, keen and painful, through Kate. She was an outsider. They had not missed her or heard her arrive. She moved slowly across the floor, barely making a sound. Then Sioned looked up, and there was concern in her face, but Kate did not see it. Misery held her fast.

'There is a ship,' began Kate, watching Sioned. 'It has a yellow and black sail. Ned, do you know who is its master?'

He looked up, surprised, as did Cadfael and Matilda. Sioned rose, and her fingers curled about the edge of the table.

'Kate! What is this about a ship?' Matilda came over to her sister with a whisper of skirts and put an arm about her. 'We were just beginning to worry about you. You have been down to the river? It is a good place to go when one feels sad.'

Kate did not bother to correct her sister. She had found out what she wanted to know. Now that Sioned knew the ship was in Chester, would she go to meet the Welshman? Had she asked Cadfael to come to Chester solely for that purpose? Perhaps he was a spy for Llewelyn, who had known that Sioned had married an Englishman in Edward's army. Kate had ceased to think straight or sensibly. Or was he an old lover? It seemed that perhaps she and her brother were not fated to find happiness in love.

'You are tired?' Matilda sat Kate down on the bench and poured her a cup of wine.

Sioned watched them, her brown eyes concerned, and she twisted the stem of her goblet. She would have thought Kate had enough on her mind with meeting her mother again, but it seemed that she had not forgotten what she had seen yesterday. Why had she asked about the sail? Fortunately, nobody had taken much notice of Kate's words. Sioned took a gulp of her wine. She must see Owain, but how could she contrive to get out alone? As it was, matters arranged themselves quite easily after all.

'I wish to spend time with my mother, Sioned.' Cadfael's hazel eyes were sombre. 'I need to discover exactly where I might find Rhys, so that no time will be wasted.'

'I understand,' she assured him. 'You would not mind if I went to pray in the abbey for your safety—and the outcome of your search?' Her heart had quickened its beat.

'Of course not!' Cadfael smiled and squeezed her hand gently. 'But you must not go alone.' He hesitated a moment. 'Take Kate with you. If anyone is in need of prayer, I think Kate might be.'

Sioned's heart gave a lurch, but she managed to murmur agreement. Cadfael spoke across the table to his sister, and Kate glanced swiftly at Sioned, smiled and nodded. It was arranged.

It had been raining, but the shower had ceased by the time Sioned and Kate came out of the house. There was a breeze, rich with the tang of the river. They came to the abbey and passed inside.

'I would pray alone, if you do not mind, Kate,' Sioned whispered. 'I seek St Winifrid's aid. If you finish before me, do not wait. I have much to ask of the saint.'

'Ay,' said Kate. She had every intention of making it easy for Sioned to slip out of the abbey if that was what she intended. She passed like a shadow into a distant corner near the door, and knelt. Images rose in her mind as she gazed through her linked fingers. Owain ap Rowan's bright blue eyes, and the feel of his strong firm hand on her claw of a hand. Her mother's thin, ivory face. Her fingers tightened. She pushed that memory out of her mind as tears caught her throat.

Kate lowered her head as she heard soft footsteps, and shut her eyes as Sioned passed. After five minutes, she, too, rose and left the abbey.

It had begun to rain again, and the wind sent Sioned's cloak flying, tugging at her braids. She almost ran through the half empty lanes and was soon at the river. Walking quickly along the bank, she scanned the ships, looking out for the *St Winifrid* with its distinctive black and yellow sail. The sail was furled, but the name was clearly written on the side of the ship. A man sat beneath an awning, eating bread and cheese, his tangled wet curls not quite concealed by his blue coif.

'Owain!' Relief surfaced inside Sioned like a bright bubble.

'Sioned!' Her brother got to his feet, putting down his food to hold out a hand

and help her aboard. 'I did not expect to see you in such weather, sister.'

'Cadfael leaves on the morrow to join the host in Wales, and I wished to make you known to him before he goes.' Sioned looked about her. The wooden deck was wet, as were the covered boxes and barrels lashed down with ropes.

'A new cargo,' said Owain, following Sioned's eyes. 'But come out of the rain and explain yourself.'

'You are going to Ireland?' Sioned allowed herself to be led to the awning.

'Ay, I take cheeses, horns, and hide. Oh, and salt from the wich houses.' Owain pulled his sister down on a huddle of blankets. 'Now what is this about making me known to your husband? I doubt there is time, if he leaves on the morrow.'

'We were seen yesterday. Cadfael's sister followed me, and she told him. He had the sheriff's men out looking for you and those outlaws last night. He was soaked when he came in, and furious.'

'You did not tell him about me? Or give my name?' His brow knitted, as he took a bite out of the bread and cheese.

'Of course not. I gave my word! But I did not like avoiding his questions.' Sioned pushed aside a damp wisp of hair. 'Let me make you known to him, Owain.'

He grimaced. 'Not yet. Sorry, little

sister. I would go from Chester without awkward questions.'

'You mean about being with the outlaws? If only Kate had not followed me! He sounds a terrible one, that black-bearded man. Cadfael says that he is a murderer—and other things!' Sioned moaned.

'I am not one of them—if that is what worries you!' Owain took another bite of his bread. There came a mewing, and a wet furry body suddenly landed on his knee. He gave a yell as the cat's claws sank into his leg. He grabbed it by the scruff of the neck and put it firmly to one side.

'Will you be able to come and see me on the morrow after he has left? We can talk then, Sioned. I haven't much time now, as I must see a merchant on business.' Owain took a gulp of ale from a pitcher.

Sioned gazed at him, exasperated. 'I would ask you what your business is, brother, but I vow you have trained that cat to get you out of awkward questioning!' The cat jumped on to her lap at that moment, and began rubbing its wet bedraggled head against her.

'Of course!' He grinned. 'And it is awkward questions from Ned and Sir Cadfael I wish to avoid just now. But I will explain on the way. I must see that merchant.'

Sioned nodded. 'I must not stay long, anyway. I might be missed.' She uncurled herself and plonked the cat on her brother's lap.

He winced, then, grabbing the cat, he tucked it under his arm and got to his feet. 'We will have our talk tomorrow, Sioned.'

She nodded, accepting her brother's hand. Tomorrow, Cadfael would be leaving. The thought pained her. Owain walked alongside her telling her a little about Ireland and his ship. They did not look back as they talked. If they had, they might have seen Kate following them with her gaze.

CHAPTER NINETEEN

Kate stood for a moment in the rain after Sioned and Owain had gone, and then, oblivious of the puddles forming in her path, she went back to Matilda's house by a roundabout way.

Was Owain a spy—or a lover? There had not been very much of the lover in his manner towards Sioned. Even so, she would tell Cadfael what she had seen. Her brother was not going to be cuckolded a second time. She would see to that! What a fool she had been not to see through Isabella and Jean all those years ago! Kate paused for a moment. Could Cadfael have told Sioned anything of the king's plans? There was a certain amount of secrecy about them, so Gwenllian had been told by John. Even he did not know what the king planned in order to bring Llewelyn to his knees. Kate came to Matilda's door, pushed it open and went in.

The hall's smoky warmth enveloped her. Matilda and Sioned were both sewing.

'Where have you been, Kate?' Matilda put aside her sewing, and approached her sister. 'You are so wet!'

'I like the rain.' Kate's eyes slid away from Matilda to Sioned. How innocent she looked, sitting there sewing! She had not even guessed she had been seen.

'Where is Cadfael?'

'He's with your mother,' Sioned answered her.

'I think I will go up and have a word with him.'

'You are not planning to leave, are you, Kate?'

'Leave?' Kate had given no thought to the length of her stay in Chester or what she planned to do. 'I have given it no thought, Sioned. Do you not wish me to come home with you?' There was slyness in the question.

'I did not say that,' replied Sioned. 'Cadfael would have us be friends, Kate. He is leaving in the morning, and I just wondered whether you wished to stay here and see more of your mother—or to return home.' As she looked at Kate, there was something in her face that caused her to feel ill at ease.

'Cadfael is leaving?' Kate seemed to be taken aback.

'Ay. He has been sent for by the king. Besides, he would be leaving anyway because of needing to seek out Rhys.' Sioned bent her head to her sewing. 'That was part of the reason for our coming here, Kate.'

'I see.' Kate was remembering now that it was before she and Sioned had gone into the forest that Cadfael had mentioned going to Chester. Had it been purely an idea of Cadfael's, this journey to Chester? She turned away from Sioned and Matilda and went upstairs to seek her brother.

Cadfael looked up at the knock on the door. He rose to his feet, glancing down at his sleeping mother as he did so, before going to open the door.

'Kate! You have come to see Mother? She is sleeping. Whatever the physician gives her seems to be causing her to doze more and more. But perhaps that is best for her, now. The pain is sharp at times.' He frowned down at Kate. 'But you are wet!'

'It is of no matter. I wished to speak to you, Cadfael.'

He stilled, his eyes suddenly hard. 'What about?'

After a minute, she said, 'Sioned. She does not know, but I saw her again today with that Welshman.'

'What are you talking about?' Cadfael's voice was harsh as he gripped Kate's arm tightly.

'I am saying that I saw Sioned with the Welshman I saw her with yesterday. They were on his ship under an awning.'

'You're lying!' he growled in a dangerously low tone.

'I am not! Why should I lie?' Kate glared at her brother. 'His name is Owain, and he is extremely handsome with dark curling hair and the bluest eyes you have ever seen.'

'You must have got very close to see that much, sister. I don't believe you!' Cadfael released her and turned away, running a hand through his hair.

'Perhaps he is a spy for Llewelyn,' she blurted out.

'A spy?' Cadfael whirled round. 'What could he hope to learn from my wife?'

'Men—men sometimes tell women things when ...' Kate licked her lips nervously. 'And the king's plans are very secret, aren't they?'

'Very secret, Kate. Too secret for me to speak about ... even if Sioned had asked me, which she hasn't. So he can be no spy.' As he spoke, he realised with a sharp stab of pain that he had begun to believe in Kate's Welshman. There had been something about Sioned last night. She had evaded his questions.

'I do not want you hurt.' Kate had begun to tremble. 'He did not act like a lover today. They talked.'

'You don't want me hurt?' Cadfael gave

a low rasping laugh. 'You don't think your words hurt me now! This boat—it is the one with the sail, I suppose, that you mentioned earlier?'

Kate nodded.

'The man's name again, Kate!' he exclaimed.

'Owain ap ...'

'Owain?' There was a strained painful note in Cadfael's voice. Not by the flutter of an eyelid did he betray his recognition of the name. He was silent for a long time, while Kate fidgeted with her fingers. Then he looked up at her. 'I will leave you to sit with Mother, Kate. I am going to take Sioned home. If she has arranged aught with this man today, there will be little chance of his going through with it.'

'You are going home? What of me?' Kate whispered.

'You will stay here.' He opened the door. 'If you had come to stay earlier, this might not have happened.' He shut the door behind him as he went out.

He ran down the stairs and walked swiftly into the hall. Sioned looked up from playing with Edward, and the smile faded on her face.

'What is it? Your mother?' she asked.

'My mother? No, I have forgotten something I need, and must go home again. You will come with me, Sioned.

Kate will stay awhile with Mother and Matilda,' he replied in a steady voice.

'But will you not miss the tide if we do not stay here, Cadfael?' Sioned handed Edward to Margaret, trying to hide her dismay.

'I will have a word with Ned, and he can ask the master to pick me up at the place we sail from, not far from the house.' Cadfael watched Sioned's face keenly. He had come to recognise the changing expressions that flitted across her face.

'But it is raining. We will get soaked!' said Sioned, lowering her eyes from his gaze.

'What is this?' mocked Cadfael. 'A mountain maid who fears the rain? I want to go soon, Sioned—before night falls. So be quick. Borrow a cloak from Matilda, if yours is wet from going out before.'

She looked at him, puzzled—there was something in his voice.

'Make haste, Sioned. Now!' His voice had hardened.

She hesitated barely a moment before she moved.

Matilda was shocked that Cadfael should want to take Sioned in this dirty weather all the way to his manor, but she knew her brother's determination. She did not argue with Sioned, only sympathised. 'Come back soon,' she whispered at the door.

Sioned nodded wordlessly. She had not even had a chance to say farewell to Cadfael's mother, and she had seen no sign of Kate. She gave a sigh. When would she be able to see her brother again? It could be weeks now, and he would wonder what had happened to her.

The rain was of the heavy drenching variety. Relentlessly cold, it was flung into their faces by a driving wind. By the time they reached home, Sioned was almost soaked through and mud-splattered. To make matters worse, Cadfael had not spoken a word the whole of the journey. He helped her to dismount, and they both felt the full force of the stormy weather before they stabled the horse, then ran into the house.

'If this doesn't stop, you will not be able to sail on the morrow,' shouted Sioned as she ran up the steps, the rain-filled wind snatching at her skirts.

'Then you will just have to put up with me for another day—won't you?' snapped Cadfael, easing the knot at the back of his neck.

'Put up with you?' She paused, one foot already on the top step. She turned to him, her heart sinking, still puzzled by his strange manner.

'Move, Sioned! We are wet enough without delaying on the steps.' He gave her a push in the back.

Sioned felt anger stir within her. 'And whose fault is it that we are wet? Yours!' She began to fight against the wind as she climbed the step. The door was locked.

'Have you the key?' Her teeth chattered, as the wind snatched her words away.

'Ay! Gwenllian must have gone to see her daughter. She will be back in the morning.' Cadfael had forgotten John's words until that moment. He put the key in the lock and turned it, opening the door as the wind caught it and slammed it against the wall.

Sioned walked in out of the storm, thankfully. It was dark and no fire burned. Unless Gwenllian had only covered it for safety. Her eyes grew used to the dimness, and with a confidence born of familiarity she walked over to the hearth. Wrapping her cloak round her gloved hand, she lifted the cover. The fire smouldered. She went to get some wood, but Cadfael was before her. It did not take long for it to catch and flames to spring up, bringing heat in their dancing tongues.

'Praise the saints,' murmured Sioned, dragging her cloak from her shoulders.

Cadfael loosened his cloak and dropped it on the floor. 'Help me with this!' He put a hand up to the knot of his sling.

Sioned moved wearily towards him. He had borne the full brunt of the wind and rain, his body protecting hers somewhat, as she rode pillion. She pulled off her gloves and eased aching shoulders before reaching up behind his head. Her fingers were stiff and awkward as she pulled the sling over his head. She could not undo the knot, it was so wet.

His breath was warm on her cheek. 'Blankets,' he muttered, as she moved away from him.

'Of course. There will be some in the chest.' She walked over to it with a slow tread and found a couple.

Cadfael had managed to peel off his surcoat, and drag his tunic down to his waist.

'You'd better undress.' He took a blanket, pulled it about his shoulders and stripped off the rest of his wet clothes, flinging them out of the light of the fire into the shadows. His eyes were on Sioned's face. 'Would you like some ale? We could warm it, and add nutmeg and honey.' His voice was emotionless.

'I—I'll do it.' Sioned was suddenly nervous. Why had he insisted on bringing her home?

'No. I will.' Cadfael's eyes surveyed her bedraggled, sodden figure. 'You'll get a fever if you don't get out of those clothes.'

'I'll get out of them.' She turned her back and began to unfasten the ties with shaking fingers. She jumped when Cadfael spoke.

'Shall I put some cushions on the floor by the fire? We might as well make the most of the heat.'

'It makes sense,' Sioned dragged off her surcoat, then her undergown, before wrapping a blanket about her chilled body. She turned to the fire, where already Cadfael had a pot of ale mulling. He had spread cushions on the floor, and she sat down, her feet towards the fire.

The ale was good and warming as it went down. Sioned had a couple of cups, and Cadfael had more. Sioned's eyelids began to droop as Cadfael began to sing. She blinked them open. It was a marching song.

'Don't!' she muttered. Tears pricked her eyes. 'I don't want to have to think of your going yet!'

The song ceased. 'Don't you? You would rather go yourself, I suppose? Back to the homeland? Well, I paid your amobr and you're not going anywhere but here!' There was only the slightest slurring of his words. His eyes glistened darkly in the firelight.

Sioned stared at him. 'You're drunk!'

Her pulses jumped erratically.

'Drunk? Hardly!' He shifted on the cushions, drew closer to her and flicked open the blanket before she could prevent him. He laid the palm of his hand flat on her bare stomach.

Sioned caught her breath. 'Cadfael ...' she began.

'It is a nymph. Naked and eagerly waiting to be bedded by her husband—or are you, woman?' There was no mistaking the anger in his voice.

'Don't call me "woman",' cried Sioned, quivering as he ran a hard hand up from her stomach to her breast.

'What would you have me call you? Would you have me whisper words of love, sweeting?' He pulled her closer to him with both hands, bringing her body hard against his. 'Love! Sweeting! My heart!' he whispered against her cheek. 'There, I will say them, but do not take them to heart. I vowed after Isabella I would never tell a woman that I loved her. And, by God, I won't.' He kissed her hard and long so that her lips were crushed and bruised when he lifted his mouth.

'Let me go!' gasped Sioned. A cold desolation had her in its grip, and she struggled, but Cadfael grabbed her by the hair and forced her head back. He pressed his mouth against her outstretched throat, nipping her neck with angry, small kisses. She aimed a blow at him.

He laughed, and forced her down against the cushions.

'No!' she cried, trying to push him away with quivering hands. She would not be forced! But his mouth was against hers, and there was no escape. His hands moved insistently, stroking, caressing. She dragged her mouth from Cadfael's. 'No, no,' she gasped in a trembling voice. 'I hate you!'

'No again? You are mine! And by all the saints in England I will have you before I leave,' he said huskily.

She tried to force him away from her, but he held her tight. Then she realised his increased strength. 'Your splint! Where is your splint? You should not have taken it off!'

Cadfael's hands slackened. 'You would prefer this ravaging wolf maimed, perhaps?' His eyes were dark and unfathomable as he stared down at her.

'You will spoil the healing, fool. Fool!' She glared into his shadowy face.

Cadfael laughed unsteadily. 'You sound almost as if you cared, Sioned.'

'Shouldn't I care? You are quite mad to do such a thing!'

'Mad? Ay! But allow me my madness, wife.' His voice was curiously fierce as he caught Sioned to him. He began to kiss her again—caressing, arousing even as she strove against him in despair. She would not succumb. Yet she feared to damage his arm, and his lovemaking had taken on a skilled sweetness so that she found herself moving, responding to a dancing insistent music in her veins. She was giving, wanting, drowning in a pleasure that took her utterly unprepared. She cried out Cadfael's name, whispered words of love—despising herself for her weakness, and hating him for his power over her when he laughed in triumph and called her a wanton.

The bed was empty when she woke the next morning. So was the room. How had she got here? She sat up abruptly as the memory of last night flooded back. The sun was beaming into the chamber, and a cold chill suddenly gripped her. She flung back the covers and scrambled out of bed, taking the first garment to hand and flinging it on. She pulled open the door and ran into the hall.

'The master's gone.' Gwenllian looked up from the fire.

'Gone?' Sioned stared at her, her legs suddenly without bone as she swayed.

'There, my pet.' Gwenllian put an arm round Sioned's shoulders and helped her to the settle. 'You must not worry—he will come back! He was never one for being waved off.' She poured out some ale and pressed it into Sioned's hand. 'I'll get you some bread. Perhaps I can find you an egg and some smoked ham. You must be hungry. Sir Cadfael said you had nothing to eat after your journey. You were so wet and tired.'

Sioned paid little attention to her, but took a sip of the ale. Kate had invaded her dreams. Kate had gone to see Cadfael when he was with his mother. What had she talked to him about? Why did Kate hate her so? Surely it was not only because of Isabella? She felt again that painful ache inside her.

'Gwenllian! What was Isabella like?' Sioned lifted her head and looked towards the little Welsh woman.

'Isabella? Goodness, why are you thinking of her, my lady?' Gwenllian came fussing over. 'A long time ago, it seems now, since Sir Cadfael came home from the crusades to discover that his wife and the child were dead and his sister badly burned. Poor Mistress Kate! She was inconsolable, and it was all that woman's fault!' She handed Sioned some bread with honey spread on it.

'That woman?' Sioned nibbled at the bread and honey, with little appetite for it.

'That Isabella! The names she called

Mistress Kate—and she herself little better than a whore! I suppose it made matters easier for the master, knowing that the child wasn't his, but sired by that Jean.'

'What?' Sioned sat up straighter, staring at Gwenllian.

'Didn't you know?' Gwenllian paused as she dropped Cadfael's wet clothes into a basket. Sioned shook her head. Gwenllian gave a tsk. 'There, the master has put it behind him, although it took some time. No man likes being made a fool of—and Sir Cadfael is a proud man.' She smiled. 'I was so glad when he brought you home. John thought he had run mad, but I knew when I saw him with you. I knew he had come to his senses.' Before Sioned could ask her what she meant, she had bustled away ... out of the door and down the steps with the basket of dirty clothes.

Sioned took a big bite of the bread and honey. Her heart still ached, but now it was a different kind of ache from before, and she had some thinking to do. Kate! She must see Kate, but it would have to wait until later. She was far too tired to travel that day.

Kate walked along by the river. She was feeling guilty and confused, wishing Cadfael had not gone with Sioned to his manor. Ned said he would not be returning—that the master of the ship taking him to Deganwy was picking him up further along the river. She realised with a shock that she was missing her brother and Sioned. How strange! She had spoken to her mother that morning, and was wondering what to do about what she had told her. When in doubt—ask! Had Cadfael asked Sioned who the Welshman was? She wished she knew. She pushed back her veil and looked up at the ship with the yellow and black sail. It was ready for sailing, it seemed. Suddenly her gaze was arrested so that she could not look away. It was Owain ap Rowan, smiling down at her. She flushed, and turned away.

'Wait!' Owain was off the ship in a trice and had taken her arm.

'Please let me go!' Kate tried to pull away from him, but he kept a tight hold.

'Not before you tell me your name, lady.' The brilliant blue eyes smiled into hers, and she felt a gentle stirring in her breast.

'Kate,' she whispered, unable to tear herself from the power of his eyes. 'Kate Poole.'

'Kate Poole, did you say?' His brow crinkled. 'Then you must be of some relation to Sioned?'

'I am her husband's sister. Are you looking out for her? She has gone from

Chester.' Kate, discomfited, made to turn away.

'Where has she gone? She thought she would still be here today!'

'She ... My brother took her back to his manor last night. He was sailing this morning for Deganwy.' Kate attempted to pull her arm away, and he released her, letting out a sharp breath. 'I see! A change of plan. I shall have to see her on my return. I, too, must go soon.' He tapped his nail against his teeth.

'You would still see Sioned, even though you know she is married to my brother?' She stepped back, a curious disappointment deep within her.

'Why not? Matters will most likely have arranged themselves by then. But for now, Mistress Poole, I must bid you farewell.' He lifted a hand. 'Perhaps we will meet again, before too long. I look forward to it.' He smiled, and had gone back on board before she could speak another word.

Slowly Kate turned away and walked back through the lanes to Matilda's house. She must speak to her mother and see what she made of the whole affair. It was much too much for her to understand. Owain ap Rowan did not seem to care a penny that Sioned was married to her brother ... and yet his parting words made it seem that he wished to see herself again!

CHAPTER TWENTY

'Sioned!' Elin Poole's face lit up with pleasure. 'I did not expect to see you so soon.' She glanced at Kate, who stood silently against the wall. 'We are glad to see Sioned—are we not, Kate?'

Kate nodded, her eyes on Sioned, who looked pale and tired.

'I beg pardon about that.' Sioned half smiled. 'But I am back again, and I have brought Gwenllian with me.' She sat down on the edge of the bed.

'Gwenllian!' Elin's eyes shone. 'It will be good to talk of old times with her.'

'Would you like me to fetch her for you, Mother?' Kate moved away from the wall.

'I would deem it a favour, Kate.' Her daughter went out swiftly, and she turned to Sioned. 'I am glad to see you, for a special reason. Kate has been telling me something about a man called—Owain ap Rowan. She says that you know him. Do you?'

Sioned's fingers curled tightly on the scarlet coverlet. 'How does Kate know my brother's name? Did she ask Matilda about him?'

'Your brother? Ohhh!' Elin leaned back against the pillows, a smile on her face. 'But what is this about Matilda?'

'Matilda knows Owain. I thought Kate might have asked about him. She has taken a lot of interest in my affairs lately.' Sioned's tone was cool. She rose to her feet, unable to sit still any longer.

'You must forgive Kate, Sioned, please.' Elin's faded eyes were concerned. 'She has suffered, my dear. But she is changing, and though she will never be the old Kate, she might become a nicer person.' She smiled ruefully. 'She met your brother by chance—or perhaps it was fate, who knows? The first day she came, she saw him. He helped her, and later she learnt his name, but she did not know he was your brother. I doubt it was just jealousy that sent her to Cadfael.' Elin moved uneasily in the bed. 'They were both betrayed by Cadfael's first wife, and she was concerned.'

'She should have come to me!' Sioned gave a small, bitter laugh. 'Your words make some things clear!'

'You did not tell Cadfael that Owain was your brother?' There was a worried expression on Elin's thin face.

'He did not ask me. He was only ...' Sioned paused. 'He was not gentle—he was angry, and I did not know why. Now I think I know.' Her throat tightened with emotion.

'It will come right, Sioned. Believe me!'

'Of course,' she replied, not adding what was in her mind. It would come right only if Cadfael returned.

There was a knock on the door, and Kate and Gwenllian came in.

'I will leave you all together,' murmured Sioned, feeling that she had had enough emotion for one day. 'I will see you again this evening, Mother Elin. I plan to stay a few more days, and then I must go home. It is where Cadfael will expect to find me.' As she went out of the room, she realised that Kate was just behind her, and they exchanged glances as Kate closed the door behind them.

'Sioned ...' Kate began nervously, pleating a fold of her gown with unsteady fingers.

'He is my brother, Kate. Owain ap Rowan is my brother! We met by accident, and he did not wish me to mention the meeting to Cadfael. I gave my word.' Sioned's face was taut, her eyes cool. 'So now you know all there is to know. Except, perhaps, that I had not seen my brother for several long years. We were happy to see each other. He is not a long-lost lover after all, you see!'

Kate could not reply. Sioned's brother! Her thoughts were confused, but the overlying emotion she felt was relief, tinged with a sense of remorse.

As Sioned made to go down the stairs,

Kate held her by the sleeve.

'I—I ask you to forgive me, Sioned. But ...'

'I am tired, Kate, and I do not wish for explanations.' Unexpectedly her anger eased. There were many things she could have said, but there seemed little point, with Cadfael gone. 'Shall we forget what has gone before? It is what Cadfael would wish, I think.'

Kate hesitated. She would have liked to explain, or at least to excuse herself. But perhaps Sioned's way was best. She nodded, and they went downstairs together.

During the next few days, if their dealings with each other were not always received immediately with understanding, they did at least manage not to quarrel and to rub along together.

Sioned planned to return to Cadfael's manor. September had come in, and she thought she should be at home. Then Cadfael's mother's condition worsened, and she stayed. No word had come from Cadfael, and a gnawing sense of apprehension and a feeling of desolation coloured all Sioned's thoughts. Surely, if he was still alive, he would have sent word—or have come himself if he had found Rhys.

Then, one night, when Sioned had taken her turn at sitting with Elin, she dozed off, and when she woke with the dawn it was to find her dead.

'But—but Cadfael has not come with Rhys. You should have waited,' she found herself whispering. Tears ached in her throat, but at last she rose and went to tell Matilda and Kate.

'I do not understand!' Kate's face was blotchy with tear-stains. 'She was so sure she would not die until Rhys came.'

'This time she was wrong,' Matilda retorted crossly, pressing a scrap of linen once again to her brimming eyes. 'What are we to do?'

'There is little point in Cadfael bringing Rhys if Mother is dead,' said Ned. 'We must get word to him somehow.'

'He could be on his way home,' said Kate.

'He might be at Deganwy still?' Matilda gazed at her husband.

'Or he might be on Ynys Mon!' exclaimed Sioned. 'We need a ship, Ned!'

Ned frowned, and tapped his fingers on the table. 'There is a ship due in from Ireland. Owain knows the waters well. If any man would go on our behalf at such a time of uncertainty as this ...' He grimaced ruefully.

'Owain? My brother's ship is due in?' Sioned sprang to her feet, her face bright with relief.

'Well, it is overdue, so if all is well with him he should be here any day.' Ned smiled. 'Perhaps even today. We could go and see, and if no word comes from Cadfael by this evening, maybe ... Maybe, if your brother does arrive, you can persuade him to go, Sioned.'

Sioned nodded. 'I will go with him. He does not know Cadfael. I will be guided by his wisdom. Surely, if he has passed the shores of Gwynedd and Anglesey, he will have some idea of where the army is.'

It was with a sense of overwhelming disappointment that Sioned returned from the riverside that afternoon and evening. She slept fitfully that night, but the next morning before they had even broken bread, a knock came on the front door. Kate went to open it.

'Is my sister here?' Owain ap Rowan smiled. 'I looked for her at Poole Manor, but they said she was here.'

'Aye, she is here.' Kate's heart was beating rapidly. 'Come in. We have looked for you the last day, praying you would return.'

Sioned had already risen, and hurried across the floor and flung her arms about Owain. 'Oh, it is so good to see you, brother!' She hugged him tightly.

'And you, Sioned! You are well?' Owain

held her off from him a little. 'You are rather pale, but ...'

'It—it is Cadfael. We are worried about him.' She took her brother's hand, and with Kate on his other side, led him over to the table. 'You will have a bite to eat?'

Owain nodded. 'What is it? What is wrong?' He sat down on the bench next to Sioned.

'My mother ... is dead, Master Rowan,' Kate answered for Sioned. 'Cadfael, we think, is with the army. But he was also seeking our half-brother on Anglesey. We have had no word from him, and would send him a message.'

'I see!' Owain frowned. 'There are many ships anchored in Anglesey waters. It could be that you will find Sir Cadfael on the island. What ...'

'Owain!' Sioned put a cup of ale before him, and a hunk of bread and salted pork. 'Would you ... Could you take me with you on your ship? Could you help me to seek out Cadfael?'

Owain took a gulp of ale. 'I am truly sorry about the lady Elin. She possessed a rare spirit, not only of courage, but of humour, and I regret her passing. But you are certain this is what you wish, Sioned? It could be dangerous.'

Sioned's eyes were bright, and she

nodded. 'I am not frightened! We are Cymri, you and I. Our land holds no fear for me.'

'I was not only thinking of going ashore, Sioned, but I see you are set on it.' Owain chewed some bread with a pensive air. 'I will have to check the unloading—and wait for the next tide. This evening, if that is your wish, Sioned, we will go.'

Sioned flung her arms round his neck and kissed him. He gazed over her shoulder and winked at Kate. She blushed, but returned Owain's smile. No longer would she run away from all that life could offer her, despite the fearful anxiety that was, she knew, a part of caring about people.

The night was clear, and the breeze tugging at Sioned's cloak was kindly and blowing favourably.

'If you tire, go and rest under the awning,' Owain told her.

Sioned nodded, gazing up at the stars, and then at the dark outline of the shore sliding past. She thought of how Cadfael had brought her to Chester after paying her amobr, and she was glad that she carried his child. It had been for the best that she had kept her secret, otherwise Matilda and Kate might have been against her going with Owain.

Sioned yawned, and bid her brother good night. Taking a blanket, she wrapped it about her, and within moments the cat came to join her and she was glad of its warm company. Gradually the motion of the ship and the purring presence of the cat soothed and relaxed her, and she drifted into sleep.

When she woke in the morning, they were lying at anchor. She stretched before stumbling sleepily to her feet and going to join her brother at the side of the ship.

'See the ships at Deganwy!' Owain waved a hand holding a chunk of salted pork towards the far shore.

Sioned narrowed her eyes, barely recognising Deganwy's green knoll with its half-ruined castle on one side and The Cistercian monastery on the other side of the arm of the sea. 'It looks different from here,' she murmured.

'Everything looks different out at sea! Perhaps being on the sea is what made Edward think of using ships to deal with Llewelyn,' said Owain casually.

'What do you mean?' Sioned stared at the hills, knowing that they rose much higher further inland, until they soared to the peak of Yr Wyddfa, the mightiest. For a moment she suffered a pang of longing.

'Over there, Edward has a contingent of men, and a few ships. Enough to convince Llewelyn that his aim was to invade the valleys.' Owain took a bite of his pork.

'Please go on.' Sioned frowned, holding her face up to the breeze. She was feeling nauseous, but did not want to give in to the sensation.

'All Llewelyn's warriors ready to attack the English are over there. And he has natural defences.'

Sioned exclaimed. 'Ay! The Conwy river at his front, and behind him the heights of Penmaenmawr.'

Owain nodded. 'Also on his right is the castle of Dolwyddelan, guarding the upper vale of Conwy, and beyond is the great mountain of Snowdon itself. Do you think, as they still do, that Edward is fool enough to try to defeat Llewelyn the old way?'

'What are you saying?' she asked slowly.

'They still speak of Edward's exploits in France, you know. He is a soldier—and has been since his youth. If he did not intend to win, he would not have put so much time and effort into this campaign.'

Brother and sister pondered Owain's statement.

'In the mountains, Edward can never win. So ...' Owain gazed at the isle of Anglesey, 'there have been rumours coming out of the island.'

'Owain! Tell me!' Her fingers gripped the side of the ship.

'It seems that Edward's men have

overrun the island and seized the harvest. Billowing smoke has been seen, so at first it was thought he had destroyed it, but I doubt a man of his sense would do so. Food is vital to life, isn't it, Sioned?' He put his hand over hers. 'To tell the truth, I know they are more than rumours. I landed on the island to have a look for myself!'

Sioned swallowed. 'I see!' She was thinking suddenly of the lady Elin's words: smoke—ships—men running. 'There will be no food for Llewelyn to feed his men or the cattle in the winter,' she said in a trembling voice. 'He will have to surrender. So—so that is why Cadfael was so sure that Llewelyn would be brought to his knees.' Tears sparkled in her eyes.

'Why cry, Sioned? Is this not the best way? At least Cadfael should be safe ... And there will be less loss of life.' Owain rested a hand lightly on her shoulder before turning away to shout to one of the men.

Sioned stood motionless, staring across the waters to the mainland, and for a long time she did not speak.

Owain had been waiting only for slack water, and a short time later they landed at a quiet spot not a great distance from the priory of Penmon.

Sioned had decided that perhaps the best place to start searching for Cadfael was

Rhys's manor. She had had the name from Matilda. Once on the island without her brother, she would have had great difficulty in finding it, because apparently there was a whole parcel of Ynys Mon from where the mountains were visible. On a clear day, he had told her, they could even be seen from the far side of the island.

Sioned and Owain left the ship in charge of the two men Owain had brought with him. The English ships they had caught sight of had been too far away to be any threat, or of any help, if that was needed. They walked for some time up the shore keeping silent, thinking that the wisest course to take. At last Owain called a halt, and Sioned sank thankfully on to a fallen tree-trunk. He handed her some bread and a wedge of Cheshire cheese, and she ate it with enjoyment now that the sickness had passed.

An eager apprehension gripped her when she thought of seeing Cadfael, yet she did not build her hopes too high. 'How much further?' she asked.

'Not far, now. I have been keeping to the trees to avoid any prying eyes. Another mile, perhaps, and then we shall be there. I thought it best to eat now, as we might not get the chance later. We do not know what we shall find at Rhys's place. We might not be so welcome, now that the English are here. Or Cadfael might have been and gone.'

Sioned nodded, and her heart suddenly seemed to quicken its beat. She would not think that Cadfael was not on the island. Whether he was still angry with her or not, she yearned to see him.

Owain rose to his feet and helped her up. 'We might as well go on now, if you have rested enough?'

The mile was swiftly covered, and soon they were approaching a small stone building a short distance away. In the field in front of it, thistles and gorse fought for dominance among straggling unscythed corn.

'It looks deserted,' murmured Sioned in a weary voice. 'Cadfael will not be here.'

'I think you're right!' Owain grunted, gazing about him. 'Still, we might as well go on to the house and see what is there.' They were surprised to find the one small window shuttered with new wood, and a door that was strong, with a latch. 'Someone has been here recently,' he said.

Sioned stood listening to the wind in the corn and trees, and the constant chirping of insects. 'How peaceful it is!'

Then, even as she spoke, there came the clumping of hooves. They both turned in the direction of the sound, and Owain's hand went to the dagger at his girdle. A horseman came into view, long in the stirrup, the wind tugging at the dark hair revealed by the mail coif pulled down on his neck.

Cadfael stared at them both—and they at him. Then he slid from his mount in one swift movement.

'Sioned! What are you doing here?' There was a flush high on his cheeks and a tightness about his mouth.

'Cadfael! Thank God!' She held out both her hands to him. She seemed to sway, and without thinking, he caught her hands, and his arms went slowly about her trembling body. Sioned began to cry. She cried and cried, dampening his surcoat and filling him with a sense of helplessness.

He did the only thing he could think of, and just held her. Often, since leaving her, he had thought of this moment, words forming in his mind. Now they were of little use.

At last her tears abated, and gently she touched his cheek. Cadfael caught her hand and pressed her fingers to his mouth.

'Do not let my presence be a hindrance!'

Cadfael lifted his head and saw Owain, thinking there was a familiarity about him. There was a stillness about his face as old uncertainties flickered through his mind. 'Sioned, who ...?'

'It is Owain, my brother!' She was having no more misunderstandings. 'I could not tell you, because I gave my word.'

'Your brother? I did not know you had another brother?' Cadfael gave a great sigh. 'But I remembered the name Owain, and how you seemed fond of its owner.'

'So you thought him my lover?' Their eyes held, and hers teased him.

'Only for a while! I feared that your longings for your home ... that you would leave me. I was jealous ... loving you ... not wanting to be parted from you.'

'Loving me?' she whispered, her eyes soft with adoration.

'Ay!' Cadfael smiled deep into her eyes.

Owain, watching them, felt suddenly in the way. 'I will start back, Sioned. If you and Sir Cadfael need me, I won't be leaving until the next tide.'

'Owain, wait!' She turned quickly, but her brother only waved a hand before striding away through the knee-high corn and weeds.

'Sensible man!' said Cadfael in a satisfied voice, pulling her back into his arms.

'If you did but know him ... But you will, I pray. But, Cadfael ...' Sioned did not know how to tell him.

'What is it?' His smile began to fade. 'Mother?'

Sioned nodded wordlessly.

'She is ... dead?'

'Ay.'

Cadfael was silent, and the expression on his face caused a lump to rise in Sioned's throat. They held each other tightly.

'When?' he asked at last in a choked voice.

'Two days ago. We came, thinking to prevent your bringing Rhys.' Sioned cleared her throat. 'It seems that he is not here.'

'Rhys is dead. He has been for the last four years. Apparently he lived like a hermit here after Grandmother died. Folk never knew that he had kin.' Cadfael sighed. 'I've been coming here when I could. It is a peaceful place, away from all thought of war. Today was to be the last time, and I was going home tomorrow.'

'So your mother was wrong about Rhys. Not about ships and smoke and men running.' Sioned said slowly. 'All that time searching in the mountains was wasted.'

'Wasted?' Cadfael stared steadily down into her face. 'It brought you to me,' he murmured with some emotion.

She tried to speak, but could not for a moment. She was deeply moved. She traced the outline of the emblem on his surcoat with an unsteady finger. 'Why did you pay my amobr? I always wondered why you did not just take me.'

Cadfael put a finger under her chin and

tilted it up. 'I have heard of men like you who take what they want without asking or payment,' he quoted softly.

There was a short silence.

'You were mad!' Sioned whispered, understanding lighting up her face. 'Quite, quite mad! You could have been killed.' She paused. 'Yet still I am glad you did what you did ... I—I love you. How I love you, Edward's man!' Sioned smiled into his face. 'Despite what your king has done to my pendragon.'

Cadfael pulled a face. 'I hope you will come to think that this way was the better. But ...'

'You are alive! And, despite my words, that is of the greater importance to me.' Sioned hesitated. 'I—I am carrying our child.' Her voice was low.

He stared at her, then he pulled her as close as close could be before he kissed her. Such a kiss that Sioned never forgot the intoxicating joyful feel of it as long as she lived.

They stayed there a long while, talking, reassuring, loving, in the place where the quest for Rhys had ended. Then Cadfael swung Sioned up on his horse before him, and they went in search of Owain.

This Large Print Book for the Partially sighted, who cannot read normal print, is published under the auspices of

THE ULVERSCROFT FOUNDATION

THE ULVERSCROFT FOUNDATION

. . . we hope that you have enjoyed this Large Print Book. Please think for a moment about those people who have worse eyesight problems than you . . . and are unable to even read or enjoy Large Print, without great difficulty.

You can help them by sending a donation, large or small to:

The Ulverscroft Foundation,
1, The Green, Bradgate Road,
Anstey, Leicestershire, LE7 7FU,
England.

or request a copy of our brochure for more details.

The Foundation will use all your help to assist those people who are handicapped by various sight problems and need special attention.

Thank you very much for your help.